DEADFREEZE
A ZOMBIE NOVEL

ANTHONY GIANGREGORIO

DEADFREEZE: A ZOMBIE NOVEL

THE DEAD KNOW NOT ANYTHING

Ecclesiastes 9:5

CHAPTER ONE

SNOW, AS FAR as the eye could see in every direction, nothing but white, clean, snow.

Dr. Mark Simmons continued walking across the low rise in the bleak landscape, his feet knowing exactly where to land. He had walked this path so many times he could do it with his eyes closed.

Over the next snow drift was the purpose of his trek. An eight foot metal pedestal, similar in shape to the Eiffel Tower in Paris, stood alone in the middle of the plateau, with a telescope perched on top.

The Antarctic sky was as clear as always. Due to the atmosphere over Antarctica being virtually unpolluted, Mark was able to obtain an especially clear view of the sky.

He climbed to the top of the rise, readjusted the telescope, and then scurried back down, his boots sinking into the snow past his calves. Withdrawing his shoes from the ice-encrusted snow, he turned and headed back the way he'd come.

The sky was darkening overhead, and with a frown across his chilled visage, he knew the sun would be leaving the sky for the next four months. The Antarctic winter lasted from around the beginning of May to the end of September, with the sky being dark for about the same amount of time.

He knew he could handle it, though, as this would be his second winter at the James-Amusen Station. It was named after a famous Antarctic explorer, one he had never bothered to do research on.

This winter would also be his last because when his two year tour was over, he'd already decided he was going to pick a warmer climate for his next assignment. Just thinking about warmer climates gave him a warm glow inside, despite the minus 0 degree temperatures he was walking in, the wind dropping it another ten below.

As he came over the last snow dune on his trek back to the station, he could now see the dome of the large building coming into view. The bright lights surrounding the station were a beacon for him to follow, the wind whipping snow into his face like a living entity.

For the thousandth time since arriving to this desolate climate, he thought of what went on inside that dome.

Though a lot of the happenings inside were exactly what you'd expect at a research facility in the Antarctic, there were a few mysterious programs operating in secrecy.

The Antarctic Treaty of 1959 allowed people and countries to use the Antarctic only for peaceful purposes, such as exploring, tourism, and of course, scientific research. The same treaty forbids military forces to enter Antarctica unless they are assisting scientific expeditions.

That was the perfect cover for the United States government's black ops to set up a private-funded research facility right in the middle of the South Pole without so much as a tremor being made in the scientific community.

But Mark knew something was off about Dr. Theodore Fredericks and his research staff.

For one thing, the staff never left the building. Now, how the hell can you research anything without leaving the building even once? Not to mention the soldiers that were now supposedly stationed here.

He'd heard rumors from the other researchers that some of the soldiers were volunteers in some secret experiment for the military. He couldn't put much stock in rumors, but he had to admit since they had arrived four months ago, they had acted suspicious, albeit not suspicious enough for him to make any official inquiries into their true mission here at the top of the world.

As he came closer to the station, he could make out the dome much more clearly. The dome was two-stories tall with the rounded roof allowing snow to slide off. The building contained about eighty researchers and support staff in all, with laboratories scattered throughout the building.

The north side of the building had been off limits ever since Dr. Fredericks and his flunkies had shown up and claimed it as their own.

The generator was on the west side of the building, housed in its own structure with a small corridor connecting it to the main building. There was also a twenty foot large dish on the roof, used for communications and research.

Now that he was almost on top of the building, it always reminded him of some form of giant insect, with the head being the generator room, the dome being the torso, and the radio tower being its antenna.

The main doors were in sight now and he could make out a figure standing in front of them.

As he approached, the figure waved to him. He yelled something in return but it was lost on the wind.

When he was within ten feet of the figure, he yelled again.

"I said, what the hell are you doing out here, Saunders?"

"I'm grabbing a smoke. What's it to you?"

"Weren't you supposed to finish up collating the latest readings and have them ready for me by five?"

"Yeah, yeah, relax, Simmons; don't get your panties in a bunch. They'll be ready," Saunders said; the sarcasm clearly audible over the wind.

Mark didn't rise to the verbal bait. Instead he continued past him and entered the front foyer of the building and the warmth waiting within.

He and Saunders had been butting heads ever since he'd been promoted to Director of Research for their department. They had both been in the running for the position, but only one of them could receive it.

And as luck would have it, he was the one.

So now, not only did Saunders hold a grudge about not getting the position, but he had become Mark's subordinate, too, and that made him very unpleasant company. Especially when you were trapped with said person in the middle of the Antarctic in a building that wasn't as big as you'd like it to be.

Mark passed through the heavy doors and was immediately blasted with warm air when he entered the building. With a weary sigh of relief, he began taking off the giant parka he'd been wearing and unwrapping the scarf wrapped around his face, stamping his boots on the floor to release any snow that had accumulated on his boots the entire time. He resembled a ten-year-old who had come in after sledding all day after a snowstorm had closed the schools.

When he was stripped of his weather gear, he headed down the corridor to the cafeteria to grab a hot cup of coffee.

As he passed a fork in the hallway, he paused and stared at the doors at the end of the hall to the right of the fork. The doors had two cameras on the top of each one with the words **Authorized Personnel Only** stenciled on the door in bold yellow letters. On the right side on the wall was a card reader. Mark also knew from past experience an armed guard was posted on the opposite side of those doors twenty-four hours a day.

As he entered the cafeteria, he took a quick look around, scanning the crowded room for a familiar face. Once spotting the particular face he was looking for, he grabbed a cup of coffee, added some cream and sugar, and went over to the table.

There were four people sitting at the table he wanted. The one person who had really caught his attention was a striking blonde woman with blue eyes and a pale complexion. Though some would say it was creamy, others would say it was chalky. A pair of octagonal wire rimmed glasses framed her eyes. Her hair was tied into a ponytail and just brushed the shoulders of her white lab coat.

As he came within earshot of her conversation, he could hear her discussing the subject she was most passionate about, namely the ozone layer.

"And with all the fluorocarbons diffusing the atmosphere, the suns rays will intensify, not to mention global warming. Why, the statistics alone state that… Oh hi, Mark. How'd it go outside?" She asked, changing thoughts in mid-sentence and looking at Mark as he came up to stand by her side.

"Oh, fine, Sara, it's a balmy minus 22 degrees out there. If I had more time I would have tried to get a suntan."

He smiled at her and pointed to her face. "You could use a little more sun, too, you know."

"Don't go there, we've had this discussion before," Sara said with a warning tone in her voice. Then, like a light switch being turned on, she changed subjects again. "So, Mark, did you hear the new rumor about what's going on over on the other side of the station?" She asked this like a high school girl gossiping about her friends.

"If you mean the one about them making super soldiers over there, yeah, I heard it, but come on; this isn't Nazi Germany for Christ sake," he sneered.

"I'd love to get a look at what they're doing over there," said one of the other fellows sitting at her table. Mark wasn't really sure of his name, Roger or Ronny or something that began with an R.

"Well, be careful what you wish for," Mark replied. "If you found yourself over there you might find it hard to get back."

"Making up more rumors, Mark?" Sara snickered as she got up to leave.

"No way, Sara. That's your job, isn't it?" He quipped while moving out of her way so she could leave.

"Well, bye, boys, it's back to work for me. The world isn't going to save itself," she said as she turned and walked out of the room.

Mark watched Dr. Sara Edwards leave the room, admiring the way her coat conformed to her body. He knew he had a little crush on her, but tried to ignore it. There was simply too much to do at the moment to complicate things with romance. Although a one or two night stand wouldn't hurt to take the edge off. All these ideas fluttered through his subconscious without him really being aware of them.

Then he was distracted when Fredericks walked into the room. As always, the man's face was set in stone with barely a flicker to show he was human and not some kind of mannequin.

Dr. Theodore Fredericks was the project director on the north side of Amusen Station. The director of what no one had a clue and Fredericks would be the last one to ask. To say Fredericks was anti-social would be a compliment. The only time he came out of his lab was to eat, and then he would always eat alone. After a month or so everyone on the station got the hint and now no one even tried to sit with him.

Mark decided now was a good time to leave also, so he went and topped off his coffee, put a cover on it, and then headed out of the cafeteria to return to his lab. Once he'd passed Fredericks, he put the man out of his thoughts.

That was usually the best place for him to be.

CHAPTER TWO

DR. THEODORE FREDERICKS finished his lunch and returned to his lab without saying a single word to anyone along the way. Reaching the security doors separating the north side of the station, he swiped his identicard through the card reader and waited for the green light.

After a slight delay, he was approved and he entered the ingress, pausing momentarily at the desk inside the door for the soldier to get a look at him. Then he continued down the hall to his lab to check on the round of experiments he currently had active.

As he entered his lab, his breath immediately became visible in front of him due to the extreme temperature of the room. The room was always kept at minus five degrees Fahrenheit due to the chemicals and experiments presently in the lab.

Fredericks walked over to a cage on the far side of the room and inspected the animal inside.

A snake, formerly from the Nevada desert, sat on a worn, brown log inside the cage with the frigid temperature in the room obviously not bothering it in the least. Where the cold would normally make the snake go dormant, maybe even kill it, the snake acted like it was a comfortable 80 degrees in the room rather than it being below freezing. Fredericks nodded approvingly and went to the next cage.

Inside was a bird native to South America. It, too, appeared to be perfectly comfortable in the cold and was active inside the cage.

The third cage had a chimpanzee inside, but unfortunately the animal appeared to be suffering the first stages of hypothermia and was close to death.

Fredericks frowned deeply. The serum was working on lower forms of animal life but didn't appear to have any effect on higher mammals, which was definitely not good. His superiors at the Pentagon were expecting results and he knew he was running out of time before funding would be cut off and he'd be recalled back to the states. He couldn't let that happen.

About six months ago, Fredericks was approached by a representative of a covert agency funded out of the Pentagon. If Fredericks was a conspiracy nut, he would have been in heaven, but he wasn't, so it was irrelevant to him where his funding came from, just so long as the money kept flowing.

This agency had picked the perfect time to recruit him. The college where he'd been receiving funding had just cancelled his grant and he was desperate to find another sponsor so he could finish his work. He was almost at a breakthrough; all he needed was a little more time and a lot of money.

So when this agency proposed he work for them, he agreed, although little did this agency know he had a private agenda exclusive to him alone.

For you see, Dr. Fredericks worked in the field of cryogenics. For the last two years he had been working on a serum that would in effect keep hypothermia at bay in a human being.

He had a personal reason that drove him to this goal, as well. When he was two years old, his parents, who were adventurers, had died due to hypothermia when they were caught in an ice storm while climbing Mt. Everest for the second time.

After their deaths, Theodore Fredericks had then spent the next ten years in foster care, bouncing from one home to another until he was taken in by a wealthy family from New York. His new family immediately spotted his potential and nurtured his love of biology and science.

He had graduated at the top of his high school class and had then gone on to earn multiple college degrees. When his credentials were impeccable, he could then focus on what had driven him to become a scientist in cryonics.

For the past two years he'd been on the verge of the breakthrough he'd been working so hard on. By mixing a cocktail of liquid nitrogen and too many chemicals to list, Fredericks was able to lower the body's temperature enough so a person could function in zero degree weather without the risk of hypothermia, thus saving climbers who may find themselves trapped on the side of a mountain when a deadly ice storm would hit.

Although he had been slowly making progress over the years, he still hadn't found that one element that would make his serum fool-proof. Despite the few successes he'd made, there were far too many failures to count.

As he stared at the slowly dying monkey, he couldn't help but reflect on some of his failures.

One time he had injected his serum into a two-year-old chimpanzee. He unfortunately had returned the next day to find it dead in its cage. The chimp's arm had broken off and it had lain in its cage for most of the night until finally dying from side effects of the serum.

When Fredericks had reviewed the videotape of the doomed chimpanzee from the previous night, he'd watched passively as the animal had reached its arm up to pull itself onto a branch and the arm had snapped off like a twig. The animal had stared at its missing limb for hours, not comprehending what had happened until finally the chimp had stopped moving and expired.

Another time he had injected a stray dog he'd found on his way home from work one day, taking advantage of resources wherever he could procure them. That experiment had ended in failure also. Only minutes had passed after the dog had received the injection when the animal had suddenly gone crazy, bouncing around and throwing itself at the glass walls within its cage. At first it tried to bark, but when its tongue broke off in mid-yelp, only gargled sounds escaped its throat. Fredericks had then shot the animal with a tranquilizer dart, and when the dog was down, he'd investigated to find the dog's corneas had frozen, as well, rendering the animal blind. He'd then put the animal down for good and performed an autopsy. He'd found the animals eardrums had frozen and then shattered while the dog had thrashed around its cage striking its head repeatedly against its prison.

After that episode Fredericks had been disheartened. He felt he had gone as far as he could experimenting on animals. The biology of a human over an animal was vastly different and failures he'd made with animals could have entirely different outcomes with human subjects.

But his sponsors would never let him use live human test subjects.

That was when he had decided to branch out on his own, his first task would be to find a human being that no one would miss and start his experiments in earnest.

Now all he had to do was find one, but the question would be, where exactly does someone of his stature find someone no one would miss?

Chapter Three

FREDERICKS FOUND HIS first human subject quite by accident.

He was heading home from work one day when he spotted a homeless person sitting outside his apartment building. He approached the bum and asked him if he would like to come inside for a hot meal. After several minutes of explaining that Fredericks was not looking for any sexual favors from the man, the bum agreed and the two of them went inside to his apartment.

As they entered the confines of the building, Fredericks was overwhelmed by the body odor emanating off the filthy man, but Fredericks just smiled as he showed him into his apartment. It was a small, two bedroom apartment with a roomy kitchen.

Fredericks sat the bum down ay his kitchen table and prepared some hot soup. Fredericks tried to make friendly conversation, but lacked the proper social skills. Fortunately for him, the bum was just interested in a free meal and could care less about what he had to say.

As Fredericks talked about nothing specific, he reached into a kitchen drawer and retrieved a bottle of horse tranquilizers, covertly crumbling a few into the steaming bowl of soup.

He then placed the bowl in front of the bum and bid him dig in. The bum ate greedily with no regard for the temperature of the hot soup. He was finished in moments and then proceeded to devour the plate of bread Fredericks had set on the table.

Fredericks just stared at his doomed guest and waited for the tranquilizers to take effect. Within moments, the drug had suffused the bum's system and he began to sway in his chair. Before he could voice a question about this strange sensation, he pitched over onto the kitchen floor and lay still.

Fredericks could see the rise and fall of the bum's chest as it matched the rhythm of his breathing.

Fredericks dragged the unconscious man into the spare bedroom he'd set up as a laboratory, so he could work away from the prying eyes at work. In his apartment, he was the one in charge and had to answer to no one.

He then went to the refrigerator freezer and retrieved a bottle of the serum he'd worked on for so many years. The liquid inside the bottle was a dark blue, almost black, depending on how the light reflected off the bottle. Fredericks retrieved a syringe, withdrew the desired amount, and gave the bum the injection.

The man remained immobile, and Fredericks was beginning to become disheartened when he noticed small, blue lines spreading across the bum's face and arms. But other than the odd side effect, nothing was happening.

Fredericks checked his watch for the fifth time and was getting worried that the serum would have no effect, when all hell broke loose in his tiny apartment.

The bum's eyes snapped open, and as his head turned to look at Fredericks, a dry rasping sound came out of his mouth. Then the bum reached out with his hands and wrapped them around Fredericks' wrists.

Fredericks was shocked to see that when he twisted to pull away from the bum, the man's arms snapped off at the wrists. The bum tried to scream, but only managed to rasp louder. As Fredericks backed away, the bum managed to get to his feet, and then with murder in his eyes, advanced on Fredericks.

Fredericks backed away looking for a weapon and his gaze landed on a set of golf clubs poking out of the room's closet. He began inching towards the closet as the bum continued to try to grab him, which would have been comical under different circumstances as he had no hands.

Fredericks wrapped his hand around a club and used it to push the bum away. The bum lunged for Fredericks and tried to take a bite out of his face.

That's when Fredericks decided the experiment was most definitely over.

Fredericks swung the club like a bat and connected with the bum's jaw, shattering it.

Before the bum could even react to the blow, the club had come down on top of his head and sank four inches into his forehead. The bum stopped in mid-lunge and stared at Fredericks, then, as the light faded from his eyes, he slumped to the floor to remain still, the club tilting at an odd angle from his skull like a radio antenna.

Fredericks waited a few seconds and then poked him with his foot, ready for any more signs of life, but the bum stayed down.

With a sigh of relief, Fredericks noticed the severed hands across the room had started leaking blood onto the carpet as they thawed out. He filed that bit of information in his head for further study later.

He then went into the bathroom to retrieve an old shower curtain and went back and rolled the corpse onto it. When the corpse was on top of the shower curtain, he retrieved his medical kit, wanting the scalpels within mostly. What the bum couldn't tell in life maybe he could tell in death, Fredericks thought, while he prepared the corpse for an autopsy.

With the sun setting in the cloudy sky, Fredericks got ready for a long night. After he had examined the body to his content, he would then have to dissect it and dispose of the pieces.

With the light in the room growing dim, Fredericks began slicing into the fresh corpse with a great big smile on his face.

Chapter Four

Private shawn michaels sat at his desk behind the main doors for the north side of Amusen station. He had been on watch for about an hour now and had three more hours to go before he would be relieved from his post.

The traffic on this side of the station was pretty light today, only a few people coming and going to give him something to keep him occupied.

Dr. Fredericks had recently passed through with barely a nod to him. Not that it was so surprising, that guy was always in another world.

Shawn had heard some of the rumors of the stuff that went down in some of the labs on this side of the station, but still found it pretty hard to believe.

Shawn had been in the Army for a little over eight months, including the two months he'd spent in boot camp. He had really wanted to join the Air Force, but his aptitude test said he wasn't smart enough, so he was offered the Army instead. What choice did he have? So here he was, eight months later, freezing his balls off for the good of his country.

He reached down and checked to see that his pistol was still on his hip.

He did it constantly ever since he'd accidentally left his weapon in the bathroom a few weeks ago. Luckily, one of the professors had found his .45 and had returned it to him without making a fuss. He owed that guy big time. He thought his name was Summons or Simmons or something like that. It didn't really matter anyway, after all, what could a little guy like him do for a big shot professor?

He leaned back in his chair and stretched.

It could be worse, he thought. He could be on watch outside in the freezing cold like some of his buddies were. They drove around Amusen Station in these little half-tracks with skis on them. They were pretty cool even though the heating system sucked.

The vehicles were experimental and had only been used in a few places in the world, Antarctica being one of them.

Well, if you wanted snow, then this sure as hell was a good place to be, he thought.

The access buzzer sounded and a few guys in lab coats came through the doors. Most of them gave him a wave or a quick nod of greeting and then headed off to whatever lab they were working in at the moment.

Then quiet reigned over the hallway once more.

Shawn sighed, already bored out of his mind.

"Jesus, nothing interesting ever happens here," he muttered to himself.

As he stared at the wall clock's minute hand ticking away silently, he had no idea that in a few hours time, he would pray to every god he could think of that he could take that sentence back.

CHAPTER FIVE

DR. SARA EDWARDS walked down the hall with a smile on her face. Ever since she had met Mark Simmons, she'd felt an attraction to him.

Unfortunately for Mark, she didn't have any time in her life right now for romantic entanglements. She grinned politely to the people she passed by in the hallway as she headed back to her own corner of the station.

She had been at Amusen Station for a little over a year now and had really felt the time had been well spent. Her work was continuous, so she had no deadline to produce results.

She had received a small research grant from her hometown college back in Boston, Massachusetts, and for the last year, had really been showing advances in her research of the ozone layer and how man was slowly destroying his environment due to fluorocarbons in the atmosphere.

It wasn't just a job to her either; she was passionate about what she believed in and lived her life the same way. Right down to the car she drove in Boston and the hairspray she would use on her hair

She wasn't an environmentalist nut, but just believed each person on the Earth needed to do their own small part in saving the planet.

When she reached her lab, she smiled at Jenny, her assistant.

"Hi, Dr. Edwards, how was lunch?" Jenny asked.

"Nothing special, the cooks in the cafeteria are definitely not going to win any cooking awards anytime soon. So, did you get the new pictures developed yet?"

"Yep, they just came back from the photo lab," Jenny said. "Dr. Simmons got some great pictures with the telescope. You wanna see?"

"In a few minutes. I have a few other things to take care of first." With a slight grin, she headed off to the back of the lab to finish up some paperwork.

"Okay, I'll put them on your desk," Jenny called to her while she walked away.

Sara waved her hand as a sign of consent as she continued to the back of the lab. She felt a feeling of contentment suffuse her mind as she settled down to finish her paperwork.

All was right in her little universe.

Unfortunately, it wouldn't stay that way for long.

CHAPTER SIX

DR. MARK SIMMONS put his cold weather gear on and prepared to head outside and reposition the telescope.

He was taking extra care to bundle up as an hour ago a bad storm had come down on their little station and the staff was getting prepared to be snowed in for a few days until they could be dug out.

He was hoping he could get to the telescope and adjust it one more time before the full force of the storm hit the station, and then hopefully, his work and Sara's wouldn't come to a halt as it so often did due to the harsh weather conditions.

He was just putting his hat on and was ready to open the doors when three soldiers stumbled into the foyer.

The one man in the middle didn't appear to be conscious as he was slumped down between the other two who had apparently carried him.

As the three men fell to the floor in heap of tangled limbs, Mark ran over to them.

"My God, what happened to you guys, are you all right?"

The soldier on the right looked up at Mark. His face was covered in snow and there were signs of frostbite on parts of his face.

"The half-track broke down, we had no heat, and the damn radio didn't work. When the storm hit we stayed put like the manual says, but that doesn't do any damn good when no one knows you're missing." The soldier stopped talking as he was out of breath, and while he sat there gasping for air, his buddy continued the story.

"After a few hours had past, we couldn't feel our hands or feet anymore," the second soldier said as he checked on his unconscious friend. "We decided we had to chance walking back to the station even though the storm was picking up. We've been out there for hours I think, I'm not really sure, it was hard to keep track of the time without the sun or a watch."

Finished with his story, the soldier slumped to the ground, expelling the last of his energy.

Mark reached down and felt for a pulse on the unconscious soldier. His neck was like touching ice. As he searched for a pulse, he noticed that almost all of the man's face had frostbite.

After a few moments of fruitless searching, Mark had found no pulse so gave up.

He stood up and went over to the phone on the wall to call for help. There wasn't anything more he could do for any of them.

Within minutes a first aid crew had arrived to help. Amusen-Station was equipped with only a rudimentary of medical services. Any real medical emergencies would be transported to Kryton Station, which was about fifty miles north of their position. Kryton Station housed over one-thousand people in the summer and only about two-hundred and fifty or so in the winter. Kryton Station sat on Ross Island off the coast of Antarctica and relied on ships called icebreakers to bring in supplies and to leave with waste materials and scientific samples. The station was also equipped with runways and a helicopter pad. Although the weather would restrict activities, scientists were still able to record weather data and study earthquakes and solar radiation. Simmons had many colleagues at Kryton Station that he frequently collaborated with on similar projects.

As the medical team examined the three men, Mark stood back and gave them room, but paid special attention to the unconscious man.

The medic turned the unconscious soldier on his back and slammed a needle into his chest and pushed the plunger. The epinephrine filled the man's heart, and the medic hoped that would be enough to jumpstart the man's frozen heart.

Then he started doing CPR, but within a minute or two realized what was wrong with the soldier and ceased working on him.

"How's he doing, I couldn't find a pulse, is he gonna make it?" Mark asked, even though he was pretty sure of the answer.

"I'm afraid he's dead. He's suffered extreme hypothermia. He probably succumbed about an hour ago. These men never knew they were carrying a corpse. I was pretty sure of the outcome, but I still had to try."

"Wouldn't of mattered if he was dead or not, Doc. We don't leave a man behind," one of the soldiers whispered from the floor.

The three men were lifted onto gurneys and wheeled away.

"How are the other two going to be?" Mark asked the medic.

"They'll pull through, they have some frostbite in some of their extremities and they too are suffering signs of hypothermia, but in a day or so we'll transfer them to Kryton for more intensive care."

"That might be easier said than done. Have you seen the storm brewing outside?

We may be stuck in here for a few days until we can get dug out," Mark informed the medic.

The medic frowned, went over to the front doors and looked through the window. Outside the doors, the howling wind was whipping the snow around, causing a white-out effect, and the temperature had already dropped to minus five degrees Fahrenheit with more to come.

Nothing was going to be coming or going until this latest storm had blown itself out.

"Well, we'll just have to make due with what we have here. After all, it wouldn't be the first time, right?" The medic asked Mark as he turned to leave.

"That's true, you let me know if there's anything I can do, okay?" Mark asked.

"Sure, sure, I'll tell you. See ya later," the medic said as he walked down the hallway to go check in on his new patients.

Mark waved to him and then got ready to head outside on his original task.

One look outside and he knew that wasn't going to happen. The storm had doubled in size since the soldiers had arrived and would probably have blown him off of his feet if he had been out there. As he turned to leave the foyer, he had a morbid thought. What would have happened if those soldiers hadn't made him stop and not go outside?

It could have been him on a hospital bed instead of them.

He put the thought out of his head and decided to grab another hot cup of coffee before heading back to his lab. He had some paper to push to pass the time until he could knock off for the day, as without the telescope, he was pretty much left with not a lot to do.

As he walked down the hallway, he didn't notice Fredericks standing against a side corner. If he had, he probably would have been even more creeped out than usual by the man if he had seen the devious smile on Fredericks' face.

CHAPTER SEVEN

FREDERICKS HAD BEEN standing off to the side, away from all the commotion that was going on in the foyer of the station. He'd watched the medics wheel the three men away and had seen one of the medics detour from the hall leading to the medical ward and head for a room the station used as a makeshift morgue.

Fredericks waited for Simmons to leave and then hatched a plan that would answer all his problems.

As he went back to his lab to retrieve his medical bag, he recapped what he'd seen and what he planned to do in his mind.

He had been walking down an adjacent hall when he'd heard the yelling coming from the front of the station. He'd crept up and watched as the soldiers tell Simmons about what had happened to them and he had taken special interest when he'd heard one of the soldiers was dead due to hypothermia.

That was when an idea had hit him. He'd been trying to make his serum work on a live subject, but what would happen if he injected a specimen who had just perished from hypothermia? He couldn't resist the opportunity fortune had put in front of him.

Reaching his lab without incident, he retrieved two vials of his *cold serum*, as he had named it, and then went to the morgue to fulfill his plan.

Only one time on the way there did he come close to being discovered, as he had no business in that part of the station to begin with. A medic had been leaving the morgue and had almost walked right into Fredericks when he'd walked around a corner.

Fredericks had put on his most serious face and had mumbled something about getting lost. The medic had looked at him like he was a total idiot and had redirected him on the best way to go.

Fredericks listened to the man like he actually cared, put on his most sincere smile and thanked the man.

The medic then went off in another direction on some errand Fredericks could have cared less about. He then made sure the hallway was empty and opened the morgue's door and slipped inside.

As he brushed through the open door, his lab coat caught on a loose screw on the door frame and he felt a slight tug when his body was slowed from forward motion. Turning, he could see the problem, so he quickly backed up to remove himself from his predicament and then entered the room. He casually noted the seam of his lab coat now had a slight rip in it. He ignored it for more pressing concerns.

The morgue was nothing more than an empty storage room with the heat turned off. One advantage to being in the Antarctic was that any room in the building could be a freezer if you just turned the heat off. Fredericks wasn't a fan of the cold despite where he presently worked, so he turned the thermostat back up to a comfy seventy degrees.

After all, he doubted the corpse would complain.

As he studied the room, he noticed some boxes piled in a corner and a hospital gurney in the middle of the room.

The room was lit with nothing more than an extension cord running from a wall outlet to a hanging construction light. He walked over and turned the light on before the door closed and thrust the room back into darkness.

Fredericks could now see the obvious outline of a body under a white sheet.

He pondered for a second why dead bodies were always put under white sheets. Why not blue or red? After all, couldn't death be colorful?

Shaking the wasteful thought out of his head, he walked over to the body. His boots echoed off the walls of the empty room and his breath could be seen in the air in front of his face when he exhaled.

He set his black bag down on the side of the bed and peeled back the sheet.

The man's face was frozen in a state of pain, as if instead of being dead, he'd just stubbed his toe and was then frozen at that exact point in time.

Fredericks looked down at the man and saw the ever present toe tag on the corpse's foot. He leaned down to read it.

"Private Joseph Baker, serial # 223-56-8770," he said, the information written in neat script on the tag. "Huh, okay then. Pleased to meet you, Private Joe Baker," Fredericks said as he stared down at the frozen face and pulled a bottle of his serum out of his bag.

He paused for a second when he heard a noise in the hallway. His heart jumped into his throat with the threat of being discovered, then the noise moved away down the hall and he began to breathe freely again.

He finished pulling the syringe out of his bag and loaded it with the murky blue fluid. Then he picked up the corpse's arm and plunged the needle into it.

Now he knew the wait would begin. He pulled some boxes over to the bed and used them as a makeshift chair while he waited for something to happen.

When ten minutes had ticked by with no results, he began to panic. He knew he couldn't stay in here forever before someone came in to check on poor old Joe laying here.

He was growing more desperate after another five minutes, so he pulled the other syringe he had out of his bag and loaded it with another dose that was larger than the first one. Then he changed tactics by plunging the needle into the corpse's chest, aiming for the heart. He then did chest compressions to try to get the serum flowing through the body.

After five minutes of compressions, he was getting winded, as he wasn't a very physical man, so he gave up.

The corpse had no reaction to the serum. He waited around for a few more minutes, his passion fueling his patience, but finally gave up and gathered his things and left the room, making sure everything was exactly the way he'd left it He took particular attention with the body. But in his haste to leave, he forgot to turn off the light and lower the heat.

Cracking the door enough to get his head through, he poked his head into the hallway to make sure the hall was clear, and then he walked out like he was going for a stroll, leaving the room behind him, the corpse already forgotten.

"Oh, well," he mumbled under his breath. "There's always next time."

He knew sooner or later he would find the proper sequence of chemicals to add to the liquid nitrogen. And when he did, he would finally solve the dilemma that had been driving him crazy for more than two years.

*   *   *

The room was now empty.

There was no sound except the wind howling outside the far wall and the soft ticking as steam went through the heating pipes.

In the middle of the room lay the late, Private Joe Baker, his body frozen from the frigid temperatures it had been exposed to.

The epinephrine the medic had pumped into his chest had sat there inside his heart, inert as his heart had stopped beating hours ago. Fredericks had then pumped his liquid nitrogen cocktail into the heart .The epinephrine reacted with the serum and began to suffuse the body with the new chemical cocktail.

But still nothing happened.

Then the window in the storage room suddenly shattered as the wind blew some stray debris into it. As the wind howled into the room, blowing snow everywhere, the light began to sway, casting shadows on the walls. The snow began collecting on the light and then it sagged as the extension cord stretched and the wind continued to cover the room in white crystals. The weight of the snow melting on the light caused it to droop down onto the corpse until the light finally shorted out as the melting snow permeated the housing. Unfortunately, the outlet the light was connected to was incredibly out of date and it didn't trip like it should have when the light contacted water. Instead, a power surge shot up through the extension cord and into the light, which was now lying on the corpse. The electricity surged through the corpse, jump starting its brain and stimulating its muscles.

The electricity also had an adverse effect on the chemicals in the body, mutating it so that it began self-replicating on its own inside the host body.

The corpse that had once been Private Joe Baker opened his eyes. He tried to speak, but only gargling sounds emitted from his frozen vocal cords. The liquid nitrogen flowed through his body, now amplified by the other chemicals.

Joe Baker was gone and had been replaced by something that knew only two things.

He was cold and he was hungry.

And not necessarily in that order.

CHAPTER EIGHT

GEORGE SAMUELS WAS whistling a tune as he turned the corner in the hallway on his way down to the morgue. There were a few more things he needed to do before he could put his newest acquisition out of the way until after the storm died down. Then he could transfer the corpse to Kryton Station.

As he approached the doors to the morgue, he thought it odd to see water coming from under the door.

He opened the door and couldn't believe the condition of the room he had left less than an hour ago. The room was covered in snow and slush, the wind continuing to blow, and drifts had begun to form under the window.

From the light cast from the open doorway, George could see the burn mark on the wall from the wall outlet as well as the empty gurney in the middle of the room.

Wrapping his arms around himself to keep warm, he entered the room to investigate further.

"Now, where the hell is the body?" He asked under his breath. He couldn't hear the words as the wind was howling through the broken window.

As he surveyed the room a little more, he took in the stack of boxes and the fallen construction light. There was nothing in here but them.

"That's odd," he said. "People don't just get up and walk away after they're dead."

Then he felt funny talking to himself so he remained silent.

While wandering around the room, he stopped in front of the window where the snow drifts were the worst in the room. One drift was almost four feet tall and the bottom was melting all over the floor.

As his eyes wandered over the drift, he paused.

Did he just see movement in the snow? Nah, that would be ridiculous.

He walked closer until he was on top of the drift and then peered straight at it.

All of a sudden, in the middle of the drift, a set of eyes appeared.

As George watched, the eyes transformed into the head and torso of the dead man, and all of it slowly emerged from the snow, the mouth trying to form words that wouldn't come out.

George stared in horror and shock when the man's tongue broke off from his mouth to fall to the floor, where it landed like the sound of an icicle hitting a hard surface.

George was paralyzed by what he was witnessing, and when the frozen ghoul began advancing on him, he finally snapped out of his stupor and tried to turn and run.

Unfortunately, his first step landed on the broken tongue, his foot went out from under him and he pitched forward to the floor head first. The force of his landing knocked the wind out of him for a second and he blinked the white lights from his vision.

That was all the time the frozen zombie needed. The ghoul was on top of him before he could move. He put his hands up to try to push the man off of him and could feel how cold the dead man was. He felt like ice. The frozen zombie slowly leaned closer to George and he didn't have the leverage to push it off him.

The ghoul's teeth sank into George's neck with the sound of tearing cheesecloth. At first all George felt was the cold press of the cold teeth on his neck, like thirty-two little ice cubes. But then the pain hit him when the teeth sunk deeper into his flesh and the blood from his severed jugular sprayed across the room, where it froze on contact with the surrounding walls.

He had time for one startled scream before the blood in his throat muffled his voice. While he lay sprawled on the floor in his last seconds of life, the frozen ghoul still feeding on him, he wondered if this was all some sort of sick dream he was having thanks to the meatloaf he'd eaten for dinner or that black and white horror movie he'd watched the night before about the dead coming to life and trapping a group of people in a ramshackle house.

That must be it, he thought while pain stifled his vision and his heart began to slow. *I'll just close my eyes, and when I wake up, it will be morning and everything will be fine again.*

With a subtle grin on his face, satisfied he had explained the unexplainable, George bled out his last quart of blood he needed to live onto the floor and slowly closed his eyes, letting oblivion take him away forever.

Only minutes had past since George closed his eyes for that eternal sleep, but the endless rest of death would be denied him for just a little longer.

George opened his eyes and looked around the room.

The ghoul feeding on him abruptly stopped eating when he saw his eyes open again, as if it could sense the change in George. That it was like him now. The zombie got up and backed away as George slowly climbed to his feet.

The *cold serum* suffused his body, flowing through his veins and George's hands became like ice. He noticed that if he tried to bend his fingers too much, they reacted as if they would snap off.

Suddenly he felt cold, very cold, and he also felt hunger. Not the kind of hunger you feel when you're a little hungry for a snack, but that insatiable hunger a person would feel if he hadn't eaten for days.

The wound in his neck stopped leaking blood as it froze over and the open chest wound he now sported stopped leaking fluids. His limited brain function reasoned the door was the way out and that there was more meat out there just waiting for him.

Stiffly, with frozen legs, he stumbled to the door with the other ghoul following behind him, and together the two entered the hallway to find more prey.

CHAPTER NINE

THE CAFETERIA WAS located in the middle of the building, so that it was easily accessible from any part of Amusen Station. The two chilled ghouls stumbled through the hallway, some part of their past memories steering them toward that specific area. They knew that would be where most of the people would be congregated.

The halls were silent as they shuffled along, one frigid foot in front of the other, until a woman came around a bend in the hall and walked right into them.

She stopped cold in her tracks, speechless at the sight in front of her. Then, when her senses came back to her, she tried to turn and run, but it was already too late.

The two ghouls grabbed her with their cold hands and forced her to the floor.

As a team they ripped into her flesh, frozen fingers ripping away her skin to gain access to the moist, juicy organs underneath. The dead man named George had his face buried deep in her chest as he gorged himself on intestines, bile and gristle squirting from between his teeth.

The dead man who was once named Joe had gone for the woman's soft neck, his teeth ripping her throat out as she feebly struggled, the last of her life force draining away and spreading across the floor.

Then voices could be heard from down the hall as more people moved in their direction.

The two ghouls looked up in time to see two men in custodial uniforms round the bend the woman had just passed by only moments before.

"What the fuck?" One of them gasped. "What the hell are you guys doing to that woman?"

Before anything else could be said, the two ghouls jumped at both of the men's legs, tangling them so the men tumbled heavily to the floor.

The two, blood-soaked ghouls began to crawl on the floor, inching their way up the two janitor's bodies until they were in a position to attack.

One of the janitors kicked his attacker in the face, and was horrified when the cheek shattered like glass, bits of frozen flesh tinkling to the floor and covering his legs in frozen gore and skin.

The ghoul paid it no mind and continued clawing his way up the man's body until his face was even with the janitor's groin. Then teeth ripped open the man's pants and sank into his penis, severing it with one firm bite from the ghoul's frozen jaws.

The janitor's screams echoed down the hallway as he fought to escape, but the ghoul's grip was too tight and now the man was going into shock from blood loss.

Then, from behind them, the disemboweled woman sat up and began crawling over to the two screaming men, her hands slipping in her own blood still pooling on the floor.

When she reached the man who was screaming the loudest, she sank her teeth into the side of his neck, thereby silencing his pleas for help and killing him in one fluid action.

As the janitor gasped his last breath, his friend was faring a little better next to him on the floor.

The second janitor had been holding off his ghoul with a hand under its jaw and one on its chest. The man could feel the cold radiating through his hands as they touched the frozen ghoul's body. It was like holding a block of ice barehanded. As the zombie flailed at him, its fingers were being broken off like twigs, the loose appendages tinkling like bells when they struck the floor.

The man could still barely fathom what was happening, fighting back by pure instinct. He was able to get his legs under him, and he kicked back with all his might, sending the ghoul flying back against the wall.

Finally, with a second to catch his breath, he struggled to his feet and prepared to run. Unfortunately, his foot landed in the woman's blood spread across the floor and his feet went out from under him. His head connected with the floor with a resounding crack, sending the man into unconsciousness.

He didn't feel a thing as the three snarling ghouls turned on him and began feeding, ripping his stomach open and plunging their hands into his warm insides.

The man didn't feel a thing until moments later when the serum revived him.

Then all he felt was cold and hungry.

He stumbled to his feet, his intestines hanging out of the gaping wound that was his stomach, the entrails swinging back and forth like a half dozen spent garden hoses. As he began walking down the hallway, following the other ghouls, his blood stopped leaking out of him as it froze inside his body. Soon the intestines became affected and they snapped off to lie on the floor like dead snakes, left behind and forgotten.

In the hallway the carnage had taken place in, the severed fingers and other pieces of the ghouls that had been separated in the fight began to thaw, quickly becoming nothing more than raw meat and blood.

The group of frozen ghouls, now five strong, continued moving down the hallway, their destination now the multiple voices that could be overheard coming from nearby.

Their ice encrusted mouths opened wide, bits of frost falling to the floor, the cold and the hunger they felt driving them forward towards new prey.

CHAPTER TEN

MARK LEANED BACK in his office chair and rubbed his eyes. He'd been working at his desk for about two hours now and was really feeling the weight of the day catching up to him. Feeling a kink in his neck, he got up from his chair and stretched. After a minute or so, he decided to go down to the cafeteria for a fresh cup of coffee and maybe a light snack.

As he headed out of his office door, he decided he would swing by Sara's office and see if she wanted to accompany him.

When he arrived at her office, he stuck his head inside the room, a slight grin on his lips.

"Hello, anyone in here?" He called from the doorway.

"Back here!" Sara's voice called out from the back of the room.

Mark walked to the back until he came upon a supply closet, where Sara was rifling through some papers on a shelf.

"Hey, there," he said. "I thought you might like to go with me to the cafeteria to grab some coffee."

"Coffee, huh," she said as she mulled the idea over in her head like it was the solution for world hunger. "You know what? Yes, that would be great. I could use a break."

With that said, she pushed the papers back on the shelf and walked out of the closet, shutting the door behind her.

"Shall we?" she inquired with a smile.

"Yes, ma'am, we shall," he grinned back as he held out is elbow to escort her to the cafeteria.

She put her arm in his and together they left the office, looking like a young teen couple on their way to the prom.

They didn't talk much on the way, that awkward silence hanging between the two of them. When the doors to the cafeteria came into view at the end of the hall, Mark was thinking to himself he could really use some kind of an icebreaker to get them talking when they began to hear screaming coming from the other side of the cafeteria door.

"Oh my God," Sara said. "What's going on in there?"

Mark's visage took on a look of puzzlement as he tried to understand what he was hearing.

"I don't know. You stay here and I'll take a look," he told her as he slowly moved to the cafeteria doors.

When he was right in front of the doors, he could hear the screaming and banging coming from inside. Slowly, he pushed the door open to peek inside.

What he imagined he might find when he peered inside the cafeteria paled in comparison to what he actually saw. The visceral tableaux in front of him was worse than any nightmare he could have ever concocted, the grotesque scenario unfolding like something out of the worst, or perhaps best, horror movie he had ever seen.

There was blood everywhere in the large room and the few people that were screaming were either on the floor or on the tables with other people on top of them. To Mark's horror, the people appeared to be getting *eaten*.

As he watched in abject horror, the cashier for the cafeteria climbed on top of one of the researchers, her hands digging inside the researcher's chest. Mark stared in shock when the cashier pulled the man's still beating heart from his chest and began eating it.

Mark looked over to his left and saw a man with more than half his throat ripped out suddenly sit up and crawl over to a woman who was still alive and being held down by two other men who also had similar wounds on their upper bodies.

Mark couldn't believe it when he saw the man with the ripped throat descend on the woman and take a bite out of her left breast like he was eating a piece of chicken. The woman screamed for all she was worth, but no sooner had her scream left her mouth then another man descended on her and began tearing her throat out with his teeth, the arterial spray going straight up like a fountain until the blood ran out of her body.

Mark couldn't see the woman anymore when a swarm of bodies enveloped her, completely covering her from head to toe, their hands clawing at her like wild beasts.

Mark was staring at the carnage in dumb shock, trying to decide if he should go in and help when Saunders jumped out from behind the door, his arms reaching out to grab Mark.

Mark jumped back, startled into action as Saunders stumbled after him into the hallway, leaving the cafeteria door open as he advanced on Mark.

"Mark, what's going on in there, what's wrong with Saunders?" She asked, the panic obvious in her voice.

"Everybody in there's gone absolutely crazy! They're eating each other for Christ sakes!" Mark yelled as he kept backing away from Saunders. "Saunders, man, what's wrong with you?" Mark yelled at him. The man's complexion had taken on an odd, light-blue color, as if the man had splattered his hands and face with blueberries and cream.

Saunders didn't answer, but continued advancing on Mark, his hands reaching out in front of him, the fingers bent at odd angles.

When Mark's back hit the far wall of the hall, he knew he was going to have to fight Saunders.

Mark wasn't a violent man, but had taken boxing in college and knew how to defend himself if he had to. This definitely seemed to be one of those times.

As Saunders got within arms reach of Mark, he swung his right fist into Saunders' jaw. The punch landed dead on and Saunders' head turned with the blow, but other than that, he kept advancing on Mark.

Mark landed two quick jabs into Saunders' chest, but that, too, had little effect on slowing him.

Mark was now out of options and Saunders was within grappling distance. The man lunged at Mark, his jaw open wide as he went for Mark's exposed neck.

Mark was able to get his right hand under Saunders' jaw and keep it barely away from his neck as he used his other arm to repeatedly punch Saunders in the ribs and kidneys. The blows had no effect. He could feel Saunders' breath on his face. What was odd, was instead of his breath being warm, it was ice cold, like someone had opened a refrigerator on a warm summer's day.

Mark could see Sara over Saunders' shoulder and he called to her.

"Sara, get me a weapon, anything, but stay away from the cafeteria!"

Even though she was scared out of her mind, she had enough of her wits left to do as he asked. She dashed back down the hall, looking for something Mark could use as a weapon.

There was nothing around, the hall was bare.

Finally, as she rounded a corner, she came upon a supply closet. Quickly, she opened the door and looked inside for anything she could use to help Mark. Her eyes scanned the small closet in less than a second, and just when she thought she was going to have to move on, her eyes spotted a plunger in the corner.

She debated if she should grab it.

Could you use a plunger as a weapon?

But then she heard Mark's cries from down the hall and knew she was out of options. She reached down and grabbed it and ran as fast as she could back to Mark.

When she returned to Mark, she saw he had Saunders at a distance again and was using his feet to keep Saunders at bay.

Mark looked at her. "Oh, thank God," he said. "Quick, give me what you found. I can't hold this bastard off forever," he breathed, sounding winded.

Sara got as close as she dared and tossed him the plunger, "Here, catch," she called.

Mark reached out and caught it and then just stared at it in between fending off Saunders.

"Are you fucking serious?" He yelled at her. "Just what the hell am I supposed to do with this? Plunge him to death?"

"I'm sorry, Mark, I couldn't find anything else. What do you want me to do?"

He sighed, "Just stay back. At the moment he only seems to want me."

As if to illustrate his point, Saunders took the opportunity to lunge at Mark again.

This time Mark was ready and he hit the man over the head with the plunger.

The rubber end bounced off Saunders' head.

Mark frowned at the result, but what did he expect? He was fighting what appeared to be some kind of zombie with a goddamn plunger for Christ's sake! As Saunders moved in again, Mark took the plunger and jammed it over Saunders' face, now at least keeping him at bay.

Saunders' arms flailed in front of him, but he didn't seem to be able to reason about what to do about the plunger over his face.

Then Mark saw people or cannibals or zombies or whatever they were stumbling out of the cafeteria door. The first one out was the woman he'd seen get her throat ripped out. If he wasn't sure what was going on before, then he definitely knew there was some bad shit going down inside of Amusen Station now.

Others were in a similar state of disrepair. One man had half his face torn off, while another had a massive hole where his chest used to be, the internal organs pulsating like a toy anatomy set. Another woman had both her arms missing, only jagged bone sticking out of the nubs attached to her shoulders.

None of these people should be breathing, let alone walking around and all had what appeared to be acute cases of frostbite, their complexion blue and their edges of their bodies blackened from frostbite, ice crystals building up wherever an orifice existed.

Mark had only seconds to escape the hallway before they would be on him and Sara, so he pulled the plunger off Saunders' face with a sucking sound, and with a skillful twist, spun it around.

When Saunders advanced on him again, he jammed the wooden tip of the plunger handle into his right eye. The point of the plunger shattered the eye like an ice cube and then continued deeper into the man's cranium, piercing the brain and moving forward all the way through brain matter until the handle stopped at the back of the skull.

Saunders swayed for a moment, not understanding he'd just been killed for the second time that day, and then he went down, landing with a crunch as his outstretched arms snapped off when they struck the floor.

Mark didn't have time to admire his handiwork, though. Turning away from his fallen adversary, he grabbed Sara and pulled her after him as he began retreating back down the hall, away from the crowd of what appeared to be mortally wounded people.

"Where're we going?" Sara asked, running behind him, her sneakers slapping the tile floor.

"I have no idea, but right now anywhere is better than here!" He screamed, his eyes searching for anything that might help them in their plight for safety.

Then he picked up more speed and practically dragged her behind him.

They kept running until the sounds of the frozen ghouls faded into the halls behind them.

Chapter Eleven

Private Shawn Michaels was walking down the hall, minding his own business.

He had just been relieved from his duty station and figured he'd grab a bite to eat down in the cafeteria. After he'd eaten, he planned on going to the recreational room to watch some television, when all of a sudden, two people came running around the corner of the hall and plowed right into him.

The three of them tumbled to the floor in a pile of flailing arms and legs.

As Shawn landed under the pile, his breath was squeezed out of him and he whacked his head on the floor.

Before he could react, the man who was now on top of him raised his arm like he was going to strike him. Shawn raised his arms in front of his face and yelled.

"Wait, wait, what the hell did I ever do to you?"

The man hesitated for a fraction of a second and Shawn used the time to get his feet under him and kick the guy off him. He then jumped to his feet so fast he felt a little light-headed. He shook it off and raised his fists in front of him, in the heat of the moment forgetting about the pistol strapped to his waist.

By this time Mark had figured out that Shawn wasn't one of the people going crazy that he'd left behind him and had calmed down a little.

"Shit, I'm so sorry, I thought you were one of those people," Mark said through gasps in his breathing. "I just panicked, you all right?"

"Yeah, I guess so," he said as he glanced over to Sara and reached a hand down to help her up. "Dr. Edwards, right?"

"Why, yes, it is, do I know you?"

"No, ma'am, I don't think so, but I've seen you around the station, that's all," he said to her while his face turned a little red from blushing. "Are you okay?"

"I think so," she said while checking herself over. She found she had scraped her elbow when she'd fallen, but other than that seemed to be fine.

"Come on, Sara, we've got to keep going," Mark told her as he began to walk down the hallway again.

"Wait, what's going on? What was it you just said about *those people?* What are you talking about?"

"You don't know?" Sara asked him.

"Know about what? Look, sir and ma'am, but with all do respect, what the fuck is going on?"

Mark was just about to attempt to explain when the three of them heard muffled voices, and the sound of people moving from down the hallway Mark and Sara had just vacated.

"Oh, shit, they're coming," Mark said as he began backing up again.

"Who's coming?" Shawn asked, wondering if these two people in front of him had somehow gone crazy.

"Them!" Was all Mark said as he pointed behind him.

Shawn turned around and just about had a heart attack. He couldn't believe what he was seeing. It was like a bad horror movie.

The hallway was jammed with people who were trying to get through, but they kept getting tangled in each others arms and legs. When one would fall the others would simply walk over him or her.

The most horrifying thing to Shawn was the way they looked. Necks were ripped open and chests were spread wide with gaping wounds, ribs and bones protruding at odd angles. Parts of them were hanging out and falling to the floor where they would get kicked around by shuffling feet.

But the thing that really got him was when he saw familiar faces mixed in with the group of frozen walking dead. One of them was one of his buddies from his squad, except the man's head was hanging on by his spine and a few threads of skin still left from the almost completely severed neck. The man's head would swing back and forth as his body would take another shuffling step forward.

"Don't just stand there!" Mark yelled. "You've got a gun, shoot the bastards or they're gonna rip us all to shreds!"

Shawn fumbled with his gun and got it out of its holster. Then he brought it up and aimed it at the first ghoul in line. He lined up the head and squeezed the trigger, but nothing happened.

He tried again, but still, nothing.

Then he realized in his haste he'd forgotten to take off the safety. He flicked the switch on the side of the weapon and then brought it back up to try again.

This time when he squeezed the trigger, the gun bucked in his hand and a bullet went flying into the crowd. Shawn didn't even see where it had gone, as he had already turned his aim slightly and shot another round as the group of undead got within reaching distance of him.

The bullet entered the chest of a ghoul and blew a fist-sized hole out its back, the exit wound spraying the ones behind it with frozen gore. The ghoul just leaned back a little as the momentum of the bullet pushed it back, but then regained its balance and continued to keep walking forward, now only inches from Shawn.

"Forget it, there's too damn many of them!" Mark yelled from behind him.

"Come with us, we're going to try to find someplace safe to hide!" Sara called to him.

At the moment, with a crowd of walking corpses ready to overwhelm him, that sounded like a damn good idea.

So he started backing up, and when he turned to run away, he could see the backs of Mark and Sara already halfway down the hall. He took another quick look over his shoulder at the monstrosities behind him and then took off after them.

He ran like the minions of Hell were after him and he had know idea that wasn't far from the truth.

Chapter Twelve

M ARK, SARA, AND Shawn dashed down the hallways, not really knowing where they were going. During their escape, they stopped other people in the halls and tried to explain what was happening, but no one believed them.

The people would just laugh at them and tell them how funny they were and then continue on up the hallway, blindly walking to their death.

"What's wrong with these people?" Shawn asked as they jogged down the latest corridor. "Why don't they believe us?"

"Would you believe us if you hadn't seen it happen with your own eyes?" Mark asked as he stopped to try another door they came upon.

"I see your point," Shawn replied back.

They could hear the sounds of screaming coming from behind them now.

"Look's like those bastards found them," Sara said, referring to some of the people they had warned.

"Not our problem, we tried, that's all we can do," Mark said.

"Do you have any kind of a plan to what we should do now?" Shawn asked.

"Hell, no, I've just been making it up as I go," Mark retorted.

"Well, I think we need to get out of this station, maybe try to get to the coast. If we could make it to another outpost, then we should be able to get someone to listen to us," Sara suggested.

"Only one problem, there's a really bad storm going on outside. If we left now, we wouldn't make it two hundred feet before we were buried up to our armpits in snow," Mark answered back. "Even the trucks wouldn't last too long out there. No, we need to go to ground and wait out the storm, then either we can try to get out on our own or help should come for us."

"Great, but where do we go?" Shawn asked as he paused to look over his shoulder. For now it was clear, luckily the dead didn't seem to move that fast.

As they continued running, they soon found themselves at the end of the station.

The only way out from where they were now was the double doors for the generator building and another door that basically looped them back to the cafeteria.

Mark stopped when they reached the double doors. He was bent over with his hands on his knees, trying to catch his breath.

"Shit, it's a goddamn dead end, we're trapped," Shawn said as he paced around in a circle. Looking like a caged animal.

"He's right, Mark, where do we go from here?" Sara asked with a worried look on her face.

Mark put his hand up in a stopping motion. "All right, all right, wait a minute. Just give me a second to think, please." He looked around, trying to figure out their next move when it came to him.

"What about the generator building?" He suggested, "It's got only one way in or out and it's heated thanks to the ducts for the exhaust for the generator."

"But what about the windows? Couldn't those people just get at us from outside?"

"No, of course not," Mark said. "If those people really are dead, however unlikely that may be, then it would be reasonable to assume that if they went outside they would freeze up and become immobile."

"Make's sense," Shawn said from the corner. He'd been staking out the hallway so that nothing would sneak up on them. "I say we go for it. I know I can't think of anything better."

"Agreed," Sara replied. "We should try to get any food and water we can find before we go over there. There's no telling how long that storm could last."

"You two go, I'll stay here and keep an eye on the hallway. I'll yell if I hear anything," Shawn said as he fingered his handgun."

Mark and Sara both nodded and took off to the nearest offices and rooms to see what they could find.

Shawn stood watch alone and the ominous quiet was a little overwhelming. He leaned against the wall with his gun in his hand, his ears straining to hear anything that shouldn't be there. Every time the wind howled and snow and ice struck the building, he jumped.

Now with a respite in the action of the past twenty minutes, he had a chance to digest what had just happened to him.

He had been going to get some supper and had been plowed over and then saved by two scientists who had stopped him in the nick of time from becoming a meal for what sure as hell looked like a crowd of zombies. He shook his head from side to side. Real life honest to God zombies.

He felt like a character in one of those horror movies he used to watch in high school. He thought about that for a moment, in those movies, the good guys always shot the zombies in the head. Well, if he had another chance, he'd try that out. What the hell, it couldn't hurt.

His ruminating was cut short when he heard definite sounds coming from down the hall.

The same shuffling and moaning was a dead giveaway as to who it was.

"Shit," he muttered as he ran back to the intersection where Mark and Sara had gone.

"Guys, we're gonna have company real soon! Please hurry the hell up!" He called down the hallway.

Then he saw Mark stick his head out of a side doorway.

"Just another minute, Shawn. I found some stuff we could really use."

"Look, man, if it was up to me you could take all the time you wanted, but those people are gonna be on us in a few seconds!" He yelled back.

"Understood, I'll be right there." With that Mark's head disappeared from the doorway.

Moments later, Sara showed up with a piece of carpet slung over her shoulder.

"I found some food and water and would you believe I found a gun, too?" She smiled at Shawn, pleased with herself.

"That's great, but if your boyfriend doesn't hurry up, we're all gonna be dead meat," he said as he went down the hall to look for Mark.

"He's not my boyfriend!" Sara yelled down the hallway to Shawn's back.

Shawn arrived at the doorway he'd seen Mark at and was about to go in when Mark came running out and almost knocked Shawn over.

"Whoa, man, once is enough for one day," Shawn said skipping out of the way.

"Come on, man, we've got no time left, we've got to move now or it's not gonna matter anymore," Shawn said as he grabbed Mark's arm.

Mark didn't argue and the two of them ran toward the doors for the generator room. Mark was falling behind due to the box he was carrying.

By the time they made it to the double doors, the first ghouls were coming into view.

Shawn had his pistol ready, but didn't want to use it unless he had no choice as he didn't have extra ammunition on him.

Sara ran to the doors and opened them up, frantically waving for Mark to hurry. Mark almost duck-walked due to the weight of the box in his hands, but he eventually made it to the doors, as well.

Shawn was backing up, trying to keep the ghouls in his sights as he kept edging closer to the doors. Finally, he felt Sara's hand on his shoulder and knew he'd made it. Just before they were inside the doors, the first ghoul lunged at him. He pushed it away and the zombie lost its footing and fell to the ground, but then began crawling towards him. Shawn decided it would be quicker to dispose of this one with a bullet than to keep trying to fend it off with his hands, so he aimed his gun and put one straight through the back of the ghoul's head.

The skull exploded, spraying frozen bits of brain and bone over the floor. As the frozen bits of meat slid across the floor, they slowly began to melt once they came in contact with the warm floor, leaving a trail of gore to mark the passage.

With the ghoul now down, Shawn jumped through the double doors. As he went through the opening, Mark and Sara were ready and slammed the doors shut after him.

Mark grabbed an old mop handle that had been lying against the wall with a few other pieces of janitorial supplies and jammed it through the door handles, making a temporary lock.

"Come on, that's not going to hold them for long. Once we're through the main doors for the generator room we should be able to keep them out," Mark said as he wiped his hands on his pants.

Mark picked his box up, and together the three of them headed down the small hallway to the generator room, and hopefully, safety.

Outside the station, the storm continued to hurl its fury at the lone structure in the middle of nowhere.

CHAPTER THIRTEEN

AS THE THREE survivors dashed down the hallway, the ghouls arrived at the double doors. The first ones in line immediately began banging on the doors, but soon stopped when the pressure from those behind started to crush them against the doors. Within minutes, the weight of the bodies was enough to snap one of the handles off of the door and the mop stick went skidding across the stone floor.

As the mass of bodies flowed into the hall, some of them stopped at a set of doors that led to the outside. When one of them leaned on the push handle on the door, it popped open a little, but stopped due to the snow that had piled up outside the frame. Immediately other ghouls wandered over to the door as the wind blew into the hallway. The cold snow that flew in through the crack in the door revitalized them. The same chemical that had raised them from the dead also needed cold to thrive. The mass of bodies now began pushing on the door and soon had it open enough for them to squeeze through. One at a time they exited the building and went into the frigid temperatures the storm had brought with it.

The cold revitalized them further as they walked deeper into the storm. Some of them fell over in the snow and were soon covered by snow drifts, while others wandered around the station. While the cold felt good on their soon to be rotting flesh, the hunger still screamed inside of them. The frozen creations of death now roamed outside the station looking for prey to feed on.

Others continued to follow the three survivors and were stopped quickly when they reached the end of the hall, another set of doors barring their way. Unlike the first set of doors, this one was made of sturdier stuff and would not so easily be broken down. Still, in the limited capacity to reason, they knew food was on the other side, so they continued to pound on it, and once again the ghouls in the front became crushed as the ghouls in the back attempted to push their way through.

The frozen ghouls were patient, however. They didn't sleep and were tireless. Sooner or later they would accomplish their goal.

One way or another.

Chapter Fourteen

DR. FREDERICKS' MOOD had changed drastically after he had left the corpse in the morgue. By the time he'd made it back to his lab, his positive outlook on things had changed as the failed experiment sunk in.

The corpse on the table kept haunting him.

"Damn, it should have worked," he muttered under his breath.

For over two years of his life he had worked to fulfill his dream and once again his hopes had been smashed. When he arrived at his lab, he had grabbed a chair and rolled it over to the cages.

Sitting down, he'd stared at the snake and lizard, his only real successes, for what seemed like hours as he sunk deeper into the depths of self pity.

Why didn't it work? Surely something should have happened.

He was snapped out of his revelry by the sound of crashing coming from the hallway outside his lab door.

"Simpson, where are you!" he yelled and then waited impatiently for an answer.

"Right here, Dr. Fredericks, I was organizing your files in the back room," Mathew Simpson said, the man who had the misfortune of being Dr. Fredericks' lab assistant for the next month and a half. All the assistants took turns assisting Fredericks and unfortunately it had been his turn. Fredericks had a reputation of being an overbearing ass. When Simpson had seen Fredericks come into the lab with a sour face, he knew it would be a good time to become scarce, so he'd gone into back of the lab to shuffle some files for a while. At least until he had been summoned by Professor Asshole.

"What can I do for you, sir?" Simpson asked politely, even though it made him cringe inside.

"Go see what all the noise is about out in the hall, it's disturbing me," he ordered him with a wave of his arm, like a king dismissing his subject. He then turned his back on Simpson and continued studying the animals.

"Yes, sir, I'll get right on it," Simpson said while flipping the back of Fredericks' head off with his middle finger.

He then went out into the hall to tell whatever jackass was out there to shut the fuck up, his majesty was contemplating the meaning of the universe.

As he entered the hallway, he couldn't see the duty desk as it was around the corner, but he could hear all the noise.

Then a gun cracked, the bullet coming so close to his head he swore he felt its passage. He immediately flattened himself against the wall, and though his instinct was to run, his curiosity had a better hold on him and he slowly began inching his way down the hall. There didn't seem to be anymore gunfire so he figured it should be safe.

Slowly he crept to the end of the wall and then peeked around the corner.

His jaw dropped when he saw the strange tableaux in front of him.

The desk guard was spread out on the desk with his head hanging over the side.

There were three men in red-stained, white lab coats standing over him. One had his face buried in the guard's neck as he ripped it to pieces while the other two were leaning over his torso. The guard's chest was ripped open, and as Simpson watched, one of them was pulling out organs while the other one pulled out intestines like a clown pulling a trick hanky from his sleeve.

But when the man began eating them, well, that was when Simpson lost it. He bent over and vomited the contents of his stomach all over his shoes.

With Simpson dry heaving in the small hallway a couple of feet from the ghouls, it didn't take long for them to notice him. In perfect synchronization, the two ghouls who had been working on the guard's chest stopped and moved towards Simpson.

The one who was eating the intestines still had them in his hands, and as he got further away, the intestines played out behind him like some kind of bloody rope, dripping gore all over the floor. As the two ghouls approached him, he could see the damage their bodies had sustained somehow. One had the entire front of his throat ripped out while the other one was missing half his face, the socket for his left eyeball nothing but a ghastly red hole. There was no way in this world the two men could still be alive which could only mean one thing, as far-fetched as it sounded.

That was enough for Simpson.

He quickly began backing up to get away from the shambling trio and then ran all the way back to the lab. Upon entering the lab, he saw Fredericks was still sitting near the cages. He ran over to him, not even knowing where to begin in describing what he'd been witness to.

"What's the matter man? Speak up," Fredericks snarled, disturbed by the interruption.

That's when Simpson lost it. He leaned down and grabbed Fredericks by the shoulders so that he had to look him directly in the eyes and shook him violently.

"Wake the fuck up, you stupid piece of shit, there are dead people walking outside in the goddamn hallway. We have to get the hell out of here, right now!"

Fredericks just looked at him, assuming the man had somehow gone mad between the few moments from when he'd left to his rather loud return.

"What the hell are you talking about, Simpson? Dead people? That's ridiculous."

With that said, Fredericks stood up from his chair so as to be on eye level with Simpson. Before either one of them could say another word, though, the two ghouls had made it to the door and had started to enter the lab.

"Shit, they're here!" Simpson yelled as he ran behind a desk to try and stay away from the two attacking zombies.

Fredericks actually kept a level head as he immediately discerned what was going on around him and took the appropriate steps. Quickly, he scanned the room for a weapon, his eyes falling on the cage behind him.

Carefully, he reached inside the cage, grabbed the snake behind its head and took the four foot python out of its cage. When one of the ghouls was close enough, he threw the snake at the dead man. The snake hit the man in the chest and knocked him backwards. The snake immediately began wrapping its coils around the dead man's torso, squeezing tighter with each second.

The ghoul tried to take a bite out of the snake, but his teeth just bounced off the frozen scales. The snake continued to squeeze ineffectually as the ghoul didn't need to breathe. The two continued to wrestle on the floor, but Fredericks ignored them. For now, that ghoul was out of the fight.

The second one had its eye on Simpson and was trying to reach him from across the desk the lab assistant was hiding behind. While the ghoul couldn't get him, neither could Simpson get away; thus a stalemate.

Then, two more ghouls came stumbling into the lab, both of them heading straight for Fredericks.

Fredericks backed away, trying to figure a way around them. He took the chair he had previously occupied and slid it across the floor as hard as he could.

One of the ghoul's legs got tangled up in the chair and went crashing to the floor. Fredericks watched with renewed interest as the zombie's outstretched arm snapped off at the elbow and pieces of frozen flesh sprinkled across the floor.

The other ghoul ignored its brethren and continued advancing on Fredericks.

As Fredericks backed against the wall, his hand brushed against the fire extinguisher mounted there. He turned around and pulled it from the wall just as the ghoul was upon him. Panicking, he swung away as hard as he could and broke the ghoul's grip on him. Then he raised the extinguisher and sprayed it into the zombie's face.

The frozen dead man sputtered as the foam filled his nose, mouth and covered his eyes. Blinded, he began swinging his arms wildly, not understanding what had happened to him.

Fredericks took this opportunity to get behind the man, and then he brought the extinguisher down on top of the ghoul's head.

But instead of the skull caving in as Fredericks expected, it shattered into a hundred frozen slivers. The pieces rained down onto the floor where the frozen brain matter quickly began to melt, leaving the floor a slippery mess of ice and blood.

Fredericks slipped and slid his way around the mess and was about to leave the room when he caught Simpson in the corner still fending off his attacker.

He was about to go help when he saw the other ghoul had wrestled free of the snake and was now also advancing on Simpson. Fredericks weighed his options and decided to save his own ass instead of helping Simpson and headed for the door.

"Fredericks wait! Where the hell are you going? Help me, for Christ sakes!" Simpson pleaded.

Fredericks just shrugged sorry and ran out of the room.

While he was leaving, the other ghoul had gone around the desk and the two of them now had Simpson in the middle. Simpson made a last ditch effort to try and jump over the desk, but was grabbed by the ankle and yanked back.

Simpson barely felt the ice cold teeth when they ripped into his flesh, the rage he felt for Fredericks abandoning him overwhelming any other thoughts as to what was happening to him.

"You bastard!" He screamed at the top of his lungs. "You bastard! I hope you rot in Hell, so help me God I'll get you for this, I'll...."

His last words were cut off when his jugular was torn out and the blood flooded into his throat. His last living thoughts were of finding Fredericks and killing the bastard. Then the darkness overtook him and he thought no more.

Fredericks heard Simpson's yelling cease abruptly as he dashed down the hallway. He decided he needed to try to find help, or if necessary, figure out a way out of the station.

But as he continued running down the hall, a smile crossed his lips.

Whatever was happening in the station may be impossible, but in the end he knew he would survive.

Anything else would simply be unthinkable.

CHAPTER FIFTEEN

MARK, SARA AND Shawn ran through the door at the end of the hallway with a sigh of gratitude. Once through the doorway, Mark slammed it and then locked the deadbolt, sealing them inside, but also keeping their frozen attackers out.

For now, at least, that seemed like a fair tradeoff.

The three of them collapsed onto the floor, as each tried to catch their breath.

Slowly, in time, their heart rates went down and it became easier to talk.

"Holy shit," Shawn gasped. "I can't believe we're still alive."

"Believe it, Shawn, and we're gonna stay that way, too," Mark told him.

Sara took a moment to look around the room they were now trapped in. The room was about forty feet by forty feet with the generator in the middle. Wan light streamed through the frosted windows on both sides of them, thin rays of light crisscrossing where the windows were more ice free. The exhaust for the generator went up at an angle and then exited through a hole in the side of the building near the roof. There were some old rags and cleaning fluids near the corner where an old desk sat, and she assumed that was probably where the engineer would write up his maintenance log as he maintained the generator.

When she stood up and began to walk around a little, she could hear her boots echoing off the walls. She hugged herself, the reality of their situation sinking in.

Mark walked over to her and put his arm around her.

"Hey, you all right?" he asked softly.

"No, not really, but thanks for asking," she said as she looked into his eyes and smiled.

He gave her shoulder a gentle squeeze and smiled back.

"Come on, let's go through the stuff we grabbed and see how we're set for a while."

She nodded and together they walked back to Shawn.

Shawn had already been busy at work unloading the box Mark had brought in with them. Mark and Sara joined in, and after a few minutes of doing inventory, everything was spread out on the floor. Sara then opened the sack she had brought with her and the three of them did a proper count of what they had managed to scavenge in the limited time before being attacked.

Mark had done the best for food. He'd found a desk drawer full of snack foods and candy from someone's office, the owner obviously having a sweet tooth. He had also grabbed a leftover sandwich and a half full bottle of water from a small, college dorm room refrigerator. There were also miscellaneous items like pens and a stapler.

"Why'd you grab a stapler?" Shawn asked curiously.

"I don't know, really. I was just grabbing whatever I could find, as fast as I could."

Sara held up the best find of everything they had retrieved.

"At least I found this," she said with pride in her voice. Shawn reached out his hand to receive it.

"May I?" He asked her.

She handed him the .22 caliber handgun she'd found in the coat pocket of a jacket in one of the offices she'd ransacked. When she had seen the jacket, she had immediately added it to her pile of pilfered items.

Shawn popped the clip and counted the bullets.

"Not bad," he said. "Almost full." He punctuated his sentence by sliding the clip back in with a click.

"How many bullets do you have left in your gun?" Mark asked Shawn as he pointed to the gun on his hip.

Shawn pulled it out of his holster and checked the clip, he didn't even remember how many times he'd shot his gun, but it looked like he had about half a clip left, as well. He pushed it back in and slid the gun back into its holster.

"Half a clip," he said. "So, what do we do now?" He asked as he gazed up at the frosted windows.

"Now we wait," was Mark's answer as he stood up and walked over to the generator to inspect it.

"But for how long will that be for?" Sara asked while she followed him.

He frowned as if he was giving her question some thought.

"Unfortunately, I have no idea, for as long as it takes I guess."

It wasn't much of an answer, but they all knew it would have to do for now.

As they got to work getting their safe house organized, none of them noticed the shadows floating across the frosted window panes, or the sound of multiple footfalls crunching in the snow and ice, each step lost in the howling maelstrom of the storm.

CHAPTER SIXTEEN

THE HALF TRACK rolled over the snow as the wind howled around it. The two soldiers in the front seat were anxious to get back to Amusen Station. They had spent too long on patrol and had been caught by the storm.

The driver just hoped the vehicle would make it before the snow did them in.

They'd heard what had happened to the other patrol earlier that morning and didn't want to be two more casualties.

"Hey, Bobby, how much farther do you think we are from getting back to base?"

The soldier in the passenger seat inquired.

The driver squinted through the snow that had built up on the windshield. The wipers just couldn't handle the amount of snow and ice that had already accumulated from the last time he'd scraped the windshield. The defrost was going full blast and could barely keep the window from frosting over.

Private Bobby P. Boone looked at the soldier sitting next to him.

"Jesus Christ, Tommy, how the hell should I know? I can't see shit out there, with all that goddamn snow on the windshield. In another minute you're going to have to go outside and scrape it off again."

"Christ, again? These damn trucks were not meant to be in the fuckin' snow. I'd love to get my hands on the asshole who thought it would be a good idea to put skis on half-tracks and send them to Antarctica."

"Yeah, well, you're still going out there in a minute."

Tommy swore under his breath again. Join the army, see the world, they told him. So far all he'd seen is boot camp and a whole lot of snow. For the hundredth time in the past six months, he wondered what the hell he'd been thinking when he decided to join the Army.

Suddenly, the vehicle came to a stop.

Bobby looked at him and said: "That's it, man, I can't see shit. It's time for you to clean the windshield again. Come on, the sooner you do it the sooner you'll be back inside again and we'll get back to the base. The station can't be too much further away."

Tommy hesitated for a moment, swore again, and then began putting his hat and gloves on to go outside.

When he opened the door to the vehicle, the door immediately flew out of his grip and slammed into the side of the half-track. Bobby was behind him, yelling at him to shut the door, but his voice was lost in the howling of the wind.

He was immediately coated in a thin coating of ice and snow as he managed to shut the door and climb out on the hood. Visibility was no more than a few feet in front of him as he leaned over the hood and began scraping the windshield.

As he was scraping away, he thought he saw movement out of the corner of his eye, but shrugged it off as a trick of the storm. Nothing alive could be out in this storm. As he finished scraping and prepared to go back inside, he saw movement yet again, and when he looked harder this time, he could make out what looked like a man walking around in the storm.

He jumped down and walked a few feet to where he thought the figure was.

It was hard to see anything as the wind whipped by his face and the ice crystals in the snow kept stinging him and getting in his eyes. He was just about to give up and crack it up to some kind of mirage when a man came into view and began walking towards him.

Tommy couldn't believe what he was seeing. This man didn't even have a jacket on, and it had to be at least minus five below out here. He walked over to the man to see if he needed help, but before he went two steps the snow drifts around him exploded, pelting him with clumps of snow. He turned his face away from the brunt of the impact, and when he cleared his eyes, he saw what looked like people coming out of the snow drifts.

They had surrounded him and had blocked off his retreat back to the half-track. He tried yelling to Bobby, but his voice was lost on the wind. As the people in front of him got closer, he could see something definitely wasn't right about them. From head to toe they were covered in icicles. There skin was a faded blue color due to the frigid temperature it was exposed to. And their faces were slack-jawed and dead like they weren't really focused on what they were doing.

Tommy took all this in at a glance and immediately pulled his gun from his holster to defend himself. Unfortunately, the bulky gloves he had on did not facilitate this maneuver, and no sooner did he have his weapon out, than it fell from his gloved hand and into the snow. Quickly, he ripped off his glove and retrieved his weapon, the frigid air already numbing his hand. Now in a state of panic, he didn't think about whom these people could be; he was scared and he felt threatened. So he aimed his weapon at the nut job with no jacket and fired point blank into the guy's chest. The bullet went in and out without doing much damage to the frozen corpse. A small hole was now in its chest that you could bend over and look through if the weather allowed it. Tommy fired again and again without doing much damage to any of them. When he ran out of bullets, he tried to run, but it was too late.

He was now completely surrounded and when the first one got too close, he threw a punch at the face, connecting with the nose. The nose shattered and pieces dropped to the snow-covered ground, quickly becoming lost in the ice. The ghoul's face now had a hollow place on its visage where its nose used to be, and as Tommy watched dumbstruck, the ghoul advanced on him with its arms out and mouth open wide so it could bare its teeth.

As the other frozen zombies converged on him, he kicked and screamed to no avail, and he shrieked in terror when cold fingers ripped his jacket off and then proceeded to the warm flesh beneath.

He screamed for help with everything he had, but the noise of the storm continued to override his voice. As the frozen corpses began ripping into his trembling flesh, he could feel the cold from the storm penetrating into his very soul. Cold fingers had a piece of him from every angle and he screamed one last time as he was literally drawn and quartered by all the hands pulling on him. As pieces of him went off in different directions, he had just enough blood and oxygen in his brain to feel his head being separated from his shoulders.

As his head was held aloft over his dismembered body, his last thought was why he didn't get sent to Iraq; it probably would have been safer.

Then the darkness overcame him and he knew no more.

Bobby was waiting patiently in the truck for Tommy to come back in and was getting pissed off. What could be taking him so long? A few seconds ago he thought he'd heard something, but it was probably just the storm. So he sat and waited, because frankly, he didn't want to go outside if he didn't have to.

After a few more minutes had passed and still no Tommy, he decided he had no choice. So he bundled himself up and jumped out of the cab of the half-track. The freezing temperatures hit him immediately, sapping his body's warmth. He walked around the vehicle, but there didn't seem to be any sign of Tommy. He yelled his name, but it didn't carry far thanks to the storm.

He was about to give up when he caught a glimpse of a shadow about six feet high off to his right.

He started walking over to it, and as he got closer, he could see it was Tommy.

What the hell was he doing behind that snow drift? If he was trying to take a piss, he'd be lucky if his dick didn't fall off from frostbite. Bobby was going to tell him that exact thing when he reached him, until he got within a few feet of Tommy.

Bobby knew something was off when he yelled to his buddy and Tommy didn't respond.

He walked up to him and slapped him on the side of the head to get his attention, but to his shock, the head fell off the snow dune it had been sitting on and rolled down to stop by his feet.

Tommy's dead face stared up at him with frozen features that were locked at the time of death. As Bobby squinted through the snow at Tommy's frozen visage, he could tell Tommy didn't die well. He began retreating to the half-track, knowing there was some bad shit going down, when he bumped into something behind him. He turned around and stared directly at a man with no nose.

Bobby let out a yell and jumped back, right into the arms of another ghoul who had come up from behind. The arms wrapped around him and before he could break free, **No Nose** leaned down and chomped right onto Bobby's nose. Cold teeth sank into the warm cartilage, and with a few tugs, the ghoul managed to rip Bobby's nose from his face. Bobby screamed from the pain as the blood from his nose poured down into his mouth, choking him, freezing almost instantly. Before he could let out another scream, another ghoul had crawled up to his legs and took a bite out of one of his calves. Its teeth ripped through cloth and took a piece of meat from his leg, the flesh stretching like old, elastic rubber bands. Pain shot through his leg and he kicked out, connecting with the ghoul's face. His boot sank up to the shin, the frozen face shattering from the blow. Only one eye remained on the ghoul's face, the lower half now gone. Still it continued to try and bite Bobby even though it had no mouth. Bobby was just about to break free when the ghoul who had wrapped him in its arms leaned down and ripped a large piece of meat from the back of his neck, tearing through his heavy sweater like it was paper. He screamed and blew blood all over his attackers as he tried to fight his way free. Then more zombies came out of the snow banks and swarmed over him and the other ghouls holding him.

In seconds, he was lost within a white sea of arms, legs and teeth as they continued to bite and rip at him.

In all the chaos, he was able to crawl out from under the pile of snarling corpses and he kept crawling as he managed to slink away foot by foot. Within a matter of seconds, he was lost from sight from the area of the carnage and still he crawled. His strength was slowly fading from his wounds and the freezing temperatures, but he continued to drag himself along.

Escaping from those monstrosities was his only goal, and when he could go no further, he stopped to rest. He didn't want to, knowing he needed to keep moving, but he was so cold and tired. If he could just close his eyes for a few minutes, he thought he'd be fine, and then he could get up and somehow get back to the half-track and escape. His eyes began drooping, even though he wanted to fight it.

A break in the storm lifted the white-out conditions for a hairsbreadth of time.

In the time before he succumbed to the hypothermia now claiming his body, the path in front of him was clear. As the darkness claimed him, the last thing he saw was Amusen Station, the front doors no more than ten feet away from where his body now lay.

Then he closed his eyes forever.

However, forever wasn't that long and within minutes, he stood up and went to join his brethren, the cold now feeling good on his dead skin; invigorating him.

And now he was hungry.

CHAPTER SEVENTEEN

WHILE FREDERICKS RAN down the hallway, screaming could be heard coming from every direction. He moved without purpose, not really knowing where to go.

As he turned a corner in the hall, he came face to face with a group of ghouls only a few feet away, and realized the hallways had become deathtraps.

The infected people were everywhere.

Quickly backing up and running the way he'd come, he ended up back at his lab again. Although this time it was quiet, as the ghouls that had attacked Simpson had apparently moved on.

Fredericks looked down at the desk where Simpson had been when he'd escaped from the lab. Simpson's blood covered the entire area, but the man himself was absent.

Warily, Fredericks crept further into the lab, waiting for something to jump out at him at any moment, but after a few more agonizing minutes, he deduced he was safe. At least for the moment, anyway.

He dashed to the back of his lab and quickly rifled through his desk, retrieving anything he thought would be relevant to his work. Then he retrieved a knapsack that some intern had left behind at some time in the recent past. He quickly loaded it full of his research and also retrieved the other samples of his cold serum.

Maybe the antidote would be found inside one of his vials?

When he had finished packing everything he thought he would need, he was halted by the sound of a table being knocked over in front in the lab.

He quietly crawled out to sneak a peek and was quite surprised to see Simpson stumbling around the lab. Although Fredericks had to admit Simpson had seen better days.

The man's throat was utterly torn apart, to the point where if Fredericks really looked close, he could just make out Simpson's spinal cord through the hole in his neck.

Simpson was trashing the lab as if he was searching for something. Fredericks wondered if Simpson could be searching for him. Especially when he thought back to the last words Simpson had yelled to him.

That thought sent a shiver up Fredericks' back as he backed away and then returned to his desk.

His eyes scanned the room for a way out. He couldn't die here, he thought, he was way to important. No, he had to make it out. There had to be a way.

The noise from the lab was getting louder as he heard more footsteps become audible over the din taking place out front. And when he snuck another peek, he saw more ghouls shamble into the lab from the hallway.

Despite himself, he started to breathe faster as panic began to set in.

Then his eyes spotted a handle on the floor off to the side of his desk. He looked at it with curiosity, as if he had never noticed it before, but then he'd never had to escape from the back of his lab before, either.

Without a seconds hesitation, he moved over to the hatch and tried to pry it up, but try as he might, it wouldn't budge. Then he realized his desk was also on top of it and quickly pushed it off the hatch.

He cringed when the desk made a scraping noise across the floor, but it seemed his luck was holding as none of the ghouls in the front of the lab came to the back.

He pulled on the handle one more time, and with the squeaking of unused hinges, the hatch opened.

At the same time the hinges screeched their protest at being opened to the world, the noise out front paused for a fraction of a second. Then Fredericks could hear the shambling footfalls of a crowd of ghouls coming to the back of the lab.

As fast as he could manage, he dropped his feet over the edge and prepared to climb down into the blackness below him.

Warm air wafted up from below his swinging feet as he stared into the pit below him. The light of the lab wasn't strong enough to pierce the darkness below, so he was just going to have to hope he wouldn't fall too far and end up breaking a leg, or something worse.

At the precise moment he was climbing down into the hatch, a horde of ghouls arrived from around the far corner and began spilling into the room.

Fredericks let go of the edge of the hatch, but when he slipped into the dark beyond, a frozen hand latched onto his lab coat and halted his progress. For a few precious seconds, Fredericks dangled over the abyss he was imagining was below his swinging feet until the ghoul tried to pull him back up.

His arms started flailing in the air, trying to find anything to halt his upward ascent.

Then his hands struck the rungs of a ladder that began a few feet below the hatch. Frantically he latched on with his right hand and he felt a jarring when his upward progress was temporarily stopped. But he was still being pulled back up, although now at a slower pace than before. He was just able to turn his head around and look above him to see the hatch opening surrounded by frozen, pale-blue faces of death. As he was slowly brought closer to the opening, despite his grip on the ladder rungs, his mind frantically searched for a way out of what appeared to be certain death.

Just when his head was ready to emerge up into the light again, and as he was closing his eyes in expectation of the pain he was about to receive from the ghoul's hungry jaws, he was shocked to hear a ripping sound and then was suddenly jolted from the ghoul's grip as his lab coat ripped at the seam where the arm and shoulder met. Unknown to him, this same tear was the one he had picked up upon entering the room of the dead soldier.

Fredericks felt weightless for a second as his body fell through the air and then he felt a jarring halt when his feet struck the concrete of the tunnel floor.

Quickly, he gazed up and realized he hadn't fallen more than five or six feet. The ghouls milled around the opening, wondering how to climb down and retrieve their lost meat. Then one of the ghoul's feet slipped into the hatch opening and it plummeted to the tunnel floor. Fredericks quickly sidestepped the falling body so as not to get crushed.

The ghoul tumbled down the shaft, its legs catching on the rungs and flipping it around so that the body struck the concrete head first.

When its skull connected with the ground, it exploded into a thousand tiny fragments of bone, brains, and ice, temporarily spraying the inside of the tunnel walls. Fredericks raised his arms in front of his face and turned away to shield himself from the crimson spray.

After a moment passed, he was able to turn and see the now shattered corpse all over the tunnel floor. On a closer look, he could see the body had shattered, too, nothing but its clothes keeping the pieces from spraying the tunnel.

In the warm air of the dank tunnel, the frozen pieces quickly began to melt, leaving blood and gore everywhere. As the corpse began to thaw, the distinct smell of death began to permeate the atmosphere of the tunnel. Fredericks repositioned his knapsack, making sure his serum bottles were safe and then turned to begin the exploration of his escape route.

As he turned and began walking, he looked back up at the hatch. The ghouls were still milling about the opening, but were more wary of the hole now.

Before the opening of the hatch was lost from sight, Fredericks looked up and saw Simpson staring back at him.

Simpson turned his head up and screamed with rage at the ceiling and then reached out and slammed the hatch shut with a loud clang that echoed throughout the tunnel, reverberating off the walls like a giant drum.

Fredericks stood there for a moment, staring at the square ring of light that defined the hatch's edges, wondering about what he'd just seen. It was almost as if Simpson had known who he was and had been reasoning, even though these infected people appeared to have no real intelligent thought other than for a need to kill.

As he started down the tunnel, he thought more about it, his mind already trying to figure out a way to manipulate this information to his own gain.

The tunnel stretched out before him, blacker than the darkest night, only a few small, red emergency lights to show him the way, the lights resembling small scarlet eyes floating in the darkness.

Fredericks continued onward, not knowing where he was going, but knowing it had to be better than where he'd come from.

Soon, he was swallowed by the shadows, only his footsteps remaining as they echoed of the walls, small footsteps dwarfed by the artificial night.

CHAPTER EIGHTEEN

THE THREE COMPANIONS lay in the dark room listening to the hum of the generator and the banging coming from the door leading to the hallway.

The ghouls never stopped, never slowed, the banging continued hour after hour.

At first it had been hard on the nerves for the three trapped survivors, but as day turned into night and the noise continued, they slowly adjusted to it.

The generator room door was made of solid metal and was holding just fine. Knowing for the moment, at least, that they were safe, helped to ease the trepidation and worry they were feeling.

Finally, in the late hours of the night, they all drifted off into restless sleep.

Sara began dreaming almost as soon as she fell asleep, her unconscious mind processing the terrible events of the day.

She was running outside in the snow, her bare feet slapping on the ice.

All around her was desolation as the arctic wind blew across the white plains of snow. She could already feel her feet going numb as she continued to run.

The cold air bit at her exposed skin, the nightgown she was wearing doing little to protect her from the frigid air.

As she ran, her breath blew out in front of her and was then lost in the wind.

Ascending a small incline on the icy plain, she came upon small mounds of snow. As she approached them, she could see they resembled burial mounds. She walked into their midst, her eyes studying the lumps of snow. It was completely silent on the plain as she stood in the middle of this circle of snow piles, now even the howling wind going quiet.

Why were they here? She wondered. Who would go to the trouble?

They were like crop circles drawn into the snow. She stood there quietly, taking it all in with her eyes when the mound directly below her began to quiver.

She immediately began backing away from it as the shaking grew worse. As she moved away, she wandered close to another mound. As soon as she was near this new mound it began to shake, as well.

Sara turned away, wanting to try and run, just wanting to be distant from these anomalies, but every time she ran from one mound, the next one would begin to vibrate, as if the mounds themselves could sense her presence.

All the mounds were now shaking, and Sara watched in horror as the closest mound shook apart, a head emerging like a newborn baby leaving the womb.

The frozen corpse's skin was a pale blue and as it climbed out of the snow, she could see it was wearing a white jumpsuit. The ghoul's facial features were frozen into a silent scream as it gained its balance and began to lumber toward her. Its arms and legs were frozen at the joints and it walked like some crazy parody of a monster she had seen in a movie as a child. As she backed away, she screamed when something grabbed her ankle. Looking down, she saw a hand sticking out of another mound of snow. As she tried to get away, she inadvertently helped to pull the new corpse out of its frozen prison.

Glancing around the plain, she could see all the other mounds were now disgorging their frozen occupants. One at a time, the frozen zombies managed to pull themselves from their icy tombs, until they were out on the surface of the snow covered ground.

As one, they raised themselves to their feet and surrounded Sara.

She stood in the middle of this shrinking circle as the ghouls converged on her.

Though they did not talk she could hear a whisper in the wind.

"Join us."

She began to shake her head vehemently back and forth. How could this be happening? Zombies weren't real. They were characters in bad horror movies.

But as their icy hands grabbed her and wrapped her in their cold embrace, and teeth flared in the wan light of the icy plain, she realized real or not, she was going to be killed and she began to scream.

And as their frozen teeth began tearing at her warm flesh, she screamed louder.

The frigid cold of death enveloped her in its icy embrace and Sara let out one last blood-curdling scream with everything she was made of.

And was instantly transported back to reality.

She opened her eyes to see Mark standing over her. He had each of his hands on her shoulders and was shaking her awake. As the nightmare faded from her conscious thought, she put up her hands and said: "All right, Mark, I'm okay."

"Are you sure, Sara? When you started screaming, I thought we'd somehow been attacked. You just about scared the shit out of me," Mark told her as he let her go and sat back down on their makeshift bed of coats and rags.

"You wouldn't have been the only one," Shawn said askance of her as he rubbed sleep from his eyes. "Anyone know what time it is?"

"Not that it matters, but it's a little before five. But don't count on the sun coming up 'cause we're about to enter the winter months," Mark informed him.

"Great, so you're telling me we have to fight off a bunch of zombies and it's always going to be dark outside?"

"Yeah, I'm afraid so," Mark said as he turned back to Sara.

"You sure you're all right?" He asked again.

Sara gently pushed him away. "I'm fine. I guess I had a bad dream."

"Sara, the way you were screaming, it must have been the mother of bad dreams," Shawn said with a grin.

Changing the subject, Sara gazed around the room. "I have to go to the bathroom."

"All ready taken care of," Mark grinned. "There's a bucket over by the desk you can use."

Sara just looked at him. "Excuse me? You want me to go in a what?"

Mark raised his hands in sympathy. "I'm sorry, Sara, but what do you want me to do? There isn't a toilet in here."

Shawn smiled and was about to add his input when Sara pointed a finger at him and said: "Don't you say anything."

Shawn just looked down and continued smiling, amused at the situation.

Sara sat for a few more minutes until her bladder wouldn't be ignored any longer.

With a sigh of surrender, she raised herself up and went over to the desk and their makeshift toilet.

Before she got there, she turned around to check on the men and was relieved to see they were no longer paying attention to her. With a hint of mild surprise, she turned and continued on her way, impressed with the maturity of her friends.

Mark and Shawn had decided now was as good a time as any to discuss their situation, being they were both awake.

"If we can make it until the end of the storm, then we should be able to grab one of those half-tracks and get the hell out of here. Kryton Station is only about a days drive from here."

"Good idea, but you're taking into account that we can find one of the half-tracks and we have to do it while fighting zombies all the way to the loading dock. We don't even know if any of them are parked outside or inside the building at the loading dock."

"If you have a better idea, I'm more than willing to hear it," Mark said to Shawn with just a little annoyance in his voice.

Shawn's forehead grew tight in concentration. Then with a shrug he said: "Nope, Mark, I got nothin'. So when are we gonna try this plan of yours?"

"Let's give it a few days, at least until the storm breaks. We have enough food and water if we ration it and I'm not exactly ready to start running for our lives again. And maybe help will come, I mean, we can't be the only ones left."

"I hear that," Shawn agreed, he was about to say something else when he caught the faint sound of tapping. "Wait a second. Did you guys hear that?"

"Hear what?" Mark said.

"It sounded like tapping," Shawn said and got up to start walking around the large room. Between the zombies banging on the door and the sound of the generator humming, it was really hard to pinpoint where the tapping was originating.

Then he heard it again. Tap, tap, and tap. This time he was closer to the source and he was able to pinpoint its location. There was a padlocked hatch on the floor at the end of the generator room. As Shawn moved closer to it, he could hear the tapping much clearer.

He crossed the distance until he was standing on top of the hatch and knocked on it with his knuckles.

Immediately, he received a response and the tapping grew louder and faster.

"Hey, guys, I think I found something!" Shawn yelled to Mark and Sara.

The two of them came over to Shawn's position and looked down at the hatch.

"What's going on?" Mark asked him.

"I think there's someone down there," Shawn said. "I can hear them banging on the inside of the hatch."

Sara leaned against Mark, her eyes going wide with fear. "Oh, God, it's those people, don't let them in here, Shawn!" She said with obvious terror in her voice.

Shawn stood up to placate her. "Whoa, Sara, relax, I don't think its one of them. Look, I'll prove it."

Shawn leaned down to the hatch and rapped his knuckles to the tune of 'shave and a haircut', and then he waited. Before barely a second had passed, they all heard 'two bits' answered back. Shawn stood back up.

"Now if that's a zombie, I'll eat my hat," he said with a sideways grin.

Mark nodded his head in agreement. "I agree with Shawn, Sara, if it is one of those people down there it would never be smart enough to knock like that."

Sara thought about it for a moment and then jumped when the hatch began knocking again, this time repeating 'shave and a hair cut'.

Shawn stamped his foot down on the hatch in answer.

"Look, I don't care what you say, I'm opening it. If it is one of those dead bastards, then I'll blow it away," he said, while putting his hand on his sidearm.

Shawn walked over to the maintenance desk and searched around for something to break the lock with. In a moment he returned with a screwdriver and a hammer.

He smiled as he held the tools up to show his friends. "Found these in a desk drawer."

Getting down on one knee, he got to work trying to break the lock. After only a few minutes, he succeeded. As he pulled the lock through the latch, he talked to no one in particular. "This lock is a piece of shit. If it was made better, I might have had problems."

After removing the latch, he gazed up at Mark and handed him the hammer.

"I'll open it and if it's a zombie you crack it over the head. Okay?"

Taking the hammer from Shawn, Mark just nodded and spread his legs so he could get a good swing in if he had to. Shawn gripped the hatch handle and then opened it, jumping back out of the way, just in case.

For a tense heartbeat, nothing emerged from the dark opening. And then Fredericks' head popped up and into the light.

Mark stood there with the hammer raised until Sara yelled, "Mark, don't, it's Dr. Fredericks!"

For just a moment when Mark saw who it was, he hesitated. He never liked the little bastard, and now he could crack his head open and say he didn't realize he wasn't a zombie until after Fredericks' brains were splattered all over the floor.

But he stopped himself, despite all his faults, he wasn't a killer.

As Shawn helped Dr. Fredericks out of the hatch, Mark turned his back on them and walked away.

CHAPTER NINETEEN

"WHAT THE HELL were you doing down there, Fredericks?" Mark asked with annoyance as he stood back to let the man climb out of the hatch.

"I found myself in a little bit of a situation in my lab about an hour ago. Luckily, I was able to extricate myself. I've been walking for quite some time down there. With it being almost pitch black in that tunnel, I had no idea of what time it was. Then I saw the light seeping through the sides of this hatch." He turned and pointed casually at the open hatch on the floor. "I heard the humming of the generator and took a chance that someone was up here." He looked down at the disheveled clothes on his body and began to straighten them while he continued his story. "It would appear I gambled correctly in that assumption," he finished as he looked up again with a smile plastered across his lips.

"More like just fuckin' lucky, Doc," Shawn said from his side. "Those damn things are everywhere in the station. We could have just as easily been those people."

"You mean the zombies," Fredericks stated as a matter of fact.

"What the hell are you talking about, Fredericks? There's no such thing as zombies," Mark snapped at the man. He'd let Shawn use the term because he liked him, but Fredericks using the word just pissed him off.

"I'm sorry, Dr. Simmons, but there is such a thing. How do you explain what is happening to the personnel inside this station at this very moment."

"He can't," Sara interjected. "You act like you know something about what's going on here, Dr. Fredericks. Do you?"

Fredericks had no intention of filling these three in on exactly what he suspected was the truth of the outbreak of the frozen dead. No, it wouldn't serve his purposes. Instead, he would share just enough of the truth to placate them. He had learned a long time ago that the key to a good lie was to sprinkle it with some truth.

"Yes, Dr. Edwards, I believe I do know what is happening. I believe that some form of biological agent has infected the personnel on this base. And that they are now the living dead. Their bite is infectious, if the infected manage to break the skin of a victim, the contaminant will then quickly take over the host body and transform the host into another of its kind. As long as there are live bodies to infect, the cycle will continue indefinitely."

Shawn just stared at Fredericks with his jaw hanging open, but after a moment, he closed his mouth. Turning to Mark he said: "That has got to be the biggest bunch of bullshit I've ever heard. He can't be serious."

Mark shrugged. "You tell me a better idea and I'll be more than happy to listen."

"Do you have a solution to the problem, Doctor?" Mark asked. "Because frankly, I'm stumped?"

Fredericks stood quiet for a moment as if he was deep in thought. Mark was about to tell the little bastard to spit it out when Fredericks began talking again.

"I believe we are doomed if we stay here. We need to leave this station as soon as possible and try to seek help from our neighboring research station. That way this station can be quarantined and sterilized before the outbreak can spread past these walls."

"That's easier said than done, Doc. Have you looked outside lately? There's a real honey of a storm blowing," Shawn said.

"Shawn's right. We're not going anywhere until that storm dies down. Sorry, Fredericks, but it looks like you're stuck with us for a while," Mark said with disappointment and more than a little contempt.

Fredericks didn't seem to notice. "Well, I guess I'll just have to make do, then won't I? On another subject, do you have any food or water? I've been walking in circles down there for quite some time and I have to admit to being parched."

"Sure, Doc, come with me. We have some stuff over here," Shawn told him as he led Fredericks to their meager supplies.

Once Mark and Sara were out of earshot of Fredericks, Mark immediately shared his fears with Sara.

"I don't like this, Sara. That little weasel is no good. I'm telling you, he's bad news. We should dump him as soon as possible."

"Dump him where? He's a fellow human being, Mark, and at the moment that is something that is in short supply. I'll admit he's a little eccentric, though."

"A little eccentric?" Mark cut in. "He's a fruitcake. You've heard about some of the things he does?"

"Oh please, those are just rumors."

"Rumors? Rumors that are probably based in fact. Those rumors have to begin somewhere, Sara." He could already tell he was losing this argument with her.

So he decided to compromise before he lost the argument completely.

"Okay," he said. "Let's agree to keep an eye on him. What do you say?"

Sara thought about it for a moment and then nodded her head. "Agreed."

With that settled, the two of them went to join Shawn and Fredericks.

Shawn was filling Fredericks in on what had happened to the three of them and how they had ended up locked inside the generator room. Fredericks listened quietly, as always wondering how this new information could benefit him.

Fredericks had just finished his second candy bar when Mark and Sara walked up to him.

"Go easy on that stuff, Fredericks, we have to make it last."

Fredericks looked at Mark as if contemplating an answer, but instead he turned to Sara and asked: "Do you have an idea how long the storm might continue Dr. Edwards?"

"Please, call me Sara, Dr. Fredericks, and no, I'm afraid I don't know. I wasn't able to check my equipment before all the chaos broke out."

Sara waited for Fredericks to tell her that, she too, could call him by his first name, but alas, it did not come. Fredericks simply frowned from receiving her answer and walked away to look out one of the frosted windows set above his head.

Mark looked at Sara with a, *you see what I mean?*

She looked back at him with a, *don't you start again*, look.

Shawn just stared at the two of them, wondering if he was the only sane one in the room.

Outside the generator room windows, the storm continued to blow its fury at the lone station. As shadows began to pass by the windows more frequently, the group of four went about their business, unaware of the trouble to come.

Chapter Twenty

FREDERICKS WAS STANDING off to one side of the humming generator as he gazed out the windows on the far wall.

The windows were about seven feet high off the ground and were on both sides of the room at four per wall. At the moment, the windows were covered with frost and ice, only the barest hint of outside light showing through.

As Fredericks continued to stare, his eye caught movement on the far window, but when he turned to look directly at the disturbance, it was gone as quick as it had appeared. He stood still, studying the window for another second, but saw nothing more, so had just decided he must have imagined it, when he saw movement again.

A shadow slowly moved across the window, the wan light from outside reflecting off the snow giving the shape an ethereal quality. His internal debate on whether he should tell his new companions about what he saw was cut short when Mark walked up to him with a serious look in his eyes.

"Listen up, Fredericks, with all this crazy shit going down I don't feel the need to be polite anymore. So I'm gonna lay it down for you so you can understand. If you're going to stay with us then you better be prepared to pull your own weight, because there are no babysitters here. Do I make myself clear?"

Fredericks just patiently listened to Mark's little speech and then nodded his head. "Of course, Dr. Simmons, I shall do my best to as you say 'pull my own weight'."

"Good, I'm glad we understand each other. And do me a favor, will ya, just call me Mark. Hearing you always calling me Dr. Simmons is really getting on my nerves."

Fredericks just nodded his head again. "Of course… Mark."

With their conversation finished, Mark turned and walked back to Shawn and Sara. Fredericks stayed where he was. He looked back up at the window, and after only a moment, caught another shadow crossing past the glass.

When the shadow had once again disappeared from the window, he smiled.

*　　*　　*

Later that morning, the group of four was trying to find ways of entertaining themselves. As the storm continued to howl outside, the banging on the generator room door was all but ignored by the four companions.

At the moment, Shawn and Sara were playing Tic Tac Toe on the floor with a nail for a writing instrument. Mark was sitting at the desk in the corner going over maintenance logs to see if he could find anything useful.

There wasn't much in the logs to help their situation, although Mark did find the construction specs for the generator room building and he learned a lot about the layout of the structure and what was under it.

Mark found it most interesting to read about the maintenance tunnels that apparently wove under and around Amusen Station.

For as long as he'd been stationed here, he'd never known they had existed. But then why would he? He was a scientist after all, not an engineer.

He followed the schematic with his finger as he studied the labyrinth of tunnels. Maybe they could use them to escape from here when the time came.

He looked over his shoulder at Fredericks, who was off in a corner of the room on the opposite side of the generator.

Once again he cursed the fates for allowing that man to join them. He knew he was trouble. He could feel it in his bones. He shrugged that particular chain of thought away. There was nothing he could do about it now.

He was about to get up and go join the others when one of the windows on the wall shattered. Bits of ice and glass fell into the room and the wind and snow blew into the interior, immediately collecting on the floor.

Shawn and Sara jumped up and joined Mark to deal with the situation, their eyes only for the shattered window. Already the temperature was dropping, the heat sucked out of the window like a vacuum.

The three of them ran together to the window and were about to try and cover it when a frozen face stuck its head into the frame. The eyebrows and edges of the face were covered with frost, icicles hanging from the nose and ears.

The group of three stopped in their tracks and stared up at the dead face.

The eyes of the ghoul seemed to scan the room with its frozen gaze for a moment and then the face pulled back and disappeared from view.

"What the fuck was that?" Shawn said to the others.

"I have no idea, a man definitely. Did you see his complexion? It was blue, like he was frozen," Sara said in a whisper. "And all that ice on his face, how could he still be alive?"

"So you're saying he was dead? Frozen zombies? That's crazy," Shawn said back.

"Well, whatever it is, it's out there and we're in here so we should be fine," Mark said, trying to sound convincing. "We just need to cover the windows so we don't freeze."

"I'm afraid it won't be that simple, Dr. Simmons," Fredericks said from across the room. "You see, there are much more than just one of those creatures out there in the snow."

"What do you mean by that, Fredericks?" Mark inquired as anger crept into his voice. "What do you know that you're not telling us?"

"On the contrary, Doctor, I'm telling you everything you need to know."

Before Fredericks could elaborate more, another window was kicked in. More wind and snow poured in through the open portal and the temperature quickly plummeted to freezing as the rest of the heat was sucked out of the room.

"Well, whatever's going on, Mark, we can't stay here any longer," Sara said to Mark as she tugged his arm.

"She's right, man. There's no way to defend this place. We've got to go now!" Shawn yelled.

No sooner had Shawn finished his sentence then another window was kicked in and bodies began coming through the openings one at a time.

The first bodies that crawled through literally shattered on the hard concrete floor of the generator room. But as more continued to fall through, the ones who had come through first cushioned the fall of the others until they had a soft bed of bodies to land on.

Within moments, there were at least ten frozen ghouls in the room with more following them. More windows were kicked in until all eight were shattered as the undead horde continued to pour into the room.

The whistling of the wind, combined with the noise of the generator, made it difficult to hear. The snow blowing into the room made vision difficult, as well. The small group fell back to their meager supplies to gather them up before they were surrounded.

Shawn was taking pot shots at a few of the closest attackers, trying to slow them down long enough to give his companions the time they sorely needed.

When his bullets struck the frozen bodies, they would penetrate two or three bodies at a time until their velocity slowed enough for the bullets to become lodged in the walking corpses. In the wake of the bullets, pieces of bodies exploded outward in a mist of frozen blood and ice.

After Shawn fired a round at one particular group of ghouls, he was able for just a moment to glimpse the hole the bullet made as it went through three bodies that were lined up in a row. At the end of the ghastly tunnel, he was just able to make out the head of another ghoul who was climbing to its feet after falling through the window.

The three of them were now slowly becoming surrounded by the crowd of undead and Shawn was down to his last few bullets.

When he had a split second of a breather, he glanced over his shoulder to Mark and Sara and said: "If either of you guys has any ideas how we're supposed to get out of here, now would be a great time to share."

Mark and Sara just looked at him, and then at the approaching hoard of frigid ghouls that were slowly surrounding them.

Their chance for escape was slowly shrinking with every shambling footstep the zombies made and in seconds it would be far too late for them to escape.

CHAPTER TWENTY-ONE

THE WIND CONTINUED to batter the research station on the desolate plain.

As the snow became heavier, it began to accumulate against the walls of the station.

The windows of the generator room were about seven feet off the ground from the outside. At first, the ghouls merely milled around the outside, not knowing how to gain access to the building with their limited intelligence. As time went by, though, the snow and ice began growing thicker under the windows until the zombies were able to walk right up to them.

But it took an accident of fate to give them a way inside. With their intelligence incredibly diminished, none of them realized that all one of them had to do was just kick a window in to gain access to the building.

So they just wandered around outside in the freezing temperatures, the cold making them feel content in their fuzzy state of existence.

Then one of the ghouls walking too close to a window lost its footing and fell into it, shattering the glass.

After that it took only moments for the horde of frozen dead to realize what it meant and begin breaking other windows and then climbing inside to get at the warm meat hiding within.

The first ones in didn't fare as well, their bodies shattering on the generator room floor. But they didn't give their undead lives away fruitlessly, for it allowed the others to enter unharmed.

And now the small group of survivors was trapped as the undead horde slowly cornered the helpless humans.

None of the ghouls had spotted Fredericks, who had taken refuge inside the generator when the frozen corpses had begun to pour into the room.

He'd been lucky enough to discover a hollow piece of metal that was blocking some kind of an air vent.

As the undead bodies slowly crept by his hiding place, he tried to push himself back just a little more into the vent so as not to be discovered. He had no idea how he was going to get out of here, but he knew if there was a way he would think of it. He just had to concentrate.

Then he felt a warm blast of air above his head. He looked up to see an exhaust vent leading up into the ceiling. The heat of the vent was more than enough to burn his skin and he quickly debated whether he should stay where he was or try and climb higher into the vent.

His decision was quickly taken out of his hands when a ghoul spotted him.

The ghoul looked to have once been a cafeteria worker as the dead woman had on a lunchroom uniform and a hairnet. As she turned and began walking towards Fredericks, he decided that the vent was a better option than becoming dinner for this abomination of life.

Quickly, he jumped up and began climbing while the sides of the vent burned the palms of his hands. He barely managed to climb a few inches when he felt something grab his leg and try to pull him back down. He tried to free himself, but the dead woman's grip was solid and the only thing preventing him from falling into her grasp was a tenuous hold he was able to manage on a seam where two pieces of the vent had not been connected properly. The woman's hold on him continued to pull him back and he could feel his grip slipping. Then his fingers slipped and he was falling back down the vent. At the last moment, he stuck his foot out and it connected with the woman's face.

The shoe shattered her nose and caved in her jaw; pieces of ice falling away mixed with skin and blood. The outside temperatures had made the woman more fragile than if she had stayed inside in the warmer climate of the building.

Her eyes disintegrated as the sole of his shoes made contact with her head. As the woman fell away, she had the shape of a shoeprint in the middle of her face. Immobilized for now, but not down for good, she backed away from him and stumbled away, now blind.

Two more ghouls had now spotted Fredericks, but before they could wrap frozen fingers around his legs, he scurried back up the vent. He didn't know where it led, but at the moment, anywhere was better than in that room.

As he climbed higher into the vent, the sounds of the wind and the generator slowly faded away.

CHAPTER TWENTY-TWO

MARK HELD SARA close as his mind frantically tried to figure a way out of their slowly deteriorating situation. His eyes scanned the room for someway out. The windows were not an option as they would freeze to death the minute they climbed outside without proper gear, not to mention how many of those things could still be out there.

The generator door was out, as well.

If he opened that door all he would get for his trouble is more ghouls entering a room that was already filled to capacity. Then he spotted the hatch on the floor. The one Fredericks had used to enter the room earlier.

"Of course, how could I have been so stupid?" He asked to anyone within hearing.

Sara looked up at his face and asked: "What, what are you talking about?"

"The hatch that Fredericks used, we can escape through there," he said triumphantly.

"Well, whatever we're gonna do, we better do it fast or we're dead!" Shawn yelled, shooting a dead woman in the head when she got too close.

Mark nodded and turned to Sara. "Sara, grab one of those coats and help me spread it out."

The two of them took the coat Sara had found in an office earlier and spread it out in front of them, with the coat now acting like a makeshift sheet.

Mark called to Shawn as he fired his last few rounds. "All right, Shawn, get behind us. We'll throw this coat on the first ones in line, and while they're distracted, we'll make a run for the hatch."

"Are you crazy? There's too damn many of them!" Shawn yelled back as his gun clicked on an empty round. "Shit," he yelled as he thrust his now useless gun back into its holster. "We're all out of options, Doc, so what the hell, let's go for it."

Mark glanced down to Sara who now had the coat in her hands. "You ready?" He asked her.

The terror was clear on her face, but she nodded yes.

"All right then, let's do this," he said.

Mark had the hammer Shawn had found in a desk drawer earlier and used on the hatch's lock, now preparing to use the tool as an offensive weapon, as well as the stapler Sara had found. Shawn had the screwdriver. Sara would stay behind them after they had thrown the coat, as she was carrying the gear wrapped up in an old bed sheet used for painting they'd found.

Mark and Sara held the coat tightly and then went for it with a nod from Shawn.

Together, the two of them walked the few feet to the first row of ghouls blocking their way to the hatch. They threw the coat at the walking corpses and the coat landed on the first two in line. The ghouls were immediately tangled up in the material and began flailing around. They soon were plowing into their fellow dead and attacking them in their confusion.

Mark hoped that distraction would be enough for them to make a clear run to the hatch.

With a simple: "Let's move people, it's now or never," the three companions made their way across the room. It was easy to avoid the first few as they were occupied with the coat. The second row would be more difficult. Mark had the hammer in his hand, and before he'd taken four steps, he'd already cracked his first victim in the head with it. When the hammer connected with the side of the ghoul's skull, it sank almost all the way in. He saw the ear was demolished, and as Mark pulled back on his weapon, for a moment he feared it wouldn't come out. Then with a sound like breaking crystal, the hammer popped free, spraying Mark with ice and bits of scalp. He didn't even get the chance to admire his handiwork, as no sooner did he have his weapon clear of one ghoul, than another one was blocking his path, its arms reaching out to try and grab him.

He danced away from the next one and when he ducked, he whacked the hammer against the ghoul's kneecap. The zombie's knee shattered, the pieces falling down its pant leg to slowly trickle out onto its shoe. Mark saw the ghoul lurch to the side and immediately dove back inside its reach and whacked the other leg.

The ghoul wavered for a moment and then went crashing to the floor. Part of one hand and several fingers from the other broke off when it struck the floor.

The ghoul was still moving, but now had no legs to stand on. That was good enough for Mark; at least it was out of the fight.

On Mark's right side, Shawn was holding his own. He would dart in with the screwdriver and take out a ghoul's eye before it had a chance to grab him, and then quickly move on to the next one. One frozen ghoul proved too fast for him to get at its eyes, so he dropped down in a crouch and swept one of his legs out in a circle, thus sweeping the ghoul's legs out from under it and sending it crashing to the ground. As the ghoul wallowed on the floor trying to regain its footing, it was all but forgotten by Shawn. The goal was to reach the hatch not kill every walking corpse in the room.

Sara was following behind the two men, her head constantly turning back and forth, wary for any ghouls who might slip past the men. They were making good progress and in a matter of seconds they would be at the hatch, and hopefully, freedom.

A ghoul came up behind Sara in her blind spot. The men didn't know she was in trouble as she was behind them. She began weaving to stay out of the ghoul's grasp and then she took the sack off her shoulder and swung it as hard as she could.

The compacted sack was fairly heavy as it carried all their food and water and miscellaneous items. The cloth bludgeon slammed into the side of the ghoul's body and sent it shuffling away. Sara realized she had a pretty good offensive weapon and decided to stop hiding behind the men and do her part.

As all this was going on with Shawn and Sara, Mark had made it to the hatch and reached down to open it. Warm fog rose up into his face as the differing temperatures combined. He turned to see the others only moments behind him and quickly pushed another ghoul away to clear the hatch. Then another ghoul wearing a soldier's uniform came up behind Mark and tried to sink its teeth into his neck. Mark was able to pull back just before the teeth would have sank in. He turned to face it with the hammer held high, but another ghoul had come up from behind and had inadvertently knocked the hammer from his grip, sending it sliding across the ice strewn floor.

Mark watched in horror as his only weapon slid out of reach. He didn't have much time to worry about it however because the first ghoul was on the attack again and had charged into Mark. The frozen man's arms wrapped around Mark's waist as the dead man struggled with him to take a bite out of his exposed neck.

Mark could feel the cold of the ghoul as it flowed through his clothes and into his soul. He grabbed the man's neck to try to keep those jaws away from him. No sooner had he done this than he could feel his hand growing numb from holding the frozen neck in his hand.

Then he remembered the stapler in his pocket.

Desperate for any chance to stay alive, he reached down with his free hand and pulled it from his pocket. For just a moment, it caught on his pants and he feared it wouldn't come loose. Then, with a ripping of threads, it tore loose and was in his hand. He flipped it open and banged it against the man's eye. The staple shot out and stuck in the middle of the right eye. For just a second, it looked like tiny spider web sized cracks appeared around the staple as it fractured the orb. Then it didn't matter anymore as the dead man renewed his attack.

While the two of them were dancing back and forth, Mark had lost track of his position compared to the hatch and didn't realize it was directly behind him. As the two stumbled around the floor, it took only an instant until Mark's foot stepped on empty air and he dropped straight into the opening.

As one being, the two of them fell through the hole with Mark landing on the bottom. The air immediately was slammed out of his body as the six foot fall to the tunnel floor dazed him into complete submission. As he lay there wondering what had happened to him, the ghoul slowly began to crawl up his body. This was made more difficult for the dead man because when he fell, both his arms had been shattered from the impact of striking the concrete floor.

Like some sick parody of an inchworm, the dead man slowly used his feet to push up Mark's body until he could reach the dazed man's exposed flesh. While the ghoul was slowly inching its way up, Mark was slowly coming to his senses. He could hear Shawn's voice as if it was from very far away calling out to him.

As the fuzziness began to clear, he could feel a pain in his back from his hard landing on the tunnel floor. He reached up with his hand to rub his eyes when he felt something on top of him. Still dazed, he slowly opened his eyes and found himself staring at the face of the dead man he'd been struggling with only moments before. The pale blue face was directly above his and as Mark looked into the frozen blue eyes, the staple sticking out predominantly in the right eye, the ghoul exhaled onto his cheek. Mark could feel a subtle blast of cold air coming from the ghoul's mouth and he immediately put his hand up to keep the frozen face away from him, but he hadn't fully recovered from the fall just yet and was only able to put up a meager resistance to the man. As the pale face hovered over Mark's, the frozen mouth opened wider and a swollen black tongue rolled out of the orifice.

As Mark fought to keep the ghoul at bay, the tongue reached out and licked Mark's right eyeball. He tried to close his eye, but the tongue was on good and his eyelid only managed to lodge it on more. He could feel the cold of the tongue pushing down on his eye and it seemed like his eyeball was being frozen, the chill penetrating past the cornea until it felt like it was freezing his brain.

With the terror Mark was now feeling, the adrenaline began to flow and he was now recovered enough to heave the ghoul off of him. The ghoul rolled off, but immediately began to crawl back onto him. Mark sat up and shakily raised himself back onto his feet. The room began to spin for a moment and he used the ladder rungs on the wall for support. He looked down at his new armless friend who was still crawling towards him.

With disgust clearly etched on his face, Mark backed up, and like a kid kicking a kickball at the first day of gym class, he let his shoe fly at the ghoul's head. The foot connected with the face right below the jaw. The ghoul's head snapped back and was thrown against the concrete wall of the tunnel. The skull was smashed apart from the force of the impact, the body going limp.

Bits of brain matter and small pools of blood began to appear as the body parts melted from the warmth of the tunnel.

Mark was distracted from his own problems from a yell from above. He looked up to see Sara just beginning to climb down into the tunnel. He went over and took the sack she was carrying and then helped her down. Shawn was still above, trying to keep the attacking ghouls at bay. They were all around him and he wasn't able to get that one second he needed to climb down into the hatch.

"Shawn, just jump down, it's not that far!" Mark called up to him.

Shawn heard him, but didn't have the breath to answer. At the moment, the ghouls were completely surrounding him and within moments he would be overwhelmed. Just when it looked like it would be too late, Shawn stepped over the hatch opening and with a, "so long assholes," dropped down the hatch.

As he didn't quite know when to expect his feet to hit the floor, his legs weren't bent properly to absorb his fall. His whole body felt his landing and the jarring of his feet went straight up to his forehead.

Immediately after Shawn fell through the hole, Mark raced up the ladder and before a ghoul could grab him, he had gripped the hatch's handle and slammed it shut, turning the latch so it was now locked. When it slammed tight, a few stray fingers tumbled down onto the floor from a ghoul that wasn't quick enough to remove its hand.

Mark then climbed back down to see how the others were.

"How you doing, Shawn? That was a pretty good drop," Mark said as his feet touched the tunnel floor.

Shawn had his hand on his head as he answered. "Well, with the exception of a splitting headache, I think I'll live."

Mark looked over at Sara and could see, she too was, fine. He nodded to himself and then walked a few feet away from the others. In a moment he returned with a flashlight.

"Where'd you find that?" Sara asked.

"From an emergency box. If you know where to look, they're scattered around down here. I read about it in some schematics I found earlier."

When Shawn had gotten it together a little more, he asked both of them. "Did either of you guys see what happened to Dr. Fredericks? I lost track of him when all that shit went down."

Sara shook her head. "I didn't see him at all. Do you think he made it out alive?"

Mark made a sound of disgust. "I don't care if those creatures cut him up and made popsicles out of him. You see, I told you he was no good. Why wasn't he around to help when the shit hit the fan? Because he's a coward, that's why."

He wanted to say more, but after looking at Sara's disagreeable stare he decided against it.

Shawn leaned against the wall to rest. "So what now?"

Mark considered it. That was a real good question. They were now trapped in a tunnel at the bottom of the station with dozens of frozen ghouls out for their blood. There was a storm blowing outside that made escape impossible and they were low on food and water. All together a pretty bad situation.

He looked to Sara as she fumbled with the sack of their meager supplies. Even with everything that had happened, with all the smudges of dirt on her face and her hair flying in every direction, she still looked beautiful to him.

They would survive this, if for no other reason than he wouldn't let anything happen to her.

He set his jaw tight as he gazed at the two faces now looking to him for answers.

The only problem was, at the moment, he didn't have any to give.

Chapter Twenty-three

THE THREE WEARY survivors walked down the tunnel in silence.

Before starting out, Mark had been fortunate enough to find a light switch on the wall by the ladder, and when he flicked the switch, a small string of red lights had flickered on along the roof of the tunnel, bathing the three survivors in a soft red glow. They had gathered their supplies and after a small breather, had decided to head out. Deciding that the sooner they moved on, the sooner they would end up wherever it was they were going.

The tunnel echoed the sounds of their shoes as they walked along the concrete floor. While they were all glad to still be alive, their lack of hope at the moment made it hard to be positive. Their outcome looked bleak. No matter how long they could keep the ghouls at bay, sooner or later the result would be the same.

They would be infected and become like the other frozen corpses.

Every now and then as they walked down the tunnel they would come upon a hatch in the ceiling. The three had debated on what could be above them so for the time being had elected to leave them be. Although they all wanted to escape the oppressiveness of the tunnel, they also enjoyed the shallow feeling of security it now gave them, even if it was fleeting.

Over an hour had passed since they had first entered the tunnels, so Mark called a halt when they came upon another hatch set in the ceiling. The wan light could be seen as it squeezed through and around the edges of the opening.

Mark was first to break the silence. "I think one of us should stick his head out of that hatch so we can at least get our bearings. Frankly, I'd like to know where we are under the station right now."

"And by one of us you mean who exactly?" Shawn asked, curious about his answer.

"Relax, Shawn, I wouldn't ask someone to do what I wouldn't do myself. I'll go."

"Are you sure that's wise, Mark? I mean, for the moment we're safe down here," Sara said.

"Yeah, we're safe for now, but as soon as we're out of food and water we'll be right back here discussing this again. No, I'd rather just get it over with. Either we get away from this station or we die trying. And as I already said, I'd rather take the chance now while I still have the energy and the nerve."

Shawn mulled it over for a moment and spoke up. "He makes a good point, Sara," he said as he nodded in agreement.

She frowned and folded her arms across her chest while she looked at both of them. "I know. I just don't want to do this anymore," she said as a single tear crawled down her cheek.

Mark reached out and pulled her to him. She buried her head in his chest and started crying softly, her shoulders shaking.

"I wouldn't mind a good cry myself after all the shit we've seen. But it's not manly and all that," Shawn said as he watched the two of them standing quietly together.

That's when he made his decision to go up the hatch and take a look.

Before Mark could stop him, he'd scurried up the ladder and had unlocked the hatch. He was expecting it to be locked from the outside, but was surprised when it opened easily. He slowly pushed it up an inch or so and took a quick look around.

The room was quiet.

It looked like a supply room. The only furniture in the room was a small desk and chair over in the far corner. The only illumination in the room was a small lamp that was perched on the corner of the desk. Shawn felt heartened by this and slowly opened the hatch a little more. The hinges on the hatch squeaked in protest and Shawn felt his heart stop as the noise echoed off the walls in the room. After another heart wrenching moment, Shawn was reassured he was alone in the room. He quickly climbed up the rest of the way and stood up inside the room. There was only one door across from the desk and Shawn went over to see if it was locked. After he was reassured the door was secured and relatively solid, he went back to the opening and called down to his friends.

"Looks safe, the doors locked. It looks like some sort of supply room," he said in a whisper. "Come on up, it's definitely warmer up here."

Mark looked at Sara who had finished her little crying fit. "I'm sorry, Mark. Leave it to the woman to cry, right?" She said a little embarrassed.

"Don't worry about it, Sara. Like Shawn said, after all the stuff we've seen recently, I think I could use a good cry myself," he added with a smile.

As she looked up into his eyes they shared a moment of intimacy. Mark was just about to lean over and kiss her when Shawn's head appeared and yelled down the hole, which broke the mood.

"Hey, guys, guess what I found. This room has a crapper in it. Man will it feel good to take a shit sitting over a bowl again." And then his head disappeared again.

The mood had definitely been broken thanks to Shawn, so Mark disengaged the two of them, and with a polite wave of his hand said: "After you, madam."

She smiled and began climbing up the ladder, with Mark following behind with their gear.

When the two of them had reached the top and had a good look around, Mark smiled. This could work. Looking at Shawn, he ran down some of his thoughts.

"This is good, Shawn. We can use this room to check this part of the station and if we get trapped we can always fall back down the hatch. What do you think?"

"I say great. The bathroom has a sink, too, so we have running water."

"Yes, but we still need food. We only have a few candy bars left," Sara added as she walked around the room. There was a phone on the desk and she picked up the receiver for the hell of it. The phone was dead, but she'd figured as much when she put it to her ear.

"Well, I say we make camp here for tonight and tomorrow we'll see how things are," Mark suggested. Shawn and Sara agreed and the three of them began to set up for the rest of the day and the upcoming night.

After the three of them had taken turns in the bathroom, they spread out on the floor to relax.

To Mark's delight, Sara had set up right next to him, and when everyone was sitting, she'd leaned into his arms and had just sat there quietly. As he leaned his nose into her hair, he could smell the soap she had used to clean up with in the bathroom. Even though he had used the same soap on himself it smelled a whole lot more intoxicating after it mixed with the scent of her hair.

He felt himself getting aroused from her warm body pressing against him and the smell of her hair, but realized this was certainly not the time. He quickly shifted position and tried to think about something else to take his mind away from carnal images.

Then they heard noise coming from outside the room. Someone was running down the hallway, screaming. Before any of them could even consider getting up to help whoever was in need, the screaming stopped. There were a few muffled noises and then all was silent again.

The three of them looked at each other knowing what had just occurred outside the door. Another human being had just been slaughtered.

Mark realized his hard on was completely gone. And he was pretty sure it wouldn't be back again that night.

They sat quietly after that, not wanting to make a sound and be discovered.

Minutes turned into hours and before Mark knew it, while holding Sara close to him, he felt himself nodding off as the exertions of the past hours finally took their toll on him.

Within moments he was sleeping soundly, leaving the terrors of the world at bay for just a little while.

Chapter Twenty-Four

M ARK WAS DREAMING.

In his dream he was lying on a beautiful, sandy beach. The sun was shining down on his tan body as he stretched his limbs.

It was so beautiful here.

The beach was surrounded by palm trees and the clear blue water gently swelled and then retreated at the edge of the shore. He glanced over at the chair next to him and saw it showed signs of being occupied. There were feminine articles scattered on the area surrounding the chair.

As he inspected more closely, he saw a hairbrush, lipstick and one of those magazines where everyone is beautiful and they'll be glad to share their personal secrets on how you could look beautiful, too.

He gazed out at the water and could just make out a slim figure as it dove into the rolling surface. In a moment the figure emerged, and as the water rolled off her toned body, Mark realized it was Sara. She waved to him as she frolicked in the water.

He sat up in his chair and waved back. The feeling of contentment that came over him was overwhelming. He wished he could always feel this good as he closed his eyes and enjoyed the warmth of the sun on his face.

Then he heard a high-pitched scream, and when he opened his eyes, Sara was gone. He jumped up from his chair and dashed to the water's edge, all the while calling Sara's name. He hesitated for only a moment and then dove into the surf to try and find her. After frantically searching for what seemed like hours, he padded ashore and slumped down on the water's edge, crying.

It wasn't fair.

Now, when he had finally found her, to lose her so quickly? How could fate be so cruel?

Then he spotted something floating further out than he had expected in his search. He immediately dove back into the surf and swam out to whatever was out there; hoping beyond hope it was Sara. Just before he managed to swim up to the object, it dropped away from view. With his last sight of the object, he could have sworn he saw an arm. He dove below the waterline; desperately searching for any sign of what he hoped was her body.

Then a few feet below him, he saw a shape as it floated downward. He swam down further trying to catch the elusive figure. Just when he thought he would have to turn back due to lack of air, he reached it, and when he turned it over he saw that it was Sara. Her eyes were wide open, filled with fear and panic, and the look in them pleaded for Mark to save her from a watery death. Mark wrapped his arms around her and together they began to swim for the surface.

But the surface of the water looked different now. The sunlight was barely penetrating into the water. As they swam closer to the surface, he felt the temperature in the water drastically drop. By the time they were only a few feet away from the surface, he could feel his body shivering from the cold.

When their heads were finally ready to break free of the surface, he reached out with his hands and struck something hard. He pounded on it for a few moments, but it wouldn't break. Although his mind was slowly losing focus due to lack of air, he realized that the surface of the water was now covered with a thick layer of ice.

He kept banging on it for all he was worth, but to no avail, and within a matter of moments he felt the last of his air evaporating in his chest. He could feel his head pounding with the rhythm of his heart as it struggled to survive without air.

He looked over at Sara and could tell she had already succumbed to lack of air and was already drowning in the icy water. The tears in his eyes were invisible as he watched the woman he loved dying next to him. All he could do is float helplessly. She spasmed a few more times and then she stopped moving, and as her body went slack, she began to sink back into the icy depths he'd just saved her from moments ago.

As his own lungs screamed for air, and he began to blackout, he knew even though it would mean his death, he would have no choice but to exhale. As he watched the last glimpse of Sara's body disappear into the blackness below, he opened his mouth and let the ice cold water fill his lungs.

For just a fraction of a second there was relief when he exhaled and released the pressure on his chest. But then the frigid water flooded into his lungs and he began convulsing as he slowly drowned. His body began sinking into the cold blackness and he let out one silent scream, releasing the pent up anger and frustration of what was happening. As the surface dwindled from view, he caught a glimpse of a blue face looking down on him through the ice. And then his brain shut down and he knew no more.

Mark snapped awake with eyes wide open and perspiration coating his body.

His heart was pounding in his chest and his hands were sore from clenching the dirty coat he was under, but slowly the fugue of slumber passed.

The room was quiet, the others still sleeping soundly. He glanced over at his side and was relieved to see Sara curled up next to him. A wisp of his dream floated to the forefront of his mind and he pushed it away, not liking where his thoughts were going. He watched her sleeping for more than a minute, studying her flawless skin and the gentle curve of her neck. Then he stopped himself, feeling a little like a Peeping Tom.

As he extricated himself from her arms, he stood up and went into the bathroom. As softly as he could manage, he closed the door so as not to disturb the others.

He stood in front of a tiny mirror on the wall over the sink, leaning on the edge of the sink for support. As he looked at himself, he could see he was covered in sweat. Fleeting visions of his dream swept through his mind, but try as he could, they wouldn't return with full clarity, only a feeling of dread remaining. By the time he'd washed his face and had a pee, the nightmare was pretty much forgotten.

Exiting the bathroom, he softly padded to the only window in the room and he was just able to barely glimpse the outside through the snow buildup on the glass. If it hadn't been for the stations outside lights, he wouldn't have been able to see anything.

He was pleasantly surprised to see the storm had broken. The night sky was clear and the stars could be seen peeking through a few small cumulus clouds.

While he scanned the outside of the building, he spotted something else, as well. Though it was entirely covered by the newly fallen snow, Mark recognized the distinct outline of one of the army's half-tracks.

After he had seen all there was to see, he went and sat back down next to Sara, thinking about what he'd found outside buried in the snow. The storm had lifted and there was a half-track sitting right outside their window.

He decided he would discuss it with the others first thing in the morning, but he was pretty sure they'd agree with him.

At dawn they were getting the hell away from the station, one way or another.

CHAPTER TWENTY-FIVE

FREDERICKS HAD BEEN stuck inside the vent for almost twelve hours now. His arms and legs were screaming with cramps, the confines of the vent not allowing him to stretch.

He had solved the toilet problem by pulling his pants off and then urinating back down the shaft so as to keep his pants dry. But now the warm air that drifted up to him smelled like stale urine.

But at least he was warm thanks to the exhaust vent.

He was on top of the roof inside the ductwork. If he wanted to, he could crawl all the way to the end of the pipe, and if he pushed on the vent cover, he was able to open it enough to see the area outside the station. The pistol in his pocket was a reminder of the predicament he was in. When he had been eating before with the group, he'd quietly pocketed the pistol when no one was looking and had then wandered over to a corner of the room.

So when all hell broke loose at least he would be somewhat prepared. Unfortunately for the group, he'd decided to cut and run which is why he was stuck in an air vent on top of the station. He idly wondered if the others had been slaughtered or had somehow gotten away.

On his last trip to the end of the vent, he'd looked outside to discover the storm had finally stopped. The night had cleared up beautifully with only some small cloud cover to mar the night sky. As he gazed down on the ground, he could see the frozen ghouls wandering around. There weren't as many as before, so Fredericks assumed the undead had found more humans to prey on.

He had no real plan to escape the situation he now found himself in. All he could do is sit tight and hope something positive would happen.

As his stomach rumbled for the hundredth time, demanding food, he could only pray it would come soon.

* * *

The next morning Shawn and Sara woke up to find a smiling Mark looking down on them. Mark didn't waste anytime filling them in on what he had discovered the night before. Both Sara and Shawn sat there, listening to everything he had to say, and then gave their opinions.

"I think we should go for it. Once we're in the half-track, we should be safe from any wandering zombies. There should also be supplies in the truck for the soldiers when they're on patrol," Shawn said with an excited edge to his voice.

"But what if there are too many out there to hold off?" Sara asked.

"Well, we still have that pistol you found in the office," Mark said. "And Shawn's gun."

Sara looked down at her hands and said: "Oh, well, about that. There hasn't been a chance to tell you, but I can't find it. It's gone; I have no idea where it went."

"Damn," Mark said. "We must have lost it in all the confusion yesterday. I knew one of us should have just taken possession of it instead of leaving it with our stuff." He sighed heavily. "Oh, well, we'll just have to make do with out it."

Shawn thought Mark should have been more upset at Sara for losing the gun, but he'd seen the way the two of them were looking at each other and got the hint.

He smiled to himself thinking about the things a man will let slide when he likes a woman.

After they'd eaten a meager breakfast from their slowly shrinking stores of food, they all made sure to use the bathroom one last time.

Then Mark pushed the desk over to the window and climbed on top of it.

The plan was to break the window and then climb outside and make a run for the buried half-track.

Mark used a leg from the chair as a weapon and broke the window with a crash, the biting cold sweeping in instantly, turning his cheeks red.

He then quickly scraped any excess glass out of the frame, and then climbed outside. He was planning on standing watch while the others climbed out behind him, always wary of anything that might be lurking in the snow.

As he fell out of the window into the snow, some of it went inside his shirt collar. He felt the chill flow down his spine as the snow melted and then warmed from his body heat.

He scanned the area and was pleased to see it was empty, so he waved for Sara to come out. She also fell out of the window and landed in the soft snow. Last out was Shawn, who first tossed their supplies out and then soon followed. He, too, had a chair leg in his hand.

The three of them silently crept across the frozen ground. The half-track was only about fifty feet away, but it seemed like miles as the small group expected a ghoul to jump out at them from the snow at any moment.

As they walked, their shoes crunched over the frost coating the ground; the crunching echoing off the building and sounding like it could be heard clear across the continent. But it couldn't be helped, so they continued on, wary for any signs of movement

Eventually they had made it to the vehicle without incident. Shawn reached up to open the driver's door and was taken completely off guard when it exploded outward. A ghoul had been inside the truck and had waited patiently for them to come to it.

The frozen corpse fell on top of Shawn and was trying to bite his shoulder, but its teeth couldn't penetrate the heavy material of his coat.

"Jesus Christ, Mark, don't just stand there; get this fucking guy off of me!" He screamed as he continued to fight with the living dead man.

To Shawn's surprise, it was Sara who came to his rescue as she was the closest. She came running at them with a flying kick that sent the ghoul rolling off Shawn. Before the pale-blue man could regain his feet, Shawn was up and had cracked the man over the head with the chair leg. One, two, three times he whacked the skull until the ghoul finally remained still.

Breathing heavily from the exertion, Shawn walked back over to the half-track, and with a nod to Sara and a, "thanks a lot," he jumped into the now empty cab to see what it looked like inside. Mark just stood transfixed by what had just transpired. It had happened so fast he'd had no time to react.

Sara walked over to him and he smiled her way. "Damn, remind me never to piss you off," he told her with a smirk.

"And don't you forget it," he added as she swaggered away, deciding she'd see if she could help Shawn.

She then stopped in her tracks, her mouth open, eyes wide in terror, as five ghouls shuffled out of the snow piles and advanced on the half-track.

Seeing the ghouls at almost the same time, Mark ran to her side, the chair leg already raised in his hand. The two of them prepared to try to keep the new attackers at bay so Shawn could get the truck started. Because if he didn't, then they were truly screwed.

Shawn was under the dashboard trying to splice together a few wires for the ignition when he heard Mark calling his name. He looked up to see both Mark and Sara trying to hold back a group of undead who had just popped up out of nowhere.

He was about to climb out and help them when Mark pointed and yelled: "No Shawn, you stay there and get that damn truck running or we're all dead anyway!"

And then he had to turn around and dodge a ghoul who was coming at him from his right.

It killed him to do it, but Shawn knew Mark was right, so he went back underneath the dashboard to continue working.

The first thing he had to do is switch the batteries as the main one was dead.

It looked to Shawn as if the half-track had sat in the yard outside the station with its engine on until it ran out of gas. Then the electrical had stayed on until, it too, had died. But luckily, these vehicles had spare batteries and double fuel tanks. The trick was to change them over without any real tools and a bunch of bloodthirsty zombies trying to eat his ass.

As he twisted another two wires together, he thought about how they never told him about this kind of shit in the Army recruitment manual.

He could see it now. "Join the Army and see the world, oh, yeah and fight zombies in the middle of the Antarctic."

As he twisted the last two wires together, he sat up and turned the key to ON. His face lit up with a smile as the dashboard came to life. "Shit, I'm good," he said to himself.

Now all he had to do was switch the gas tanks and start the engine. He leaned over and felt around under the dash again until he found the switch he needed, then he raised the cover on the switch and flicked it with his thumb. The gas gauge on the dash immediately read full. "Yes," he said as he pumped his arm into the air.

Now was the moment of truth. He held his breath and turned over the engine as he said a silent prayer. The first few tries were failures and he was beginning to get worried that the battery was going to give out on him when the engine suddenly surged to life.

"Oh, yeah, baby!" He yelled to nobody, then revved the motor a few times to make sure the engine was steady. Then with a blast from the horn, he surged forward out of the small snow dune the half-track had been buried in.

As the truck's horn blared behind them, Mark and Sara turned around to see the ice-covered, front grille barreling down on them. They jumped to the side just in time and the vehicle moved past them to plow into the ghouls that had been attacking the two scientists.

Body parts flew everywhere as the front bumper struck and pummeled the brittle bodies, smashing them to pieces on the half-tracks hood. Then Shawn began backing up to return to where Mark and Sara had fallen.

Mark was just getting up and brushing the snow from his clothes when a ghoul came up on him from behind and knocked him to the snow.

Mark was able to turn before he landed and was at least facing his attacker as the frozen ghoul tried to get him. As the jaws came down to try and bite him, Mark stuck the chair leg into the open mouth. While the ghoul fought with him, Mark was able to see that this particular ghoul had once been a soldier. His eye caught the name tag on the breast pocket of the zombie's uniform. The name **Private Boone**, was stenciled in black marker.

However, none of this mattered to Mark while he struggled for his life. As the two of them continued to roll around on the ground, Mark felt the holster at the soldier's hip. With one hand holding the chair leg in the dead man's mouth, he reached his other hand down to the holster to see if it was full or empty.

As his hand unsnapped the holster, he silently yelled for joy when he felt the cold metal of a gun inside. Struggling, he pried the gun loose, and then after it had fallen into the snow was able to grab it again.

With a surge of triumph, he brought the gun up to the soldier's head and pulled the trigger.

"See you in Hell," he said as he expected the gun to buck in his hand.

But instead, nothing happened.

He tried again and squeezed the trigger, but still nothing. The soldier was still fighting with him, and one of its hands was ready to rip out Mark's left eye, so instead of messing with the gun anymore, he took the gun in his hand like a club and began to beat the soldier senseless with the weapon. On the fourth hit, the soldier finally stopped fighting him and Mark let go of the chair leg as it was now in a death grip in the soldier's mouth. He wasn't going to be getting it out of there without a lot of work.

The upper part of Private Boone's head was nothing but a red icy mess now spread over the carpet of snow.

As Sara joined him, he leaned on her shoulder while they made their way to the half-track. Once there, they climbed up into the cab. With a sigh of relief from Mark, the passenger door was slammed closed, locking out any future attacks. Mark looked over his shoulder, out the door's window, to see more ghoul's coming at them from around the corner of the station, but it was too late for the undead to reach them now that they were safely inside the cab of the vehicle.

Shawn put the transmission in drive and began to drive away when he heard the distinctive crack of a pistol over the rumbling engine.

"Did you guys hear that?" He asked as he tried to look out the windows at the surrounding landscape.

"Yes, I heard it, too. If someone's firing a gun then that must mean someone else is alive out here." She turned to Mark and grabbed his arm and pleaded with him.

"Mark, we have to help them. What if it was one of us out there?"

"She makes a good point, Mark," Shawn said from the driver's seat. "If it was me out there, I'd sure as hell would want you to try and help me. They sound close, too, probably just on the other side of the station."

Mark mulled it over for a moment, but in the end he already knew the answer.

"Let's go help whoever's out there," he said. "We have to."

With the decision resolved, Shawn drove to the other side of the station where they had heard the shots. A few ghouls tried to grab the half-track, but they were only caught and ground under the treads, staining the snow a dark crimson.

When Shawn banked around the edge of the station, the three survivors saw a lone man wearing a white lab coat running from at least twenty ghouls. What the man didn't realize was that there was another large group coming from the right side of him, flanking him, and in a matter of moments he would be trapped between the two undead groups. The man was doomed if help didn't find him soon. As the half-track moved closer, Mark was able to make out the features on the terrified man's face.

"Ah, shit," Mark said under his breath. "Not him."

Sara turned to look at him, seeing his distaste and not understanding it, but then she turned and stared out the window again. It was then she recognized the man heading towards them and nodded, understanding clearly.

Though there were more than a hundred personnel assigned to the Amusen Station, it appeared there was only one more survivor.

And the survivor they were racing to save was none other than Dr. Theodore Fredericks.

CHAPTER TWENTY-SIX

FREDERICKS TRIED TO work the cramp out of his leg for the thousandth time since he had climbed into the vent. Deep down, he was really beginning to wonder if he might die in here, when he heard the sound of an engine starting. As he focused his ears to the sound, he was pretty sure it was coming from the other side of the station.

As he crawled to the end of the vent, he could see the ghouls below had also heard the noise and were now heading off in the same direction. Fredcricks decided it was now or never.

He had to get to that vehicle. It was probably his only chance to survive.

As fast as he could possibly manage, he wedged the cover off the end of the vent and dropped down onto the roof of the generator room. The frigid wind bit at his exposed flesh, but he ignored it, knowing frostbite was the least of his concerns. He then dashed across the roof to a side of the building that didn't have too many ghouls below and jumped off the roof.

He aimed for a snow drift that had accumulated against the building from the storm, hoping it would be enough to break his fall.

He landed with a speed that shocked him. He lay in the mound, dazed for a second, a second he realized he didn't have to spare. As he began to climb out of the snow bank, he was shocked to see two arms rise out of the snow, one on each side of him.

In horror, he realized he'd landed on a ghoul that had been hidden inside the snow bank.

As the arms wrapped around him, he struggled to escape but the grip was too strong. And to make matters worse, three more ghouls had noticed the disturbance and were now turning to come for him, as well.

For a moment nothing but terror and panic ruled his mind, but then the analytical scientist took over and looked at his situation from a different perspective.

The first thing he needed to do was get himself disengaged from the ghoul who was now imprisoning him, so he reached up with his hand and was able to get a hold of the ghoul's fingers as they were now wrapped around his chest.

He grabbed the stiff digits one at a time and began snapping them off, the fingers sounded like breaking icicles as he cracked one after the other.

The thumb gave him a little trouble, but with some added pressure, he was able to break the frozen digit off, as well. He then began on the second hand and in a matter of seconds there was nothing left but a frozen stump. The open wounds were red, but didn't bleed due to the frozen nature of the walking corpses.

With all its fingers now gone, the zombie under him wasn't able to maintain a firm grip on him, so he was able to shrug himself out if its frigid grasp. He rolled out onto the ground and came up at the feet of the other ghouls that had been moving towards him.

As they bent over to grab him, he rolled away. And when they followed him, he continued to keep rolling. If he stopped for the split second needed to regain his footing, they would be on him.

He continued to roll away from them in the open area until he came up short against another snow drift. As his body rolled into it, the snow flowed over him, blocking his body from the chasing ghouls. His exposed skin was so cold he thought it would crack from exposure, but he ignored the pain, knowing he needed to remain still.

As the trio of ghouls dived into the snow bank to grab him, he realized the snow was basically fluff, so he began to push his way through it to escape the grasping limbs trying to get a hold of his body. The snow began to get into his nose and mouth as he tried to breathe so he pulled his shirt over the lower half of his face. That helped a little, but he knew if he didn't find the other side soon, he would die of suffocation.

He continued to crawl through the drift as the snow weighed down on him. It didn't feel so fluffy to him anymore but still he slowly pushed his way through.

When he thought he couldn't make it another inch, his head popped out the other side of the snow drift. He quickly pulled himself out of the snow, and as it cascaded off his body, it made him look like one of the frozen ghouls.

He heard a horn blare and knew he had to keep moving. As he ran in the direction of the vehicle again, he glanced over his shoulder to see the three ghouls were still digging in the snow drift. Still looking for their lost prey.

As he came around the corner of the station, he stopped. He was now behind a large group of ghouls who had been going to the source of the noise, as well.

He hesitated for only a moment.

He knew what he had to do.

Pulling the pistol out of his pants, he took a deep breath and began running into the crowd of undead.

Because he was coming at them from behind, the zombies didn't realize he was among them. As he ran into their midst, he shouldered them aside as he made a mad dash to what he hoped was salvation.

He hit one ghoul so hard from behind he knocked the zombie flat on its face. As it fell to the ground, he just ran over the body. His shoe landed on its head and pushed the pale-blue face deep into the fresh snow covering the ground. As he continued onward, the zombie pushed itself back up and sputtered snow out of its mouth, looking more like a carnival clown with pie on its face than one of the walking dead.

As Fredericks cleared the front line of the undead horde, he now realized he was now the focus of their attention. But it couldn't be helped as he put on a burst of speed to try and reach the vehicle he'd heard.

A ghoul popped out of a snow dune in front of him and he raised the pistol and fired point blank at the frozen head. When the bullet impacted with the ghoul's head, it snapped back from the force of round. With the back of its head now shattered into hundreds of frozen pieces, the body pitched backward into the snow. It didn't move again.

No sooner had Fredericks shot the gun than the ghoul was forgotten, his attention only for running. But then he slipped, his shoes not made for running on snow and ice and he pitched forward into the snow. His face dug a groove in the ice and he sputtered ice crystals from his mouth, swallowing the melting snow. Rising to his feet again, he saw he'd lost valuable time and the chasing ghouls were gaining on him. Picking up his pace, he headed off again, and when he rounded a large, ten foot, pile of snow, a military half-track came into view moving directly towards him.

A ray of hope filled him at the sight of the vehicle, but when he glanced over his shoulder to see the other ghouls still chasing him; he could only pray the half-track would reach him in time.

Chapter Twenty-seven

Shawn floored the gas pedal, the half-track swerving in the snow the result. The stabilizing skids attached to the sides of the vehicle only did so much to control its stability. He was still driving on ice and snow and would only be allowed so much maneuverability at any given speed.

And at the moment, he was going way too fast to properly control the vehicle.

When he saw the single man running across the snow, he had turned the vehicle in his direction and floored it. In a matter of seconds the half-track would be on top of him.

When he was close enough to see who it was, he was quite surprised.

"Holy shit," he said as he swerved around another bad spot in the snow. "That's Dr. Fredericks."

"Yeah, I know who it is, but go ahead and save him anyway," Mark said from beside him.

Between holding the half-track steady and now aiming for the walking zombies, Shawn missed the irony in Mark's voice.

"I'm gonna take out that group coming up on his right. When I do, you guys reach out and grab him," Shawn told them as he pointed the grille of the vehicle at the approaching ghouls. Both Mark and Sara looked at each other and then at Shawn.

"Got it," Mark said for both of them.

Shawn was aiming at the first walking corpse in line and when he plowed into it at plus forty miles per hour, the body rebounded off the grille and went flying into the air. When it finally came back down to earth, it landed on the ground in a very different state than before. Now, it was missing most of its extremities. But the torso wasn't alone for long. The half-track plowed into the other ghouls, and one at a time, they were launched into the air from the impact of the vehicle's grille.

Body parts were flying everywhere as the frozen and brittle bodies broke apart on impact with either the half-track or the frozen ground when they finally came back to earth.

Shawn watched with mild amusement at the damage he had wrought.

"Wow, did you guys see that? I guess they don't build zombies like they used to," he said with a mischievous smirk as he swerved to take out another one.

Fredericks had seen all the action taking place in front of him and breathed a sigh of relief when he saw the half-track now heading directly for him, and taking out a formidable group of ghouls at the same time.

He altered his direction so as to come up next to the vehicle when it pulled over to him. He was quite surprised to see who opened the door and reached a hand out to help him inside.

"Simmons? Well, I don't believe it. You're still alive?" Fredericks asked as he climbed up into the cab.

"Believe it. Alive and saving your ass... again Now shut up and get in or I'll leave you here to be lunch," Mark growled as he pulled him inside and closed the door.

Mark looked over at Shawn and wondered why they hadn't left yet.

"Okay, Shawn whenever you're ready. Although now would be good," Mark told him.

"I'm trying, but the damn truck won't go into drive," he said as he fought with the stick shift.

While Shawn was struggling to put the truck into drive, the vehicle was slowly being surrounded by the frozen dead.

"Ah, Shawn, have you looked outside recently?" Mark asked as the ghouls began to climb onto the truck.

"Jesus, Mark, I'm a little busy here. If you want me to look outside so…" He stopped in mid-sentence when he saw what Mark was talking about. In the time it took to get Fredericks inside with them and prepare to leave, more ghouls had shown up and now the truck was surrounded by at least fifty of them.

"Oh, shit, we are so fuckin' screwed," Shawn gasped and then began to fight with the shifter again.

The ghouls were now covering the truck, the ones on the hood banging on the windows in an attempt to gain access. In the small cab behind Mark and Shawn, Sara sat and watched helpless as the frozen dead covered the entire truck. Then she leaned over to Shawn and asked him: "Shawn, does the truck still go in reverse?"

"Reverse? Of course it does, I… Shit, how could I be so stupid?" He asked as he struck his forehead with his hand.

Fredericks, who had recovered some of his composure now that he was relatively safe was the first to add something.

"Quite easily I would imagine, Private. Now would you please get us out of here?" Fredericks pleaded from the back.

"I have to agree with the little bastard Shawn," Mark said under his breath so only Shawn could hear him. "Give it a try."

Shawn nodded and slammed the truck into reverse and then hit the gas. With an exhalation of his breath, he pressed the gas pedal and the truck surged backwards, throwing the ghouls off the truck. Shawn backed up slowly as he had no idea where he was going. The half-track crunched over bodies that weren't able to get out of the way in time, grinding and pulverizing arms, legs and heads like they were nothing more than baby food.

After a few seconds, Shawn brought the vehicle to a stop. They were out of the immediate area of trouble for the moment although they could hear footsteps walking around on the roof of the cab.

"Shit, they're on the roof!" Shawn yelled as he put the truck into park again.

"What are we going to do? We can't drive in reverse all the way to Kryton Station. It's over a hundred miles away," Sara said from the back.

Before anyone could answer, Shawn put the shifter back into drive and tried again. With relief flooding his face, the transmission made a few grinding noises and then the vehicle bucked forward, already beginning moving more smoothly with each passing second.

"Yes, yes, yes," he said as he turned the wheel to get them away from Amusen Station. "The transmission is definitely going, but hopefully it'll make it to Kryton before it gives out completely," he said as he avoided a bad patch of ice in front of him. I wouldn't want to take a chance and take it out of drive again."

"So you're saying if we stop the truck it's possible it won't go again," Mark said as he looked at Shawn.

"That's right, we either keep going or we'll probably be walking."

"Then it's simple, we keep going until we make it to help," Mark told him.

"But what about the dead guys on the roof? We can't leave them up there, especially if they're contagious. We don't want to bring the infection with us to Kryton," Sara reasoned from behind him.

Mark sighed. "I know, Sara, that's why I'm going to go out on the roof and knock them off."

"That's ridiculous, Simmons. What if they overwhelm you? If you fall off it will be quite difficult to try and retrieve you," Fredericks added from the back next to Sara.

"You could always come with me?" Mark asked Fredericks.

Fredericks just looked at him with a 'don't be ridiculous' stare and then pretended to busy himself with something in the back.

"That's what I thought," he said and then turned to Shawn. "You keep it steady, all right?"

Shawn nodded. "I got ya, but listen, I have to keep the speed at about twenty-five miles an hour or we'll get bogged down in the soft snow out here. If it wasn't for the skids attached to this thing we would've been stuck a while ago."

"I hear you. You just do your best to keep it steady," he said as he slapped Shawn on the shoulder. "I trust you."

Shawn nodded in reply, a quick gesture almost missed if Mark hadn't been looking straight at the army private.

Sara handed Mark a heavy weather coat, one of three she'd found under the seat she was sitting on, along with a few other supplies like a pair of gloves.

"Here, I found these under the seat. You're going to need them for sure out there," she told him.

With a quick nod for a thank you, Mark took the coat and shrugged into it, his mind on what awaited him on the roof of the half-track. He was just getting ready to open the door and climb out when he felt a hand on his shoulder. He turned slightly to see Sara staring at him, her eyes filled with concern for his welfare.

"You be careful out there," she said while placing a hand tentatively on his arm. He placed his hand on hers, squeezing gently.

"Piece of cake. You'll see, I'll be back in a minute."

And then Mark opened the door, and with the frigid wind cutting through the cab like a knife, he climbed out onto the roof.

CHAPTER TWENTY-EIGHT

THE DOOR BLEW out of Mark's hand the moment he opened it. Even though the half-track wasn't going very fast, the wind was amplified due to the open plain they were driving across.

The wind immediately found every open spot on his clothing, slipping into the crevices in his jacket, and he was chilled to the bone before he was fully out of the cab.

Mark looked down at the snowy ground rolling by below his feet. Shawn may not have been going very fast, but as the treads churned the snow up and then spit it out behind the vehicle; he still wouldn't want to fall underneath them. A very different chill went down his spin as he thought about that for a second.

As he began climbing onto the roof, he was wary of anything that might be lurking there. He had no idea how many were up there or where they might be positioned.

As he reached the end of the side, he slowly poked his head up over the edge. There were three ghouls sitting down on the roof. Due to the rocking of the half-track, they couldn't maintain their balance and had opted to sit down. Mark thought about this for a moment. Did this mean they could reason? Or had they just fallen down when the vehicle began moving and had just stayed there, not really knowing what they should do?

Mark watched one of the ghouls on the roof. The dead woman was sitting right on the edge of the other side of the vehicle's roof, staring at the sky like a dullard, and that gave him an idea.

He climbed back down and then went onto the hood of the half-track and then climbed over to the other side. He paused for a second and waved hello as he passed by the windshield. The others inside just watched him with open mouths, wondering what the hell he was doing.

Once he had made it over the hood, he climbed down the other side of the vehicle and got directly below the woman.

Luckily, there were numerous places for him to secure his hands while he progressed across the side. The wind was a constant problem, and if he hadn't been wearing gloves, his hands would have been numb in seconds.

Once he was below the woman, he carefully climbed up until he was in reaching distance of her. Then, when he was sure he had a good grip on the side of the vehicle with his left hand, he reached up with his right hand, grabbing the woman by her flapping white lab coat and pulling her off the truck.

The woman's arms flew out in front of her as she toppled off the roof. Mark caught a quick look at her face when she flew by him and she didn't even realize what had just happened to her until she hit the icy ground behind the half-track.

Mark watched as she disappeared into the darkness behind him, wondering if she was dead or just broken up a bit. Then he pushed the thought away from his mind because one of the other ghouls had noticed what had happened and was now crawling towards him.

Before Mark could climb away, the ghoul had reached over the side and grabbed him by the hair. As the ghoul tried to pull him up, Mark attempted to hold his ground and stay where he was. Unfortunately, the ghoul had the better leverage and was slowly winning the battle, pulling him up an inch at a time.

Mark decided he had only one option, so he turned to the front of the vehicle and yelled to Shawn. It took several tries for Shawn to hear him over the rumbling of the treads, but finally Shawn rolled down his window and yelled back to him.

"What do you want me to do?" Shawn called over his shoulder out the window, while he used the half-track's door side mirror to see Mark.

"When I say so, hit the brakes for just a second, but wait for me to say so!"

Mark called to Shawn.

Shawn stuck his hand out the window, his index finger and thumb making the sign of OK, and then got ready for Mark's signal.

Mark made sure he had both hands firmly locked onto handholds on the side and then wedged his legs into some holes near his feet, as well. Then with the ghoul still pulling on his hair, he yelled to Shawn.

"Now, Shawn, hit the brakes, now!"

Shawn hit the brakes hard for only a second, and as the half-track's momentum stopped for that fraction of an instant, the ghoul above Mark flew over the hood of the vehicle and took a hunk of Mark's hair with it when it became airborne. The ghoul's body just caught the tip of the hood and then went under the front bumper with a crunching sound like a car rolling over ice cubes. Then the corpse was lost in the darkness. Just like its now departed sister had been only minutes before. Satisfied he was finished for now, and not worried about the last ghoul still on the roof, he turned to head back inside the cab.

That was more than enough action for one day. Slowly and carefully, he made his way back around the side, then over the hood, until he was climbing back inside the cab.

When he closed the door and was once again safe inside the truck, he blew out the deep breath he'd been holding.

"Wow, that was fun," he said.

"Did you get them all?" Shawn asked as he kept his eyes on the darkness in front of them.

"There's still one left. That last one took a piece of me with it," he said as he reached up to feel his head. There was just a little blood on his fingertips when he pulled them away from his scalp. He was very surprised there was only a little blood, actually. The way it felt when the ghoul flew off the roof, he would have figured half his scalp had gone with it.

"So what are you going to do about the other one, Dr. Simmons?" Fredericks inquired from behind him.

"Well, I thought you could take care of that one for me," he teased as he turned to look at Fredericks. Fredericks simply frowned, finding the idea very unappealing.

"Why don't you just shoot the last one off with the gun you found," Shawn mused askance of him.

Mark thought about it for a moment. "I don't know, with all the bouncing around it would be hard to get a good shot at it."

"Well then, let me have a go at it. Me and you can switch places. We won't even have to stop," Shawn suggested.

Mark thought about it for only a second. If it meant he didn't have to go back outside again then he was all for it.

"Okay, sounds good to me, let's do it," Mark told him.

Together Mark and Shawn began trading places. As Sara watched from the back, she chuckled. The two of them looked like one of those buddy comedy shows on television.

Eventually, with a lot of elbows in crotches and pokes in the ribs, the two men had made the switch. For just a second, the two of them sat quietly, taking a breather.

After shrugging into one of the jackets, Shawn grabbed the gun off the floor where Mark had left it and got ready to climb outside.

"Okay, now the same goes for you, Mark. You make sure and keep it steady and try to keep it at about twenty-five mph."

Mark just nodded and said: "Good luck and watch out for the bumps. Always keep at least one hand firmly on something."

"Got, it," Shawn nodded and opened the cab door.

Shawn, too, was immediately frozen to the bone from the chill air as it found every open seam in his clothing. As he climbed out onto the side of the half-track, he gazed up at the night sky and then all around him. With the exception of the headlights, utter darkness ruled the landscape. With the winter months now here, it would stay like this for at least the next three months.

Shawn pushed such trivial matters out of his mind and concentrated on the matter at hand. As he poked his head over the edge of the roof, he could see the ghoul was laying flat on the roof, just barely holding on. The ghoul was wearing a gray janitorial uniform and Shawn actually recognized the dead man.

It was Fred.

Fred was in his late fifties and had come to Antarctica more than two years ago. His wife had died a few years ago from lymphoma and his kids were all grown up and had moved away, so he had decided to begin a new life for himself at the edge of the world. Unfortunately, it hadn't worked out as Fred had planned, what with becoming a zombie and all.

From where Shawn was located on the side, he was safe from being grabbed by Fred, so he climbed up a little more and yelled to get the dead man's attention.

When Fred heard him, he turned over and began to crawl toward him.

Shawn patiently waited until Fred was so close he could see the frozen pupils of his eyes reflecting the moonlight. Then he aimed the gun directly at said pupil and pulled the trigger.

Fred's head snapped back when the bullet penetrated his skull. The gun wasn't a large caliber, so the bullet just ricocheted inside his cranium until it lost momentum and stopped. But by then his brain was nothing but frozen slush.

As the body went slack and slumped to the roof, Shawn climbed up over the edge.

"Sorry, Fred, I really am," Shawn said to the corpse, and then with a heave, he pushed the body off the roof where it fell into the wake of the treads below. Within seconds the janitor was lost from sight.

With a job well done, Shawn climbed back down the side and then made his way to the cab.

It looked like they were finally out of the woods. They had escaped with their lives, and by tomorrow, would be at another research station where they could report the outbreak and finally relax in safety.

Yes, Shawn thought, it had been a rough ride, but it looked like they would be okay.

But if Shawn had been able to see the ground behind the back of the half-track, he might have noticed the small drops of red fluid that were dripping onto the snow.

And that small thing might have changed his opinion of their upcoming future dramatically.

CHAPTER TWENTY-NINE

THE HALF TRACK shook as it drove over another pile of ice and snow. They had been driving for at least three hours now and there was nothing around for miles but a wasteland of ice and snow. If the half-track was to breakdown now, they would be stranded in the middle of nowhere with no way of finding help.

Inside the cab, spirits were high. Sara had found a backpack full of supplies from the last occupants and she had handed them to the group. While they had a meager meal of saltines and spam, popular in the Antarctic because it didn't freeze, they talked about what would happen when they arrived at Kryton Station in the morning.

"The first thing we need to do is find the communications building and notify the mainland what went down back there," Mark said around a mouthful of crackers.

"Yes, and we need to tell the researchers to notify anyone out on the plains to stay away, as well," Sara said from the back of the cab "The station needs to be quarantined until our government can get in there and regain order.".

"What do you thinks gonna happen to us?" Shawn asked from the driver's seat.

He had taken over the driving from Mark about a half hour ago and was feeling pretty refreshed.

They had to take turns driving more frequently due to the driving conditions they were dealing with. The steering wheel of the half-track constantly fought the driver as the treads bounced over irregularities in the terrain. Plus, as they were all exhausted after their escape from Amusen Station, the constant darkness had a way of making even the most alert person tired.

"That's a good question, first we'll probably be debriefed and then there'll probably be countless interviews as the guys in charge try to figure this whole mess out," Mark theorized.

Frederick's was silent in the back of the cab. He listened to the others with a grim look on his face. He'd learned a long time ago that listening instead of talking would get you far more information. Soon the others stopped talking, each becoming lost in their thoughts as they contemplated the future.

There wasn't much to see. With the only light for miles around being the half-track's headlights, he was only able to see a few feet on the side of the vehicle as the frozen ground drifted by.

Mark leaned his head against the glass and gazed out his window.

To Mark it almost felt like he was on a boat surrounded by a sea of white.

It didn't take long for the steady vibration of the vehicle to lull him into a light daydream.

In his daydream, he was back on the beach again, except this time the beach was covered in snow. When he looked over at his side, instead of Sara next to him there was a woman ghoul sitting there. All she had on was a white bikini and her blue skin was clearly visible as Mark's eyes roamed up and down her body.

If she hadn't been one of the frozen dead, Mark admired she would have been attractive. Her legs were shapely and went up to a slim waist that then continued up to a chest with two full breasts sitting inside her bikini top.

Her face was a dull blue and her hair would have been blonde if it hadn't been discolored with dirt and ice. Her hair now carried a subtle blue tint to it, as well.

What struck Mark odd was that she had makeup on. She was wearing the kind of makeup hookers or really old women would use to try to make themselves look attractive.

As Mark stared at her, she leaned over and batted her eyes at him. For some reason, he felt the urge to kiss her, so he bent over in his chair and pressed his lips to hers.

When their mouths touched, he could feel the cold radiating off of her. As she slipped her swollen black tongue into his mouth, he was reminded of a frozen fish that had been partially thawed out in the hot sun. He tried to pull away from her, but she had his head between her hands and she wouldn't let go. As he strained to pull away, he suddenly felt the cold from her mouth spreading down his throat and into the rest of his body.

That was when he began to scream.

The screams were muffled, as she still had her mouth covering his, and try as he might, he couldn't break free.

He felt like he was suffocating, the cold totally suffusing his body. While he was locked in her embrace, he began shivering from her touch, and he realized he was slowly freezing to death. That was when he let out another scream...

And then he was awake inside the cab once more.

Looking around, he saw the driver's door was open and the frigid wind and a dusting of snow flakes were blowing inside the cab.

For just a second he realized that was why he had been so cold in his dream. He gazed out the front window and saw the hood of the half-track was up, the others gathered around the front grille in a loose circle.

Mark opened his door and hopped down into the snow. Now that he was outside, he could really feel the snow penetrate his clothes. Wrapping his coat around him tighter, he walked up to the front of the truck to join the others.

"What's going on? What's wrong?" He called to them as he came up beside them.

"Hey, Mark, how was your nap?" Shawn said with a frown.

"It was great. Now, why the hell is everybody standing out in the middle of nowhere with the hood up?" He snapped back.

"It would seem, Dr. Simmons, that we are having mechanical troubles. Would it not?" Fredericks added.

"What kind of mechanical troubles?" Mark asked again this time looking to Shawn for answers.

"Well, the best I can tell is the transmission fluid has drained out, and once it was gone, we fried the tranny."

"You can't be serious," Mark said as he looked at the three faces surrounding him. But their grim countenances said the truth.

They were stuck.

"Mark, do you have any ideas what we should do? We were just talking about that subject before you joined us," Sara said as she gazed into his eyes.

"Why didn't anyone wake me up?" Mark asked of the group.

Shawn let out a quick laugh. "Why? Unless you had some transmission fluid hidden somewhere there wasn't any reason to. No, I figured I'd just let you sleep and the others agreed with me."

Mark frowned as he analyzed the situation.

"How far do you think we are from Kryton Station?" He asked Shawn

Shawn's brow creased as he gave that some thought. "I'd say we've got about a days travel if you're thinking of walking. But hopefully, once we get closer, we might get lucky and be spotted by a research group or a patrol."

Mark nodded. "I don't think we have a choice. If we stay here we'll die of hypothermia or starvation. At least if we head out now while we're still strong, we'll have a chance, slim as it may be."

The others looked at each other for a few moments, as if trying to read what the other was thinking; then Shawn spoke up. "Makes sense, it's either walk or die."

Mark clapped his hands together. "Okay, then, let's get our gear together and pack as much extras as we can carry. We might as well head out now as it's as light out as it's gonna get. Let's take as much burnable material as we can carry. It'll be nice to have a fire, even if it's just for a little while." He was about to say more, but he caught the look on Frederick's face.

"You want to add something, Fredericks?" Mark asked the man, his tone dripping with contempt.

Fredericks shook his head. "No, Dr. Simmons, I believe you've said it all quite well."

Mark turned away and then stopped again; realizing Fredericks had tossed a double entendre at him.

He was about to say more, but Sara stopped him with a hand on his arm.

She waited for Shawn and Fredericks to go back inside the cab and then as the two of them stood in the headlights, she asked him one question.

"Mark, do you really think we'll make it all the way there?"

He looked down at her and smiled. "Sara," he said softly. "If I have to I'll put you on my back and carry you there myself."

She grinned and leaned against him. Then she gazed up into his eyes and he leaned forward cautiously, seeing what she would do. She didn't pull away and they kissed for the first time.

Out in the middle of nowhere, where death loomed everywhere, they kissed. And for that brief moment, Mark would not have wanted to be anywhere else on Earth but right here, right now.

Then Shawn leaned on the horn and the two of them jumped. Mark looked up at the windshield to see Shawn waving for him to come on and get moving.

The two of them disengaged from each other and Mark could see Sara was blushing. "To be continued?" She asked him.

"Definitely," he replied.

With the two of them feeling like teenagers at the end of a first date, they went to help the others pack up and get ready to move on.

Twenty minutes later, they were ready to go. Shawn had stripped the truck's seats of its material and had even ripped some of the headliner off the ceiling of the cab.

Anything that could be burned was packed up into a small sack. Shawn tied it to the end of a rope and was planning on dragging it behind him in the snow while they hiked across the icy plains. Both Mark and Sara had small packs to carry, leaving Fredericks with nothing. Mark was pretty sure Fredericks had maneuvered this to happen just this way and it was just one more reason for Mark to dislike the man.

The four of them set out across the white, frozen plain. Mark took point with Sara right behind him. Fredericks took the middle and Shawn the end, with his pack dragging behind him. Shawn had found a compass in the glove box and so had them on a proper heading to reach Kryton Station.

As they walked single file into the oppressive darkness, Shawn turned around one last time to look at the half-track. They had already walked a quarter of a mile and the vehicle's headlights were all he could see when he glanced back. And as he continued onward, it wasn't long before those, too, were slowly swallowed by the darkness.

Shawn gazed up at the night sky, his warm breath blowing out each time he exhaled. Despite the dire straits he now found himself in, he still couldn't help but marvel at the beauty surrounding him.

Then he looked forward and concentrated on putting one foot in front of the other.

*   *   *

The half-track sat motionless in the darkness, the last of the battery's power giving out about an hour ago, the headlights finally blinking off. The treads of the vehicle were half-buried in the snow, the wind blowing the snow against the sides. In time, the entire vehicle would be gone, replaced by a large snow dune.

From beneath the undercarriage, something dropped to the ground with a soft thud, the snow cushioning the impact.

After a full minute had passed, a body crawled out from under the half-track and raised itself to a standing position.

The zombie who was once known as Mathew Simpson gazed out on the desolate, frozen plain.

As he looked for any signs of the occupants of the half-track, he could tell immediately they were long gone.

Stumbling around to the front bumper, he noticed the footprints leading off into the distance, the wan luminance coming from the night sky just enough to navigate the frozen plains, the snow reflecting whatever ambient light was available.

Simpson began walking; putting his shoes into the tracks of the people he hunted. Or more precisely, the person he hunted.

When Simpson was being torn apart by the ghouls, and Fredericks had just shrugged and ran away, leaving him to die, the anger, loathing and betrayal he'd felt had somehow transcended the void between life and death.

Simpson's need for vengeance was so powerful that when he came back after dying, only one thought dominated his now shattered mind.

To find and kill Fredericks.

When the half-track had run over the crowd of ghouls the day before, he had been plowed underneath the undercarriage with the others, but he'd not been hurt and had reached up and insinuated himself in between the spare tire and the fuel tank. He'd stayed there quietly, waiting for his chance to get Fredericks, but it had never come. As the hours wore on, he had remained perfectly still. For the dead don't need to stretch or go to the bathroom or get cold.

So now he would follow the tracks in the snow wherever they may lead.

And when he found the man who caused him to become an abomination of nature, he would kill him slowly. Or better yet, make him one of the walking dead, as well.

As the lone walking corpse trudged alone in silence through the heavy snow on the vast desolate plain in the middle of Antarctica, frozen lips cracked just a little as Simpson smiled in anticipation of what was to come.

CHAPTER THIRTY

ONE FOOT IN front of the other; that's all Mark could think of.

They had been walking for hours and although Mark liked to consider himself fit, he was really testing the limits of his body on this trek across the frozen wasteland of Antarctica.

He turned slightly, glancing over his shoulder to check on Sara. She was trudging along behind him, her face a blank slate as she concentrated on walking.

The footing was treacherous, none of them knowing what lay underneath the thin layer of snow. Each footstep had to be lifted out of the snow and then placed more forward than normal to avoid tripping, it was like walking in knee-high water, only thicker.

Sometimes they had found themselves walking on sheets of ice that were frozen over small bodies of water. Luckily, the temperature stayed well below freezing and the ice was safe to walk on. But the same temperatures that saved them from falling through the ice were also damaging their faces, fingertips and toes.

Already Mark could feel some of his fingertips becoming numb from the frigid cold. And he didn't even want to think about what his face looked like.

He knew they would have to stop soon and build a shelter or else probably freeze to death from the cold or perhaps just drop from exhaustion.

As he looked back at the end of their small line, he could see Shawn wasn't doing any better than the others. He caught a quick glimpse of Fredericks behind Sara and the man looked about the same.

At least when he looked at Fredericks, he received a modicum of satisfaction at seeing the man suffer.

He turned forward again and concentrated on walking. The sky was clear for the moment, but off on the horizon he could discern clouds heading their way. In a matter of a few hours they would be in for another storm.

All around him was nothing but blackness. It was like the sun had exploded and left the planet in utter darkness. Without even a flashlight to help them on their way, it was a constant battle to stay on course, as they had no marker ahead of them to follow. Many times in the past few hours, Shawn had caught them going off course and had to correct their path. Mark always wondered how many wasted footsteps they had made before they were put back on course again.

An hour later, Mark could feel a drop in the temperature as they continued walking and decided it was time to stop and hunker down. The drop in the temperature signaled a coming storm and unless they had shelter, there was no way they would survive exposed out on the frozen plain.

Quickly, he called a halt and explained to everyone how to build a small igloo.

The four of them began forming blocks out of the snow, and one at a time they piled them on top of the other until they only had a roof to cover. It wasn't pretty, and certainly didn't look like what someone would imagine a standard igloo should look like, but it would do the job well.

It was Shawn's idea to cover the roof with the seat covers from the half-track, thus saving them time and energy in trying to fashion a roof out of snow.

By the time they were finished with the igloo, over two more hours had passed.

The wind had now picked up and snow was falling. Within another hour the storm would be right on top of them. One at a time they crawled into the igloo, with Mark going in last and pulling clumps of wet snow behind him to block out the blowing snow and wind.

Once inside, there was barely enough room for the four survivors. Mark crawled next to Sara and she snuggled close to him for warmth.

"What do you think, Mark, should we build a fire?" Shawn asked from directly across from him.

Mark only gave it the briefest of thought before he told Shawn his opinion.

"I think we should wait a while. I know we're all cold, but I think the temperature's going to drop even lower, and when it does, that's when we're really going to need that added warmth.

"Too bad, I was hoping we could roast some marshmallows," Fredericks facetiously said.

Mark chose to ignore him and continued talking to Shawn.

"Now, when the storm hits, we have to make sure we keep a small hole in the top of the igloo open or we'll suffocate from carbon dioxide in here. Got it?" He asked Shawn as he pulled Sara closer to him.

Shawn just nodded and pulled his arms tighter around himself.

Fredericks just sat quietly thinking to himself. And that was just fine with Mark.

Less than an hour later the storm hit; the wind pelting the little igloo with ice and hail. For the moment, the four survivors huddled down, safe in their small shelter as the Antarctic storm threw all it had at them.

Sitting in the dark there wasn't much to do but sleep, so in no time Mark and the others had fallen into a deep slumber brought on from exhaustion and stress.

Thankfully, no dreams intruded on Mark's restless slumber.

*　　*　　*

Miles away from the lone igloo, the frozen corpse named Simpson continued trudging through the storm. Although the cold didn't bother him, the inclement weather did slow him down. At the rate he was walking, he was moving at half the speed of the survivors. Unfortunately for him, as the snow and wind continued, it was slowly obliterating his quarry's trail.

Still he continued on, the heat of revenge warming his frozen heart.

He would find Fredericks or die again trying.

CHAPTER THIRTY-ONE

WHILE THE FOUR companions slept precariously in their ice shelter, the storm howled relentlessly outside. Hours had passed since they had crawled inside the frozen cube and sealed themselves in.

Inside the small igloo, the four companions were now deep in sleep, the exhaustion of the day's activities hitting them hard.

As Shawn slept, he began to toss and turn in his corner of the small shelter as nightmares intruded on his restful slumber.

Moments later, Shawn opened his eyes inside his dream world. He had that feeling of knowing he was dreaming, but yet unable to stop it or control it.

He was in the forest. And as he looked around, the sky was clear and he could hear birds singing from inside the majestic treetops.

He didn't know what he should do, so he began walking deeper into the woods.

As he walked, the tree tops became thicker above his head and soon the sun was all but blocked out by the thick entwining branches.

The forest began to take on an eerie quality as he wandered aimlessly, a preternatural silence descending over the land. And then he spotted a break in the tree line and light shining through. He began running for the light, and within moments, found himself standing on the edge of a massive cliff.

As he gazed out across the open expanse, he could see another cliff on the far side a good half mile away. In between the two cliff edges was a small rickety bridge. It creaked as it swayed back and forth in the air currents that floated up from below. As Shawn looked down, he saw a drop that had to be at least a thousand feet or more, ending in a raging river of rocks and water. Off to the side, at the opening to the bridge, stood a sign with a skull and crossbones painted on it in red. As Shawn investigated more closely, he reached out and touched the paint. Rubbing it in between his fingers it felt smooth, and when he put his finger to his nose, he smelled the distinct odor of copper. If he was right, this sign was painted in blood; and recently.

Swallowing the knot in his throat, he put his first foot out in front of him and began to traverse the bridge. Deep inside his mind, the part of him that knew this was a dream, yelled at his dreamself to stay on the cliff.

Don't step out on the bridge of death!

But it wasn't heeded. Shawn's foot pressed down on the first worn piece of wood on the rickety bridge and he strode forward. The bridge creaked in protest as he started across; the bridge now swaying with the motion of his footsteps.

When he gazed down below his feet, through the slats in the wood, he felt a rush of vertigo and quickly looked back up and straight ahead.

In a matter of a few minutes, he had made it to the middle of the bridge. The swaying of the bridge was the worst here and he struggled to hold on to the thin rope that meandered along with the bridge on either side at about waist height.

Then his foot came down on a rotted piece of planking and his legs fell through the slats, taking the rest of his body with them.

He had just enough time to reach out with his arms and halt his descent so that now his lower body was swinging in midair and only his fragile grip on a piece of rope was keeping him from plummeting to his death.

As he held on for dear life, and his body swayed with the air currents, he desperately tried to pull himself back up, but his arms were at such an angle he just didn't have the muscle mass to haul himself back up.

He stayed there for what seemed like hours until he saw shadows blocking the sun and then moving in a circle and returning. As he crooked his neck to look up, he saw what appeared to be buzzards floating on the air currents above him.

After another hour or so the birds gained the courage to come closer and landed near him on the bridge. The two buzzards slowly walked up to him to investigate their find.

When one was right on top of him, it poked its beak at Shawn's hand. If he tried to pull away, he would loose his grip on the rope and fall to his death, so he spat at it and yelled: "Fuck off, ya filthy bastard!"

The birds jumped back for a second, startled, but when nothing else threatened them, they quickly ignored him and went back to poking his hand.

One at a time they darted in and took a bite out of Shawn's flesh.

Buzzards were basically cowards and preferred dead flesh, but when their prey was alive and helpless like Shawn, they would make an exception. The birds darted in again and again, taking pieces of his hand with them. Shawn yelled and screamed at them, but to no avail.

It was when one of the birds went for his face that Shawn knew he was in real trouble, not that he was in great shape as it was.

The bird's beak, already covered in Shawn's blood, darted toward his face, going for his left eye. He tried to turn his head away, but wasn't able to go far. The bird simply hopped closer and dove in. Shawn squeezed his eyes closed as tight as he could, but it was hopeless. As the bird started to rip away his eyelid to gain access to the juicy eyeball beneath, he screamed in agony. The bird ignored him and continued to burrow into the socket until its beak was able to get a grip on the eye and pull it out. Shawn could feel the ripping of the nerves as the eyeball was plucked from its socket, a viscous ooze dripping down his cheek. He screamed again louder, his shrieks of pain echoing off the jagged walls of the cliffs. As he dangled helplessly on the bridge, he considered letting go. At least it would be painless; better than being slowly picked apart by buzzards, anyway.

The other bird went at his other eye with the same results, except this time when Shawn yelled his pain to the empty cliffs, the other buzzard dove in and grabbed his soft tongue in its beak. Shawn pulled his head back and bit down hard just as the buzzard pulled back its beak with its price. Shawn's teeth clamped down on his tongue and sliced his tongue in two.

As the blood began to pour into his mouth, he tried to turn his head and spit, but due to his angle it was almost impossible. He tried to swallow the blood filling his mouth, but it was just too much and he began gagging.

That's when he made his decision. He was now blind and drowning in his own blood.

His situation was beyond hopeless, so he decided to let go and at least deprive these carnivore bastards of feeding on him.

It was easier than he thought to let go due to the fact that because he was now blind, the intimidation of the drop below held no meaning anymore. As the birds darted in to take another bite from him, he let go, taking solace in the fact that at least he was depriving them of a free meal.

The wind howled around him and he felt like he was flying. The cold air surrounded him and he could now feel the mist from the raging water below. He wondered when he'd hit the water as he continued to fall....

Only to be awakened by Mark a heartbeat later.

As he opened his sleep encrusted eyes, he could feel the snow and wind on his face and neck. He looked up to see the roof of their igloo had fallen in from the weight of the snow.

Mark positioned himself so they were face to face and then said: "The roof caved in, when I looked outside the storm had stopped, we should all grab a bite to eat and get moving."

Shawn nodded and tried to stretch in the close confines of the shelter, the pressure on his bladder already screaming for attention.

"Okay, just give me a second," he said.

The last images of his dream washed across his mind, but he pushed them away. It was time to deal with reality. When he stood up, he whacked his head on the edge of the igloo and swore loudly.

Sara laughed next to him as she handed him one of their last candy bars.

"I did the same thing a few seconds ago. It'll be good to get out of here. It's a good thing none of us are claustrophobic," she mused while packing up their gear in expectation of the hike to come.

"Speak for yourself, my dear Dr. Edwards. I find these conditions most intolerable. I've simply disdained from saying anything about it," Fredericks said unctuously from his side of the igloo.

"Until now, right, Fredericks? You're a real prince," Mark said sarcastically.

Fredericks simply frowned, refusing to be baited by Mark.

With all their gear gathered, and when everyone had finished a meager breakfast of candy, crackers and snow, for water; they climbed out the top of the igloo and looked around the plain.

The storm had added another thick layer of snow to the already snow covered plain.

For miles in every direction there was nothing but white. The dull night from the stars reflected off the snow and gave the three companions some form of luminescence to carry on their march. Shawn held up the compass to get their bearings and then pointed the way they needed to go.

"But first I'll be right back," he said and then trotted off a few feet away.

When he was finished urinating, he made his way back to the others with a grin on his face.

"Now we can go," Shawn said.

One at a time they began slogging on, the going twice as hard as before. Their legs sank up to their knees in the soft snow, but they ignored it, and with one arduous step after the other, they marched on.

*　　*　　*

About a half mile in front of the survivors, Simpson doggedly followed.

During the storm, he had lost the companion's trail, but had kept moving. In the middle of the night, he never knew he actually walked right past the igloo with his quarry huddling within. The storm blew around him, blocking out all visuals. The fallen snow had him walking at about a third of the speed of the others, but still he moved on, now actually in front of the very prey he was searching for.

Still he continued, his rage a driving force, pushing him ever onward.

One frozen step at a time.

CHAPTER THIRTY-TWO

THE FOUR WEARY travelers had been walking for a little over three hours when Mark called for a break.

"I think now would be a good time to use some of that stuff you brought with you to build a small fire," Mark told Shawn as they all gathered in a circle. "We can boil some snow for hot water, too."

"That would be wonderful," Sara exhaled next to him. "I could use something warm in me, even if it's just water."

"All right then, just give me a minute to set it all up," Shawn said as he got to work.

"I'll help, too, Shawn," Mark said as he began to dig a small hole in the snow for a windbreak for the fire.

Together the two men made short work of preparing the kindling for the fire, and once Shawn had his lighter out, he quickly lit the material salvaged from the half-track. The fire began to smolder and then began to burn more intensely. Mark and Sara wasted no time in putting some snow in a couple of spam cans they had saved and then melted the snow until it was water. As each can was warmed, Sara would give it to one of them who would quickly drink it.

Then they would fill the can with more snow again and start the process again.

Within a matter of minutes they had each drank their can of warm water and felt slightly better. By this time the fire had sputtered out, leaving the group in darkness once again. Shawn packed up the few materials they had left for use at a later time and then the group started walking again.

"Hey, I was just thinking. I hope none of that snow we melted was yellow," Shawn joked.

"Yellow? Why is that, Shawn?' Sara asked, perplexed.

Shawn glanced over to her, and was surprised to see she really meant her question.

"Come on, Sara, you never heard about yellow snow?" Shawn asked.

She shook her head back and forth slightly. "No, I grew up in Arizona. We never had any snow there. Until I came here, snow was just something I read about or saw on TV."

Mark chuckled then. "Yellow snow is what happens when dogs pee in it, Sara. That's why you never eat the yellow snow."

"Oh, I see, got it. No, Shawn, there was no yellow snow. I would have noticed when I was filling the cans." She said this all matter-of-factly, with no hint of humor, and Shawn began to laugh. Mark soon caught the laughter bug and began chuckling softly, doing his best to hold it in.

Sara just looked at the two of them like they were both crazy.

In the back of the line, Fredericks shook his head with contempt. "God, the both of you are acting like children. And you, Simmons, are supposed to be a respected researcher," he said in a biting clip.

"Bite me, Fredericks," Mark snapped back, which made Shawn begin to laugh harder.

With their laughter floating across the plains, the four survivors trudged on.

* * *

"Hey, Mark, how much farther do you think we have left to go?" Sara inquired as she walked up beside him. He was now on point, and he was doing his best to make sure they didn't walk over a fault line or crash through thin ice.

Mark thought for a moment as he looked off into the distance. "If I had to take a guess, I'd say we have another twenty miles or so."

"Oh, God, that many?" She gasped, not wanting to believe it.

"Yeah, I'm afraid so. That storm didn't help us any and we haven't been able to move that fast in this damn snow," he said to her as he stumbled for a moment and then caught himself.

He heard Fredericks snicker from behind him, but when he turned to look at the man, Fredericks acted like he hadn't said anything. Mark decided to let it go.

"Hey, Mark, if you had a choice, would you rather be stranded in the desert or where we are now?" Shawn asked from behind him.

Mark glanced over his shoulder to see Shawn smiling and waiting for an answer.

"Well, considering that I'm stuck here, I'd say I'd pick the one I don't know. I guess I'd pick the desert. Why?"

"No reason," Shawn said. "Just curious."

Mark stopped and looked at him for a second, wondering what the point was in his question. Shawn just kept on walking, and as he passed Mark, he just grinned and shrugged. Mark shook his head and looked down at his ice-encrusted shoes buried in the snow. By now Fredericks had passed him with barely a glance.

With a weary sigh, he began walking again, now the last one in line.

*   *   *

Simpson had been walking continuously since he'd left the half-track. At first he had a trail to follow, but now he had nothing. He was just walking around in circles.

That is until he spotted a small light coming from his right side way off in the distance. Immediately he turned in that direction and began walking towards it. After only a few minutes, the light disappeared, but Simpson had his bearings now and continued on a trajectory that would bring him straight toward it.

After about an hour of walking, he came upon the companion's trail left in the snow. Something deep inside Simpson smiled. He'd found their trail again. He turned and began walking in the path the group had left in the snow, the crushed powder making it easier for his frozen legs to navigate the difficult terrain.

He was on the right track again, and as he continued on into the darkness in front of him, the moonlight reflected off his frozen eyeballs.

From a certain angle, they seemed to glow like the stars in the night sky.

CHAPTER THIRTY-THREE

TWO HOURS LATER, the group received their first lucky break. They had been walking single file, their eyes staring down at their feet as they concentrated on putting one foot in front of the other, when Mark heard Shawn yell.

"Look, over there, headlights! Holy shit, someone's out there!" He screamed.

Mark didn't hesitate, as fast as he could manage with feet that felt like lead weights, he ran up to Shawn and unpacked the last of their burnable material.

"For Christ's sake, Shawn, help me with this stuff. We need to light a fire so they'll see us!" Mark rasped, his throat raw from the cold.

Shawn stood immobile for a fraction of a second, resembling a statue, but then he exploded into action, helping Mark get the cloth into a pile to light it.

As he held the flame from the lighter under a corner of the cloth, the wind kept blowing it out. After the second try, Mark yelled at Sara and Fredericks.

"You two," he pointed at them. "Lie down in the snow in front of the cloth and form a wind barrier, and for God's sake, hurry!"

The two did as requested, although Fredericks grumbled under his breath as he lay down in the snow.

Shawn then tried the lighter again and this time the material caught fire and began to burn. Mark then had everyone stand up so, hopefully, whoever was out there would see the fire and want to investigate.

They waited for signs that the vehicle in the distance had seen them, but when their fire began going out, and still no sign of them being discovered had shown itself, everyone was beginning to lose hope.

Then Mark took a chance and began to take off his exterior layers of clothing and put them on the fire.

"Mark, what the hell are you doing? Are you crazy? If they don't see us then you're gonna die of exposure!" Shawn yelled at him.

"I know that, Shawn, I'm not an idiot. But I'm willing to take that chance if it means it could get us the hell out of here."

Then Sara took off some of her clothing, although not as much as Mark, and she, too, tossed them on the fire.

"You people are crazy," Shawn said as he threw his hat and gloves onto the now growing flames.

The fire shot up into the air with the new fuel added to it. As the four of them watched anxiously for any signs of being seen, they all had held their breath.

Then, when it looked like the vehicle was going to turn and continue away from them, the vehicle suddenly stopped and flashed its headlights. Then it began to drive towards them.

The four of them immediately began jumping up and down with relief. After all they had been through, they were finally saved. As the vehicle moved closer, Mark could see it was a half-track similar to the one they had abandoned.

As the treads drove over the frozen ground, the stabilizing skids were the only thing keeping it from totally going out of control.

The half-track was still a good ten minutes away and Mark was already freezing his butt off. Sara saw how uncomfortable he was and took off the lab coat she'd been wearing under her heavy coat and wrapped it around him. He was so cold, he didn't argue, but only nodded in thanks, his lips trembling.

When the half-track finally pulled up next to them, a white haired old man rolled down his window and looked down at the foursome.

"Well, as I live and breathe; what the hell are you folks doing way out here in the middle of nowhere?" He asked as he stared at the group.

Before any of them could say anything, Fredericks stepped to the front of the line and started talking to the man.

"My good sir, perhaps we could talk about it inside your vehicle? Because frankly, we're freezing our asses off out here."

Mark just looked at Fredericks shocked. He had no idea the man had balls of any kind. Nevertheless, he heartily agreed with him as he stood there partially naked.

"I'm sorry for my companion's rudeness, but he has a point, we've been out here for more than a day, could we come inside with you please?" Mark asked politely.

The octogenarian seemed to mull it over for a second and then he smiled from ear to ear.

"Of course, of course, where're my manners? Come on, boys and girls, hop up inside here where it's warm," the old man offered with a mostly toothless smile.

The four of them climbed up inside the cab and relaxed as the warm air from the heater vents hit their cold bodies.

"Oh, yeah, that feels good. I was beginning to forget what it felt like to be warm again," Shawn said as he rubbed his hands over the dashboard vent.

"Where did you folks come from again?" The old man asked again.

"We're from James-Amusen Station," Sara said as she tried to get some of the vent heat herself.

"James-Amusen you say? Well then, how the hell did you get way out here then?" The old man asked.

"Look, that's a long story and right now we really need to get to Kryton Station and see the proper authorities. Could you please take us there?" Mark asked with a little impatience in his voice.

"Sure, sure, no problem there, sonny, that's where I'm from. We're about an hour away," he said as he sat there looking at them as if they were the strangest thing he'd seen in years. Then he glanced at Mark. "Where are all your clothes son? Don't you know you'll die of exposure out here like that?

Mark only nodded his flesh now a deep red as the circulation flowed back through him. "Yes, I kind of figured that one out for myself, thank you."

"Will you please go, for Christ sakes!" Shawn yelled at the old man.

While Mark didn't want to yell at the old man, he had to admit he wanted to do the same thing.

"All right, all right, hold your horses," the old man said as he put the vehicle into drive and began to turn around and head back the way he'd come.

The truck did a 180 degree turn and then drove off into the darkness.

*　　*　　*

The half-track moved across the austere, frozen plain, and from the sky above, if someone was looking down on it, the vehicle resembled a small toy in a child's backyard after a snowstorm. Inside the cab, the old man talked and kept talking.

His name was Rufus and he'd been at Kryton Station going on five years now.

After his wife had passed away a few years ago, he had come up here looking for work and had found a job at Kryton Station doing odd jobs for some of the researchers. That's what had brought him out on the plains today. He had gone out looking for a weather balloon that had gone down somewhere in the area the four of them had been found. It had a tracker on it and old Rufus was just about to turn around and head off in another direction when he spotted their little bonfire.

He told them he would bring them back and then head off again to find the balloon.

The half-track drove over a subtle incline in the terrain and Kryton Station finally came into view.

It was a sprawling little village with more than a dozen buildings surrounding the main complex. Off in the distance, the four of them could just make out the docks where icebreaker ships would moor when they arrived with supplies.

The only way to leave Antarctica and Kryton Station was by those ships.

At the moment, by the lights surrounding the docks, there were no ships in port. Rufus told them it would be at least another week before the next ship was due to arrive.

As it was now winter, there was a skeleton crew of about two-hundred and ninety or so personnel stationed at the base. The station didn't have a, actual real police force, but there was a small battalion of soldiers stationed nearby at the outskirts of the station. Only about fifteen or so men, as Kryton Station wasn't a high priority.

But Rufus said he'd bring them to Sgt. McDonald, the battalion commander, and he'd be sure to fix them right up.

As the half-track drove into the main street of the little village, Mark gazed out at the buildings, with the light posts every few feet it was almost as bright as day inside the limits of the town and many buildings had small white lights, like Christmas lights dangling from windows and doors, giving the place a cheery, down home quality.

For the first time in what seemed like ages Mark relaxed...really relaxed.

They were finally safe.

*   *   *

Simpson had also spotted the headlights of Rufus' half-track on the distant ice plain and had watched passively as the vehicle turned around and drove away, the two small, red taillights flickering in the darkness.

Now having an actual direction to head for, he renewed his pace and continued onward, and as the red taillights receded into the darkness, he continued forward, now once again following the trail of Fredericks and the others.

Hours later, he picked up the trail left by the half-track's treads. Now his path was even easier to follow. He continued walking on the crushed path of snow and ice and the hours drifted by, time meaningless to him now. A day or a year, in the end it mattered little to his rage-filled mind.

When he made it to the top of the incline, he gazed down across the open plain on Kryton Station. With all the lights spread out in streets and around the buildings, it was like it was still daylight in the tiny village station.

Simpson began moving down the light incline, continuing on to the station a mile in the distance.

Somewhere on that base was Fredericks, and he would slaughter every man, woman and child who got in his way until he found him.

CHAPTER THIRTY-FOUR

RUFUS STOPPED THE half-track next to a small building on the outskirts of the village and put the transmission in park.

"Well, folks, here you go. Go right on in that door there and Sgt. McDonald should be able to help you with whatever you need." He looked at Mark sitting next to him in his underwear and flashed a toothless grin. "He should be able to get you a new set of clothes, too."

"That would be very much appreciated, thanks Rufus," Mark said as he and the others climbed out of the truck. There were a few people on the street and they stopped and stared at Mark as he climbed out of the cab. Mark just decided to ignore them as it would take way to much time to try and explain. Not to mention that as he was outside again, and away from the heat of the cab, he was already freezing again in the frigid temperatures.

"Thanks, old timer, I don't know what we would have done if you hadn't seen us,"

Shawn said on his way out of the cab.

"Yes, thank you again, Rufus, you saved us," Sara said. Then she leaned over and gave Rufus a kiss on the cheek.

"Ah, shucks, it wasn't that big a deal. Anyone would've done the same," Rufus said as he turned beet red.

While Fredericks was climbing out of the backseat of the cab he mumbled something under his breath that no one quite heard. Then he hopped down and stood in the snow, waiting for the others. He was ready to break off from the people he'd been forced to travel with, and now that their ordeal was over, he was just waiting for the right time to leave.

As Rufus pulled away, he beeped the horn and waved out his window at them.

Mark, Shawn and Sara waved back and then turned and entered the small, one-story building.

On the door there was a simple sign that read: **Security, Sgt. James McDonald, U.S. Army**.

Mark was the first one through the door as he was the coldest. When he stepped inside, the first thing he noticed was the huge United States flag adorning the far wall. Below the flag was a desk. And seated behind that desk was the meanest looking soldier Mark had ever seen.

Sgt. James McDonald had a jaw chiseled out of rock and a strong chin to boot. His eyes were a dark blue that reflected the light from the one lamp in the room. Despite the fact there was no sun in Antarctica, the man's skin was tanned a rich brown. His dark black hair was cut skin short on the sides of his head and just a little was left on the top. It was what the jarheads called a "high and tight."

When he smiled as the four companions walked into the room, Mark could see his teeth were a clean white that seemed to sparkle in the light of the room.

To Mark, this man looked like the poster boy for the U.S. Army.

Sgt. McDonald stood up as they crossed the room to his desk.

"Now, what the hell do we have here?" He asked around the cold stub of a cigar protruding out the side of his mouth.

Mark was the first to walk forward and put out his hand.

"Uh, hi there, I'm Dr. Mark Simmons and we've come from Amusen Station and man have we got a story for you. But before we tell it, do you think I could get something to wear? I'm freezing."

McDonald cracked a smile from ear to ear. "Well, mister, if the story winds up with you telling me how you lost your pants, then I'm all ears," he said in a friendly tone that was the opposite of his appearance. "Just give me a second and I'll be right back." Mark was about to correct the man, and tell him it was *doctor*, not *mister*, but decided getting some clothing was far more important.

Finishing his statement, McDonald left his chair and walked off into a back room. Mark and the others could hear him digging around, as they heard things crashing to the floor. Then McDonald returned with a camouflaged jumpsuit for Mark.

"Here ya go, pal, try this on for size," he said as he tossed the clothes at Mark and then plopped back down in his chair. "Now, let's hear that story of yours."

Mark sat down in the chair in front of his desk and the others went over to a couch situated on the far wall. Shawn dropping down with a loud sigh.

And then Mark began from the beginning and told their entire story.

*   *   *

"And then Rufus dropped us off at your door," Mark finished. He'd been talking for about a half hour now and his throat was parched. Sara and Shawn had pitched in at times, adding things to the story when appropriate.

Through the entire story, McDonald had sat quietly behind his desk. Every now and then he would nod as he chewed on the end of his cigar. Even now that Mark had finished his story; he still sat there, as if he was still taking it all in. Then he sat up and stared Mark square in the eyes.

"Do I look like a fucking idiot to you, Doctor? That has got to be the most ridiculous story I've ever heard. Zombies are real and they're running around in the snow."

"Look, Sergeant, if you don't believe me, then try and contact Amusen Station. No one will answer because everyone's dead," Mark said, trying to reason with him

Sgt. McDonald stood up now as he looked over the foursome.

"Oh, don't you worry about that, Doctor. I intend to. Now, tell you what, why don't we get you and your people settled in. I'm sure you could use the rest," Sgt. McDonald said as he reached for the phone on his desk to get them an escort.

"All right, I'm friggin' exhausted. Man, I can't wait to sleep in a real bed tonight," Shawn said as he raised himself off the couch.

"Well, enjoy it, Private, because tomorrow morning you report to me at 0700 hours, got it?" McDonald told Shawn with a stern tone and the same hardness of his countenance that Mark had seen when he'd first entered the building.

"Ah, yes, sir... I mean, yes, Sergeant. 0700, I'll be there," Shawn said. Despite everything he'd been through, he was still in the Army.

The outer door opened with a blast of cold air and a young soldier of about nineteen walked in. When McDonald went over and discussed with the young soldier what he wanted him to do, Sara walked over to Mark and whispered quietly so only he could hear.

"God, Mark, if they don't believe us, then what are we going to do?" She asked.

"Don't worry, Sara, as soon as they send someone out there to investigate, they'll find out the truth. We'll talk about the rest later," he told her as McDonald came back over to them.

"Okay, people, this is Private Nollans, he'll bring you to your temporary quarters until we can get this mess all sorted out. He'll also fill you in on how you can get some chow."

"That would be most excellent, Sgt. McDonald. I for one am famished. Shall we go then?" Fredericks inquired as he strode out the doorway, hoping to get the others moving, also.

And it worked, as Private Nollan then led the others outside, following Fredericks.

About five minutes later, Private Nollans led them to another one-story building with a metal door as the only entrance. Nollans retrieved a key from his pocket and opened the door for them and quickly ushered them inside, not wanting to let the cold in.

The four companions walked into a cozy, two room dwelling with eight bunk beds in each room. As Mark studied the room, he could see a small bathroom with what looked like a shower stall at the opposite end.

Shawn walked in and dropped down on the first bed he came to. "Oh, yeah, that's nice," he said as he closed his eyes and stretched, but not before kicking off his boots and taking off his coat.

"Feel free to take any bunk you want. Seems that you're late for dinner, I'll have something sent over for you," Nollans said by the door.

"Whatever you send, could you please make sure it's hot?" Sara asked as she walked around the room.

"Sure, that shouldn't be a problem, ma'am," Nollans said.

"Well, all right then, thank you, Private. I think we can handle it from here,"

Mark said as he held the doorknob, preparing to open it so Nollans would take the hint and leave.

"Yes, sir, have a good night. The food will be here shortly." And then Nollans turned, waited for Mark to open the door, and then stepped out of the open doorway. Without waiting to see if the man was clear of the closing door, Mark slammed it shut, not wanting to let any more freezing air into the room.

At last they were finally alone.

The second the door closed, Shawn and Sara began bombarding Mark with questions about what they should do next.

"Whoa, slow down, we'll be fine. I hate to say it, but whatever happens now it's out of our hands. All we can do is sit tight until the Army figures out this entire mess," Mark said as he sat down on a bed.

"Well, I for one don't plan on just sitting around. I have colleagues at this station and first thing in the morning I intend to seek them out," Fredericks stated at the back of the room where he had sat down on another bed.

"Shit, at least you guys get to take a breather. I have to report for duty first thing in the morning," Shawn said as he lay back down on his bed and closed his eyes.

"I'm sorry about that, Shawn. If there was anything I could do for you, you know I would," Mark said to him.

And then there was a knock at the door.

Mark was the closest, so he raised himself up and crossed the room. Upon opening the door, he was surprised to see Nollans standing there with a large covered tray.

"Could I please come in, sir? This tray is heavy," he said as he balanced the tray in his hands.

"Yeah, sure. Wow, that was fast," Mark said as he waved him inside the room.

"Yes, sir, it is. Sgt. McDonald called ahead and had them get started preparing the food immediately, figuring you were all pretty hungry," Nollans said as he carried the food tray inside and set it down on a small, corner table set against the left wall. Then he bid them goodnight and left.

The four of them dived into the soup and sandwiches on the tray, and within a matter of minutes, had devoured everything. While they sat around and enjoyed the feeling of being warm and fed, Shawn got up and looked at Mark and Sara.

"Look, guys, I'm beat. I'm gonna grab a bunk in the other room with Fredericks. I'll see ya later," he said as he walked to the back of the second room. He stopped when he reached Fredericks and held out his hand to escort the man back with him.

"But what's wrong with these bunks?" Fredericks asked. "Why do I have to go into the back room with you?"

Shawn just looked at him. "Doc, if I have to explain it to you, it just defeats the point. Now come on or I'll carry you."

Fredericks looked at Shawn and decided it wasn't worth the fight, so he gathered his meager possessions and followed Shawn.

There was a curtain hanging between the two rooms and when Shawn crossed the opening, he pulled it closed. Mark got a quick glimpse of his face as he closed the curtain and caught Shawn winking at him. Then the curtain was closed and Mark and Sara were finally alone.

Back at Amusen, when he had imagined this scenario with Sara, he'd believed he would have been nervous about the situation he now found himself, but that would have been the farthest thing from the truth.

A lot had happened in the past two days to change his attitude to her and the way he saw himself.

He lay back on his bed and held out his hand for her to join him. She smiled wanly and walked over to him. When she passed the light switch, she hit it with her hand, plunging the room into darkness.

As their eyes adjusted to the darkness, they realized the only feeble light in the room was shining through the front window from all the lamp posts lining the street outside the building.

As she lay down next to him, he wrapped his arms around her and the two of them laid quietly, curled up in one another's arms, until sleep came to them.

This night Mark slept dreamless, with Sara cradled in his arms.

Later that night, when they both stirred in the bed, he rolled over and kissed her.

Their kiss was electric, and as he explored her mouth with his tongue, he found himself becoming aroused. More so than he could ever have imagined before. And he knew why. It was not just her physical attraction that was turning him on, but so much more. He knew it was because he respected her as a person first. She was intelligent, resourceful, and brave, not to mention incredibly attractive.

To him, she was the perfect woman, and one he had been longing for, for far too long.

And she reciprocated his attentions as she moaned into his mouth and pressed her body against his. He could feel her soft breasts against his chest and he found himself tingling all over. It was like every nerve ending, every inch of his flesh was now only receptive to her touch, to her gestures and body movements.

And then in the dead of night, they made love for the first time. And five minutes later, after they had both orgasmed together, Mark was ready to go again and when they made love for the second time, they took their time and enjoyed the feeling of each others bodies, letting their lust give way to love.

After they were finished making love for the third time, they curled up together and went back to sleep. It was still hours before dawn and they had nowhere to be but together.

Off in the back room, Shawn rolled over in his sleep and began snoring again as Fredericks lay in a nearby bed with his eyes wide open, not getting any sleep at all.

*   *   *

While the four weary survivors lay sleeping, Simpson had made it to the outer edge of the small coastal village known as Kryton Station. He had been walking continually for hours, never tiring, never slowing.

As he stepped onto the first street at the edge of the station, he was taken aback by the brightness of the area. Moving deeper into the village, he spotted his first victim walking down the street. He stumbled over to him, his legs moving easier now that they weren't bogged down by the deep snow on the plains.

And as the prey came closer to him, he prepared himself to attack.

Private Nollans had just been about to call it a night himself when he saw a stranger walking down the middle of the street. As it was a small skeleton crew at the moment staffing this part of the station, he knew just about everyone on it. And this guy did not look familiar.

Plus, he looked like he had the worst case of frostbite ever recorded. So Nollans walked over to see if he could help him, after all, he could be from the party of people who had just arrived earlier in the night, though they hadn't mentioned that there had been a fifth member with them.

As he walked closer, he could definitely tell this man was ill. The man's neck looked like it was torn out, yet it was odd that there wasn't any blood. And wow, the man's skin looked blue, like he'd been exposed to frigid temperatures for a long period of time. His clothes were covered in dark maroon stains which looked a lot to Nollans like old, dried blood.

Nollans was only a few feet from the stranger and was just beginning to get second thoughts, when all of a sudden the stranger lunged at him. He tried to back away, but lost his footing on a small patch of ice on the ground. As he went down, the man fell on top of him, and before Nollans could even yell for help, the man had sunk his teeth into the front of Nollan's throat, ripping into his jugular.

Nollans lay there drowning in his own blood and wondered how the hell this could be happening.

The sounds of the man slurping his blood came to his ears as Nollans closed his eyes and sank into the depths of death.

Moments later, Nollans opened his eyes and raised himself to a standing position on legs that didn't feel like his own. The man who had turned him into one of the frozen dead was still standing next to him, as if he'd been waiting for Nollans to revive.

And now Nollans had an incredible craving for human meat. Check that, any meat would do, but human meat would be the easiest to find.

Together, the two ghouls moved down the brightly lit street, their bodies casting long shadows behind them. There were many more victims to feed on and then make like them, and many hours until morning.

As the two ghouls turned and entered the first unlocked door they came upon, muffled screams of the residents within soon rose from the building, only to be lost in the howling winds of the Antarctic.

As the night wore on, there would be many more screams of pain and anguish to join those first few souls unfortunate enough to be slaughtered, and many more undead to assist them.

This would continue until Simpson had found and killed everyone.

Sooner or later, Simpson would find Fredericks, and with an army of the undead by his side, he would utterly destroy the man.

CHAPTER THIRTY-FIVE

FREDERICKS ROLLED OVER in bed for the hundredth time.

Shawn's snoring was driving him crazy. He was so upset he was just about ready to go over to the chugging soldier and smother him with a pillow.

But instead he decided to just get up.

As he silently raised himself from his bed, he saw the small clock on the wall read 4:30 a.m. While he walked over to the bathroom to use the facilities, he decided now was a good a time as any to cut his ties with these people. After all, the only reason he was with them in the first place was because circumstances had dictated he not be alone in his exodus from Amusen Station.

But now he was safe and would be very pleased to go back to being alone.

As he went back to his bed, he leaned down to retrieve his clothes and the purloined pistol.

As he dressed quietly in the dark, he wondered what Mark, Sara and Shawn would do when they discovered he was gone in the morning.

He shrugged the thought away, realizing the answer didn't really matter to him.

Now fully dressed, he quietly crept to the curtain dividing the two rooms. Shawn's snoring was continuing and was doing well at disguising the creaks the wooden floorboards were making with each step he took towards the front door.

As he entered the front room, the first thing he noticed was Mark and Sara curled up under the blankets together. As he snuck past them, Sara turned over in her sleep and her left breast became partially exposed to the cool air. As Fredericks walked by, he couldn't help but pause and admire her.

While Fredericks had never actively pursued a woman in a romantic relationship that didn't mean he wasn't partial to the female form.

As he stood there watching her sleep, Mark grunted and turned over in the bed, as well.

Fredericks decided that would be his cue to leave. He was pretty sure Mark would not take too kindly to him if he was to wake up and see him standing there.

So he went to the door, and with a twist of the knob, had it open and then he was through and outside.

He looked left and right on the tiny road, noticing a few people who seemed to be wandering around a little ways down the street from him. He paid them no mind as he went off in the other direction, searching for the main research building.

One advantage to working on a continent where the sun disappeared for months at a time was that people were up at all hours of the night, as it was always dark.

While he walked down the street, he thought he had heard a scream or a muffled yell, but when he waited for the sound to occur again, nothing happened. He shrugged and continued on, assuming it was probably just the wind blowing through the small streets of the research village.

If he had bothered to pause and take a better look at the people who were wandering around behind him, he may have noticed they had what would be considered multiple life-threatening wounds on their bodies.

And if he had looked closer still, he would have noticed they shuffled more than walked on the icy streets.

And if he had looked even closer, he would have noticed that the people were actually the walking dead

And they were hungry.

*   *   *

As the front door closed with a soft click, Mark opened his eyes and looked around the dark room, wondering what had woken him. As he lay there and nothing else seemed amiss, he closed his eyes again and relaxed.

He could hear Sara's steady breathing next to him as she slept. He felt around for her shoulder and put his arm tighter around her, enjoying the feeling of her soft skin next to his own. As he lay there in the dark, listening to Sara's breathing and the wind blowing outside, he soon found himself drifting off to sleep again.

With his consciousness fading, sleep taking over once more, he never noticed the slow moving shadows that began to float by the front window of the room.

So he never knew of the shadows of death now descending on the small research station in the middle of nowhere.

*   *   *

Sgt. James McDonald rolled over in his bed and turned off his alarm.

The clock read 5:00 a.m., so he jumped out of bed and walked over to his bathroom to take care of business.

After a shit, shower and shave, in that order, he went out to his front room to do his morning calisthenics. Every morning he did countless push-ups, chin-ups and sit-ups. He was a firm believer that a strong body equals a strong mind.

He'd been in the Army for a little over seventeen years and was looking forward to the last three years until he could retire. The Army was his life, and he couldn't imagine why every man and woman in America didn't want to enlist and serve their country.

After finishing with his exercises, he went over to his small desk to check on some paperwork from the previous day.

One report stated that all attempts to contact the James-Amusen Station had failed and that earlier this morning a patrol would be sent out to investigate.

McDonald smiled. He would be looking forward to that patrol's return so he could address that lunatic, Simmons', story about frozen zombies running around Antarctica.

He shook his head just thinking about it. What a ridiculous story, as if the man actually thought someone would believe him.

Dismissing that train of thought, he rose from his chair, went to the front door of his tiny quarters and put on his coat, making sure to strap on his side arm.

As he opened the front door to walk over to his office, his mind already on a warm breakfast, he noticed there were an odd amount of people on the street for this time in the morning. Although it was always dark, the research station still kept on a schedule of days and nights.

As he closed the door behind him and began to walk down the street, the people around him started to move closer into his vicinity, so he picked up his pace a little to outdistance them, not feeling comfortable with the odd way the residents were acting.

As he turned the corner of his street to continue down the next one, a man came out of a side door and blocked his path.

As the man stood there in McDonald's way, The Army veteran noticed the man's shirt was covered in blood. He was just about to ask him if he was all right when the man took a step closer.

As the man stepped forward, his head fell back like he was looking up at the stars and that was when McDonald saw how the man's neck had been ripped open from ear to ear, the jagged wound now crusted with ice and blood.

As the man stepped forward, his body twisted, which allowed the head to snap back into place again.

McDonald hadn't realized yet that he was standing face to face with a real live zombie.

As the frozen eyes of the ghoul bore into McDonald, the dead man lunged at him, catching McDonald completely off guard.

And before McDonald could say: "Just three more years to go," he found himself in a battle for his life.

*   *   *

Shawn rolled over in bed and snuck a peek at the clock on the wall between partially opened eyelids. It read 6:30 a.m. He felt like he could sleep for another ten hours as he forced himself to get up and get dressed. He didn't want to piss Sgt. McDonald off as the man didn't seem like the forgiving type.

After he finished in the bathroom, he went over to the curtain and peeked through. The love birds were still sleeping, but of course they were, it was 6:30 in the damn morning, he thought to himself.

He quietly tiptoed over to where his coat was hanging near the door when he heard Mark stirring in his bed. He tried to be quieter, but was surprised when he heard Mark say: "Relax, Shawn, I'm up, you don't have to sneak around."

"Oh, ah, okay, morning; how'd you sleep?" Shawn asked, not really knowing what to say at this awkward moment.

Mark stretched in bed and made Sara dive under the covers more as he let some cold air slip in underneath the blankets.

"Okay, I guess, you?"

"Fine, hey, I noticed Dr. Fredericks wasn't in his bed. Do you know where he is?" Shawn inquired.

Mark stretched one more time and said: "Nope, don't know and I don't care."

Shawn just remained silent at his answer and then noticed the clock on the wall and said: "Oh, shit I gotta go. I don't want to be late to see McDonald."

"Okay, good luck," Mark waved from his bed as Shawn opened the door to go outside.

Shawn opened the door and was about to step outside when he noticed someone standing in front of the doorway with his back to him. And the guy was totally blocking his exit.

Shawn reached out and gently poked the guy's shoulder with his finger and asked: "Hey, buddy, would you mind standing somewhere else? You're blocking the doorway."

The man slowly turned around and faced Shawn. But as the man was slowly turning, Shawn could already sense something was wrong, and when the guy was finally facing him, Shawn was positive.

The man standing before Shawn was missing his left eye and ear, not to mention half his cheek was gone, gums and teeth exposed to the air in a death rictus of a smile. When the man tried to talk, which was nothing more than garbled gibberish; it was then followed by a dry, rasping sound. The entire time the man attempted speech, his tongue could be seen moving inside his mouth from the torn hole where the cheek was missing.

When the man lunged for Shawn, the startled soldier quickly slammed the door in the obviously dead guy's face. A dull thump could be heard inside the room now as the frozen ghoul banged on the door, wanting to get in.

Shawn just stood there with his back to the door and then said to the ceiling.

"Oh, Jesus Christ, not again. I don't know if I can do this shit all over again."

By now Mark was up and Sara was stirring awake, as well.

"What? What's the matter, what's wrong? Who the hell is banging on the door, Shawn?" Mark asked as he quickly pulled on his pants and shirt.

Shawn just stared at him.

"Oh, man, believe me when I tell you, you don't wanna know," Shawn said as his eyes practically popped out of his head when he looked past Mark.

Mark turned to see what he was looking at and saw Sara standing butt naked. She was bending over to gather her scattered clothes off the floor and from the end of the bed, where they had been tossed haphazardly the night before.

"Shawn, do you mind?" Mark asked him pleadingly.

"No, I don't mind at all," he said absently as his eyes followed Sara as she walked to the bathroom and closed the door, the smooth angles of her thighs and buttocks now a permanent etching in his mind.

But when the bathroom door closed, it was like a switch had gone off in Shawn's head and he immediately focused on Mark again.

"Oh, ah, sorry, where was I again?" He asked Mark.

Anger was beginning to flare in Mark's eyes as he walked over to Shawn and looked him straight in the eyes.

"You were about to tell me what's on the other side of that door," he said as he pointed to the shaking door.

"Oh the door, well, you're not going to believe this but… there's a zombie out there," Shawn said.

"No, you're joking! You can't be serious," Mark said, not wanting to believe him.

Shawn nodded vigorously. "Mark, my man, I'm as serious as a fuckin' heart attack. If you don't believe me, see for yourself," Shawn said as he stepped aside.

As the two of them were having their discussion, the banging continued nonstop on the door, so Mark went to the window and peeked outside.

His jaw dropped at what he saw.

There had to be a least twenty ghouls stumbling around in the street that he could see and more shadows and shapeless forms could be seen at the far end, just on the edge of his vision. As he squinted to try and see further down the street, he could just make out the shadows that appeared and he knew there were a lot more coming with each passing second.

He pulled back the drapes with his mouth hanging open.

"It doesn't make sense. How the hell did they get here?" He asked Shawn.

"I'd say less worrying about how they got here and more worrying about how the hell we're gonna get out of here," Shawn said. Then he turned at the sound of the bathroom door opening, Sara walked out looking refreshed after a hot shower.

She looked at them both and smiled.

"Morning, guys, what's going on?" She asked as she dried her hair with a towel, the steam from her hot shower floating out of the open doorway behind her.

Mark and Shawn looked at each other and then Shawn shrugged, knowing they had to tell her.

And then they filled her in on their unfortunate discovery.

CHAPTER THIRTY-SIX

WHEN THE FROZEN ghoul lunged at McDonald, he flinched back instinctively, the ghoul's teeth biting down on empty air.

Quickly, he backpedaled as his mind tried to grasp the situation he now found himself in. Coming from behind him, he heard footsteps scraping on the ice and snow and was even more shocked to see a group of his fellow residents advancing on him. Their bodies showed different degrees of damage as they shambled towards him. Some had their throats ripped out while others had their stomachs and chests torn open to expose the red remains of their organs.

McDonald was processing all the data he was experiencing and came to only one conclusion; that crazy scientist from yesterday was telling the truth and somehow the infection had spread to his station, as well.

McDonald wasn't a man to second guess himself. When he made a decision, he stuck to it unless he was shown with proof the error of his judgment.

So the second his mind had decided that zombies were trying to kill him, he knew what he had to do, thanks to the information Mark and his friends had told him about their past adventure at the James-Amusen Station.

In one smooth motion, he pulled his sidearm from its holster and lined up on the first ghoul that came into his sights, firing at point blank range.

The bullet tore through the zombie's eye socket and blew a fist sized hole out of the back of its head. As it slumped to the ground, the others behind it were temporarily slowed while they maneuvered around the downed corpse.

That gave McDonald the chance he needed, so he swung back around and shouldered the first ghoul out of his way and made a run for it down the street.

As he turned a corner onto another small street, he immediately saw more of the frozen dead scattered about.

He set his jaw and lowered his eyes, then he began running straight at the wandering ghouls, shouldering them aside like he was a football player going for the end zone.

He kept running until he'd cleared the street and turned the corner. As he slowed down to a jog, he knew where he had to go. He needed to find the only people he knew of that would know how to handle the situation he was now in.

He kept jogging until he came upon a small one-story building with a single door. It was the building housing Mark Simmons and his friends.

*   *   *

Sara was sitting on one of the beds as she tried to process what Mark and Shawn had just told her. The towel she'd been using to dry her hair was now lying on the floor next to her feet, where she'd dropped it upon hearing the news that the station they'd thought was their salvation was now overrun with the undead.

"But how did they get here? It doesn't make any sense," she said as she stared at the shaking door. Every time the ghoul pounded on it she would twitch in fear, though she did her best to remain calm.

"It doesn't really matter how the hell they got here," Mark said while looking at both Sara and Shawn. "What matters is they're here and the immediate question is what are we gonna do about it?"

"Seems to me we do the same thing as before," Shawn said. "We find a place to lay low and then figure out how to get away from here."

Suddenly, the banging on the door stopped and after a moment continued again with twice as much force. Before any of them could even decide what to do about it, they heard a gunshot and a voice coming from the other side.

Bang, bang, bang again, then: "For the love of God, open the fucking door before those things get any closer!" The voice yelled and was then followed by another gunshot.

The three friends looked at each other for a moment and then Shawn spoke up.

"Hey, I think that's Sgt. McDonald. I'm gonna let him in," he said as moved towards the door and opened it.

McDonald literally fell into the room. His back had been pressed hard against the door as he tried to keep another ghoul at bay.

In one quick motion, Shawn kicked out with his foot and connected with the ghoul's chin, sending it flying back out the doorway where it fell into others who were attempting to get at the prone sergeant. Shawn then slammed the door in their undead blue faces and locked it. As an added precaution, he leaned his body against the door, as well.

"Shit, Sarge, that was close. What the hell were you doing out there?" Shawn breathed as he helped McDonald to his feet.

"I was walking to my office when those…people attacked me," he gasped as he tried to catch his breath. "They were everywhere, so I came here after I realized you were telling the truth about what you told me yesterday."

He jumped as the banging on the door began again as the zombies tried to get in.

"Telling the truth? Why I should…" Mark said with his hands balled into fists.

Sara jumped in and cut Mark off in mid-sentence as she looked at McDonald.

"We're just glad you're here, Sergeant. We can use all the help we can get. Before you arrived, we were discussing a plan of action. Hopefully you can help us with that," she said.

"Of course, whatever I can do," McDonald said as he regained some of his composure. He shook his head back and forth. "I just can't get over the fact that it's true, though."

Mark ignored McDonald's comment and began talking.

"Okay then, when we were at Amusen Station, we first had to get to a secure place to hide out and then we found a way to leave the station," Mark reasoned.

"Because if we stay here, there's no way we'll survive. Sooner or later we'll be overrun by those people," Mark said to McDonald, but also as a reminder to Sara and Shawn.

McDonald gave it some thought as he paced around the room, trying to think of a place they would be safe for a while. When it came to him, his eyes lit up.

"I know where we could go, we could hold up at the commissary. It only has two entrances, one in the front and one in the back where there's a small back room used for storage. And once we're inside, we'd have food and water, too. And there shouldn't be anyone there yet as its too early in the morning."

"Yeah, but how are we gonna get inside if there's no one there yet?" Shawn asked as he leaned against the door. "We'll be standing outside with those bastards trying to eat us. The thing is, Sarge, if you stay still for too long they get you."

"That's the beauty of it," McDonald smiled at them all. "There's a roof access that I happen to know is broken thanks to a sweet little honey I know that works there. She likes to go on the roof for a smoke on her breaks. And we can gain entry from the building next to it."

"Let me get this straight," Mark said, his hands waving in the air as he talked. "You want us to climb up a nearby building and then jump over the gap to land on the adjacent roof and by doing that gain us entry into the commissary by the roof access?" He said the entire thing without talking a breath.

"Yup, that sounds about right," McDonald answered him confidently like he was suggesting they all just go for a walk.

"And how far are these buildings from one another, may I ask?" Mark queried.

"Oh, about eight or nine feet I guess, I can't be certain, I never actually measured it," McDonald said as he sat down on a bed.

"Wow, that's a pretty good jump. Do you think we could make it?" Shawn asked as he went to sit down by Sara. So far, the door seemed to be holding fine.

"I don't see us having any other choice. If we try to…" Mark was cut short as the front window exploded inward, the ghouls attempting to crawl through. The drapes blew inward from the wind as the first two ghouls fell into the room. Before the friends could react, McDonald was on his feet and moving towards the disturbance with his gun already drawn and ready to fire.

He shot the first ghoul in the forehead and as it went down, he was already firing on the second one. Before it regained its footing, the corpse was already slumping toward the floor minus the upper half of its head. McDonald then holstered his weapon and turned to the three companions.

"Well, Simmons, I'd say the time for talk is over, we either move now or we're dead," he said.

Mark nodded in agreement and then went to gather his gear.

"He's right, guys, let's get our stuff and move out before we're trapped in here," Mark said as he checked on Sara. He saw her hesitating, her face filled with trepidation, and he quickly moved to her side.

"Sara, you all right? Come on, we've gotta go," He told her as he put his arm around her shoulders.

"Yes, I'm fine, Mark. Just a little queasy about everything. I can't believe we have to do this all over again," she said while she began gathering her things off the floor. The room was now freezing, the shattered window letting in the sub-zero temperature.

"Believe me, I know how you feel, but right now we just have to get out of here, all right?" Mark said to her trying to sound supportive.

She nodded and the two of them joined Shawn by the door.

"Is there a back door out of here?" Shawn asked as he pulled the gun Mark had taken off the dead soldier back at Amusen Station.

"Yeah, there is, but it leads to a small alley that would probably be a deathtrap for us," McDonald said. "No, I think we should just plow right through the bastards and then head down the street until we reach the commissary. Do you guys agree?" McDonald asked Mark as he stood by the door, though his dour expression said he was doing what he wanted whether Mark agreed or not.

Mark shrugged. "It's your station and I defer to your expertise. Lead on," Mark said as he leaned over and picked up a heavy lamp off the floor to use as a weapon. "You two have the guns so me and Sara will follow you guys and watch your backs."

Sara walked up next to Mark and he put his arm around her and spoke softly so only she could hear. "Don't worry, we've done this before and you know I won't let anything happen to you, right?"

She looked into his eyes and nodded. "I know, don't worry about me. I can take care of myself," she said defiantly, a small spark of courage appearing in her eyes. She then leaned down and picked up the dinner tray their food had been delivered on the night before, now ready to use it as a weapon.

He smiled at her and nodded. "I know you can. You ready?"

She nodded affirmatively and then looked at Shawn and McDonald.

"All right, let's do this," she said with a hard look in her eyes.

McDonald looked at his three new recruits and nodded.

"Okay, good. On three I'll open the door and we'll make a run for it. When we leave here, take a right and then follow the street down until the T in the road and then take a left and follow it until you see the commissary in front of you. The building we want is on the right side of it. There's a fire escape on the back that we can use to get up on the roof. You guys got all that?" McDonald asked as he looked at the three faces in front of him.

Quick nods of understanding was the reply

"Okay then. One... two... three!" McDonald barked as he pulled the door open and the four of them charged into the street and into the swarm of frozen dead waiting for them.

Chapter Thirty-seven

Fredericks glanced at the wall clock for the third time in as many minutes.

The clock read 5:00 a.m.

When he'd finally made it to the research building, he had found it empty. It seemed even though the station basically operated twenty-four hours a day, the researchers and scientists chose to work a more uniform day.

When Fredericks had entered the lobby, he had immediately walked over to the list of researchers presently employed at the station. He had seen at least three colleagues who would welcome him and at least a dozen who wouldn't.

Fredericks had burned a few bridges in the scientific community, or more to the point, he had put a nuclear bomb on the bridge, piled it high with dynamite and had then blown the whole thing up after spraying it with a tanker full of gasoline.

Despite being alienated by almost every colleague he'd worked with, it didn't bother him. He firmly believed all the other scientists just didn't understand his unorthodox way of getting results.

The lobby was deathly quiet, so he decided to lie down on the couch in the corner and try to catch up on some of the sleep he'd lost thanks to Shawn's snoring.

He closed his eyes and dreamed of being awarded the Nobel Peace Prize as he often did when he wanted to boost his morale.

As he closed his eyes and drifted off to sleep, he was unaware of the slowly flowing shadows that moved by the lobby windows. And even if he did, he probably wouldn't have realized what they foretold.

*   *   *

McDonald went through the open door to their room and immediately plowed into the swarm of ghouls in the street. Before Mark or the others had managed to step one foot outside, McDonald had already put a bullet into two heads and had kicked a third ghoul down to the ground where he now stood with his foot firmly pressed on its neck.

After that Mark lost McDonald from view when two ghouls came up on his immediate right and attacked him. Mark swung the lamp he was holding like a bat at the first ghoul, shattering its jaw. Bits of teeth and flesh fell to the ground across the surrounding area as the dead man stumbled back from the blow. As the second one came within range of his lamp, Mark hit it on the top of the head with the weighted end of the lamp. The blow pushed the ghoul to its knees where Mark then kicked it in the face and watched it drop onto its back on the icy ground. The first ghoul came back at him again, but now with its jaw missing, the tongue now hanging down almost to its shoulder, flopping around like some kind of grotesque slug.

Mark whacked the ghoul on the right side of the head and then forgot about it as without the ability to bite him, the ghoul was far less dangerous than the others. Another one had crawled up to his feet and tried to bite his foot, but the tough shoe leather deflected the teeth and Mark kicked it in the face. As he backed away from the prone ghoul, he left the zombie spitting out teeth onto the frozen ground.

Another came up at him from his left side and he quickly kicked it away. It fell back into the others following and caused them all to fall over as they tried to disentangle their arms and legs from each other, reminding him of a Three Stooges movie. Mark smiled as he watched the frozen zombies struggling on the ground like fish out of water.

After taking out all the ghouls near him, he felt a surge of hope. Maybe they would make it through this after all.

He looked over his shoulder to see how Sara was doing and was pleasantly surprised to see her holding her own. From the corner of his eye, he saw a ghoul come up on her and she turned and whacked it over the head with the metal serving tray. The sound from the tray clanged through the street as she then hit the ghoul again. She connected with its skull three more times until the ghoul finally slumped to the ground and remained still, its head and brain nothing but frozen jelly. She then caught up to Mark and together they continued working their way down the street.

Shawn was doing well for himself, too, as he lined up his gun and put another bullet through one of the ghoul's eyes. While he wasn't necessarily a good marksman, it was hard to miss at this range and he continued to take them out as he worked his way down the street.

He had just lined up another one in his sights, when a zombie got in under his guard and sank its teeth into the flesh of his arm. With no hesitation, he stuck his gun against his foe's temple and blew the top of the ghoul's head clean off. But the jaws stayed locked onto his arm in a death grip. Making sure he was clear for a second from any more threats, Shawn stuck the muzzle of his gun in the blood-soaked mouth and pried the jaws apart so they would release his arm.

As the corpse fell away, Shawn was horrified to see a small chunk of his arm was missing, bright red blood seeping from the wound. Shawn cradled his hurt arm against his chest and then proceeded to fire his weapon left handed at the milling mass of animated dead flesh.

As the foursome moved along the street, McDonald veered off from them when they turned at the T in the road.

Mark saw him veering away and yelled.

"Sarge, where're you going? The commissary's this way!" He called over the chaos.

"Just keep going! I have to get some thing's we'll need from my office. I'll catch up with you!" He yelled and then was lost from Mark's view as more ghouls surrounded him.

Mark turned and continued on his way with Shawn and Sara, wondering if he'd see McDonald again.

McDonald worked his way through the frozen corpses like a whirlwind. He was never still long enough for them to get a hold of him. If one did, it received a bullet in the brain pan for its trouble.

As McDonald approached the door for his office, he put his back to it and kicked it in with his foot. As the door flew inward, he jumped through the opening and then slammed the door shut. He quickly grabbed one of his office chairs and jammed it under the knob. He knew it wouldn't last long, but all he needed was a few undisturbed minutes.

He charged into the back room and began to dig through the pile of uniforms and layers of paperwork he had ignored for far too long. Finally, his hand felt the hard surface he was looking for and he pulled a footlocker from underneath the pile.

He quickly opened the combination lock on the front latch and opened the top. Inside were weapons from a dozen campaigns he had participated in. Although he had to admit, he never would have thought he would need them in Antarctica.

With speed and efficiency, he shoved hand grenades into his pockets and grabbed the M-16 he had lovingly kept preserved. He filled his pockets with extra clips and then strapped on his sixteen inch panga. The long blade would serve him well in close quarters.

He then turned and headed for the front door. As he entered the front room, the front door fell in from the weight of the bodies pushing on it. The ghoul's perseverance had finally overcome the chair against the door, and when the door opened, it banged loudly against the wall and hung loosely on its hinges.

The ghouls began to pour into the room, knowing their prey was trapped. Although things didn't go the way they might have hoped.

As they flooded into the room, McDonald opened up with the M-16, spraying the walking corpses from head to toe. The steel-jacketed rounds decimated the approaching horde as he continued to send bullet after bullet into their frozen bodies. When he was finished, there was nothing left but a mess of frozen body parts and bloody ice as the warmer temperature in the room made the meat begin to thaw out. The walls were peppered with bullet holes and blood spray, looking like a mad painter had decided to create his masterpiece in the office.

Careful not to slip on the frozen gore, McDonald strode out into the night air and headed off to meet up with his fellow survivors.

When he was within fifty feet of the others, he noticed they had done a good job of clearing out the area surrounding the alley that would lead them to the fire escape of the building they needed to get to. As he walked up to them, he took down any ghoul that got in his way.

So far, behind him, he'd left a trail of shattered corpses and decimated bodies as he had made his way through the streets.

Then he saw Mark yelling at him to turn around.

He glanced over his shoulder to see a large ghoul coming at him from behind, mouth agape and hands out in front of it so as to grab McDonald.

He smiled as he turned back to the others, and then continued walking forward again like there was no threat to be concerned with.

Mark had seen McDonald making his way towards them and he had to admit he was impressed. McDonald knew how to fight. Then Mark had seen a ghoul coming up from behind him. He'd tried to warn McDonald, but with all the gunfire and yelling, he didn't think the soldier had heard him. All Mark could do was watch as the ghoul came up behind McDonald and hope the man would see his attacker before it was too late.

Then McDonald stopped, and in one fluid motion, withdrew a long knife that was strapped to his hip and swung around and cut off the head of the approaching ghoul as it was preparing to attack him. He then side-stepped out of the way and let the body drop to the frozen ground. The head rolled the opposite way and came to rest, rolling gently until the momentum was finally exhausted.

The dead eyes still moved back and forth and the mouth tried to speak words it couldn't possibly hope to say without vocal cords.

McDonald saw the head, walked over to it and then slammed his heavy military issue boot down onto the skull. The head shattered like red carnival glass as the boot pushed it flat into the snow. Only then did he continue on his way to the waiting group. The beleaguered man took down any zombie that got too close to him and left a wake of frozen dead parts behind him as he made his way to the three companions.

When he arrived next to Mark, he saw they were all a little worse for wear, but seemed to be fine. He led them up the alley to the fire escape, constantly scanning the area for signs of movement.

"All right, guys, we're real close so let's not screw it up now. Stay on your toes," he told them as he walked down the alley, trying to look everywhere at once.

There were two ghouls who had congregated behind a dumpster, and when the group approached them, they stepped out and Shawn put up his weapon to take them out, but McDonald held his arm.

"No wait, let's do this quietly. We don't want to advertise where we are if we don't have to," he said as he retrieved his panga from his hip.

Shawn nodded when he saw the blade glimmer in the gloom suffusing the alley way from the street lamps at the opposite end

McDonald walked straight at the two zombies, and before they barely had time to attack him, he'd already managed to take the head off of one and had begun to systematically take the other apart piece by piece.

The first limbs to go were the arms. He hacked at them like a man chopping through dense foliage in the woods, the limbs flying off one at a time. Then before the ghoul could even comprehend what had happened to it, he sliced sideways at the legs, shearing them off above the knees. As the corpse pitched forward to the ground, he was ready and smoothly cleaved the skull in two. He marveled at the lack of blood as he wiped his panga clean of red ice on one of the corpse's dirty clothes.

When he finished cleaning his blade, Mark walked up beside him and asked: "You're enjoying yourself, aren't you? You didn't have to be so brutal on that one."

McDonald grinned maliciously as he slid his panga back in its sheath.

"You know what? Yeah, I guess I am enjoying myself a little. But, hey, so what, I'm just doing what I have to. I plan on surviving this shit."

Shawn stuck his head into the conversation while smiling at McDonald.

"Yeah, Sarge, but you don't have to enjoy it so much."

"Guys, can we please go? I don't like being out here," Sara said from behind them. Agreeing with her, McDonald led the group down the alley to the fire escape.

When they arrived at the metal stairs of the fire escape, Sara was the first to go up them, followed by Mark and then Shawn. When McDonald knew it was clear, only then did he follow them to the top.

Once at the top, they had a pretty good view of the station and its borders. In a few spots they could see some isolated fires sprouting up from the buildings.

Every now and then a scream would carry on the air to them, but then quickly stop.

Over the buildings themselves, they could see the docks sitting peacefully in the night air.

"There you go, Simmons," McDonald said as he pointed toward the docks. "You said you wanted a way out of here. Well, in about six days the next icebreaker ship is due to arrive. All we have to do is make it 'till then.

Mark nodded. "Sounds good, is there any way to contact them from here? You know, to tell them what's happening?"

McDonald shook his head. "Afraid not, the only way to communicate with them is from the radio house and that's at the other end of the station."

"Damn, I'd really like someone else to know what the hell's going on for once," Mark as he walked away from the edge of the roof.

Shawn walked over to McDonald and asked: "Hey, Sarge, which side do we have to jump from?"

McDonald got his bearings and in a moment waved Shawn to follow him to the opposite side of the roof. As they approached the edge, he pointed to the other roof.

"See? That jump isn't so bad, is it?" He asked Shawn as they both gazed out over the rooftop.

Shawn looked down into the alley to see at least ten ghouls milling about below with more showing up by the minute. They were wandering around and kept looking up at them, knowing the survivors were on the roof.

"Shit, they know we're up here," Shawn said quietly.

"So what if they do? Even if they could get up here I'd just blow them all to Hell anyway," McDonald said as he spit down into the alley. His spit landed on what was once a soldier, the spittle running down the dead man's cheek to then drip onto his shirt.

"So what do you say we finish this shit and jump over there so we can go inside? I'm freezing my balls off out here," he said as he walked away from the edge.

He then backed up about ten feet, and with a good run, jumped over the chasm and landed with a tuck and roll which brought him back to his feet again.

As he stood there brushing the snow off his arms and legs, he called over. "See? Nothing to it."

Mark, Sara and Shawn walked over to the edge and looked down at the ghouls shuffling about below. They kept putting their hands on the walls of the alley like they could somehow climb up. Shawn moved to the side some more, as he stared at the ghouls below, leaving Mark alone with Sara.

The jump was about nine feet, and if they came up short, they would fall into the horde of undead just waiting to tear them apart.

Mark looked at Sara as she stood on the edge and gazed down at the zombies reaching up to them with bent and cracked hands. He could tell she was deep in thought, and after a moment had passed, he saw her eyes change focus, so he asked her a question.

"You all right?" He asked while he searched her face for the real answer he was looking for.

"Huh? Oh, yes, I'm fine. I still can't believe we're going through this again. Look at them down there. That could be us if we hadn't been lucky enough to escape," she said as she looked over at him. "Mark, I don't want to become one of them. Promise me if it happens, you'll make sure I'm not walking around like them," she nodded back down into the alley at the writhing bodies.

Mark nodded to her. "Believe me, I feel the same way. But don't worry, I promise I won't let anything happen to you." He glanced down at his feet as he moved closer to her so only she could hear his next statement.

"Sara, if you haven't realized it already, I'm falling in love with you. Even before all this crazy shit started I had feelings for you, I just didn't know if I should act on them." He said all this feeling more than a little nervous, wondering what she might say in return.

She turned to him and took his hands in hers and smiled up at him.

"Oh, Mark, I feel the same way, but didn't know if I should say anything. You know, the right time and all that."

The two of them were about to kiss when McDonald called over to them from the other roof. "Hello, what's taking so long? I was right. The door's still unlocked so get over here so we can go down into the commissary. I want someone to watch my back when we go in there. Just in case some of those bastards got inside."

Mark waved at him and called back: "Okay, we're coming, relax a little, you'll live longer."

He looked at Sara again. "So, are you ready for the broad jump or what?"

"I'm ready. Let's get this over with." And then she backed away from the edge, and when she had good distance, she ran for the edge and jumped over the gap.

She landed in a heap on the other side, clearing the edge by at least another foot or so. As she picked herself up off the roof, she called over to Mark and Shawn.

"It's not so bad. Just give yourself enough clearance to gain some speed."

Mark and Shawn looked at each other wondering who was going next when Mark spoke up.

"I'll go next, Shawn, and then you follow me. Okay?" He asked as he started walking away from the edge to give himself some clearance. Then, with a deep breath, he ran for the lip and jumped. As he went over, he looked down and the feeling of flight, plus all the ghouls below, gave his adrenaline a boost so that he landed easily with plenty of room to spare. He rolled in the snow and picked himself up.

"No problem. I don't even know why we were making a fuss about it," he called out to Shawn.

Shawn looked down at the ghouls and then moved back to get a running jump, as well.

Then he heard the clanging of feet on the metal fire escape and turned to see a half dozen zombies swarming onto the roof behind him. He knew it was now or never.

When he began running to the edge, his wounded arm was throbbing with pain and it was a distraction he did not need. Cradling the arm against his chest, he threw himself off balance just as he jumped across the divide. His foot was too far from the edge to give him that extra push needed to clear the gap and he came up short, landing hard on the edge of the other roof.

Instinctively, he reached out his arms to catch himself, and as his body bounced off the side of the building, he felt the wind knocked out of him. He could already feel his hands slipping in the ice and snow and was already imagining the waiting teeth and fingernails that were waiting below to rip him apart when his descent was suddenly halted. Mark and Sara had each grabbed one of his arms. Each of them strained to pull him up and onto the roof with them. With one final heave, Shawn's body slid over the lip and Mark and Sara dropped down next to Shawn, all three exhausted from their exertions.

"Wow, Shawn, that was close. Aren't you Army guys supposed to stay in shape and all that?" Mark rasped as he lay beside him, trying to suck in a lungful of freezing air.

Shawn rolled over so he could see Mark's face, his breathing coming in gasps. "I don't know what just happened. I think I slipped on some ice or something."

Then McDonald walked over and looked down at the three companions.

"If you guys are tired of playing up here, I'd really like to have some backup when I go downstairs," he said as he turned and walked away back to the open roof hatch.

The three of them looked at each other as they lay on the roof and then began to laugh.

Maybe there wasn't much to laugh about, but they were still alive and now hopefully, they would have a place to hole up for a while.

As the three of them got up and walked over to McDonald, who was waiting impatiently, Shawn held back for a moment and checked his arm where the ghoul had bitten him. The wound was sore when he touched it and small blue lines, like veins, were coming off the wound and spreading up his arm. He tried to flex his hand, but it would barely move.

As McDonald called to him to pick up the pace, he quickly lowered his sleeve and turned the ripped part of his jacket sleeve away from the wound. Then, after putting on his best casual grin, he walked over to the others so they could go down and explore the commissary together.

CHAPTER THIRTY-EIGHT

FREDERICKS TRIED TO roll over on the couch and almost ended up on the floor. He snapped awake just before his body was going to slide off the edge and he quickly stopped himself.

Rubbing his eyes with a low groan from a sore back, he checked the wall clock and was surprised to see it read 7:15 a.m. He looked around the lobby, and realized it was empty. Why was there nobody present? Where was everyone? There should be a cleaning crew, a general staff, countless interns and researchers all arriving for another day of discovery.

While scratching his head with consternation, he stood up from the couch and stretched as his eyes scanned the lobby for a bathroom.

Spotting the signs for the men's room, he crossed the polished floor and entered through the swinging door. As his back disappeared from view, the front lobby doors opened and a group of ghouls stumbled in from outside. Not quite having a purpose, but just following the first one in line, the frozen dead wandered around the lobby looking for prey and in their own way were disappointed when none could be found. One of them went over to the elevator, and when its hand accidentally rubbed the call button, the elevator doors opened. The ghoul entered the car and was lost from sight as it was taken to another floor.

That was when Fredericks walked out of the bathroom. His hands were inside his pants as he was still tucking his shirt in and his mouth went slack when he saw what was now inside the lobby with him.

"I don't believe it," he muttered in surprise to himself, wondering how there could be infected here at Kryton Station.

He didn't get long to ponder the problem though, because as soon as he walked out of the bathroom, the ghouls saw him and began moving towards him.

He hesitated for just a moment and then went into action, knowing to remain immobile would be a painful death sentence. A small part of him was impressed by how calm he was, how practical. It was amazing really what the human mind would accept, and in the environment he now existed in, zombies were as common as the snow outside the lobby doors.

He pulled his small handgun and fired at the closest ghoul as it approached him. The ghoul was female and wore a blood stained white lab coat. The upper part of her right cheek was nothing but a mass of torn flesh and muscle, the blood now frozen to her face. The bullet hit the woman square in the shoulder, ripping muscle and bone as it passed through the frozen corpse and then lodged in the wall behind her.

The second bullet found its mark when it impacted on her nose. The force of the round snapped the woman's head back and she dropped to the cold cement floor, still forever.

When he looked around the room, he saw he still had three more ghouls to deal with. One out of the three had what looked like a broken leg as the dead man dragged his left leg behind him. That was good, he thought. He could easily out maneuver that one.

That just left the other two.

As they approached him, he noticed that one of them was a soldier. The dead man's uniform was covered in a maroon color that Fredericks could only assume was blood. He idly wondered if it was the ghoul's blood or someone else's.

The second ghoul looked to be a young woman of about twenty. She was wearing a shear nightgown that left nothing to the imagination. Fredericks noticed off-hand that she had a nice figure. Or had a nice figure, as now parts of her body were marred by rips and bite marks where something or someone had taken away the flesh exposing the glistening muscle underneath.

As the dead couple moved closer to him, he maneuvered behind the couch to keep them at bay. Then, when he knew he couldn't miss, he lined up the soldier's head in his sights and fired point blank. The soldier dropped like a rock to the floor as the bullet punctured his brain and then ricocheted around inside the skull before exiting back out his cheek.

Now all he had to do was kill the woman and then take care of the gimp.

As the woman came within arms reach, he aimed the pistol and fired at her face, already realizing head shots were the only way to put a ghoul down for good. But instead of the woman's head disappearing in a red mist of blood and bone fragments, all he received was a dry click from the gun. He stared at the gun as if he could will it to work using only his mind and then pointed and squeezed the trigger again.

Again, nothing happened.

Damn it, he thought. He hadn't kept track of the bullets and now he was empty and had a ghoul staring him in the face. But it wasn't his fault! He was a scientist not a soldier for God's sake!

As the dead woman lunged at him, her knees fell onto the couch just as Fredericks jumped back. Quickly, he dashed for the elevator. If he couldn't fend her off, then he would go to another floor where he'd be safe until help arrived.

As the elevator dinged its arrival and the doors opened, Fredericks had to jump back when another ghoul stumbled out of the car and right into him.

Jesus, they were everywhere, he thought.

For a few panic filled seconds he struggled with the elevator ghoul as it tried to bite his face and neck, both of them falling to the floor. Then he was able to push the body off of him. As the corpse rolled onto its side, he rolled the opposite way and quickly got back to his feet just as the gimp zombie reached him.

Fredericks kicked out with his right foot and knocked the ghoul's other leg out from under it, and then when the body fell to the ground, he rolled to his feet and ran away.

He was running in circles now, just trying to stay out of the ghoul's reach when he noticed a snow shovel in a corner of the lobby by a locked storage room door.

He ran for it, pausing for just a moment to inspect the padlock on the door. Even if he gained access to the room, he would then be trapped with no food or water and the frozen dead right outside the door just waiting to rip him apart.

No, he would make his stand here. Grabbing the shovel in his hands, he spread his legs shoulder wide and waited for the dead to come to him.

The woman was the first, and when she was within reach of the shovel, he swung it as hard as he could at her head. When the shovel connected with the side of her face, Fredericks could feel the bone giving way to the hard metal surface of the shovel.

She was thrown to the side where she twitched on the ground. Not quite dead, but at least out of action for the time being.

The ghoul from the elevator was next, and when it came within range of the shovel, Fredericks used it like a spear to hit it in the neck. He then began to push it back to the wall; the shovel keeping it from moving away. He was yelling the entire time, trying to keep his courage up.

When the ghoul's shoulders struck the wall, the shovel continued the pressure on its neck until the tip of the shovel began slicing through the skin until it reached the point that the head was severed from its shoulders.

When the shovel hit the wall with a dull thud, the head lost its balance on the pan of the shovel and toppled to the floor. A moment later, the ghoul's legs realized there was nothing connected to tell them what to do and they slumped to the floor to join the head.

As Fredericks watched in horror, the eyes on the severed head looked up at him and blinked with a dull-witted stare.

Pulling his attention away from the head, he began looking around the lobby to see where the gimp was. When he spotted the ghoul on his left, he casually walked over to it and slammed the shovel down on top of its head like he was banging railroad spikes into the ground for the railroad.

The force of the blow sent the ghoul to its knees and as the body slid onto the floor, Fredericks slammed the shovel into its mouth and severed the upper part of its head from the lower half. With a flick of his wrist he sent the severed head skittering across the floor, where it came to rest under a potted plant in the corner of the lobby.

As he looked around the lobby at the carnage he had wrought, he slowly regained his breath, his limbs shaking with adrenalin. Once he felt he'd recovered enough to move again, he went to the lobby doors and checked outside.

He wasn't happy about the view.

In the light of the street lamps, he could see more than twenty frozen ghouls moving about the street. Some had massive wounds on their faces and necks, while others looked to be unharmed. Some appeared to have been attacked in their quarters. Some were naked while others wore pajamas and nightgowns.

The good news was they were spread out and he was faster than them.

The bad news was even if he got away, he had nowhere to go. He racked his brain for an answer, but knew the only place he could go for help.

Back to Simmons and the others.

Squeezing the shovel handle tighter to the point he turned his knuckles white, he opened the lobby doors and charged back into the snow covered streets of Kryton Station.

This time running toward Simmons and the others.

CHAPTER THIRTY-NINE

THE FOUR WEARY survivors climbed down the small ladder that connected the roof to the attic of the commissary. Once Shawn had made it down, they all inspected their new environment. The attic was full of old, discarded boxes and at least two years worth of dust. As the group walked along the floor, tiny dust balls shifted underfoot, and when one of them would rub against one of the boxes, dust would fill the air, causing them to cough or sneeze.

"Jesus, it's filthy up here," Mark said to the group. "What do you say we head down to the main floor before we suffocate," he said as he waved dust away from his face.

McDonald took one last look around and then moved to the top step of the stairs leading to the main floor. "Mark's right, there's nothing for us up here. Let's go downstairs," he said from the top step.

The others followed him and soon the group was slowly walking down the stairs. McDonald was first, followed by Sara and Shawn. Mark took last place as he constantly glanced over his shoulder to make sure they had no surprises from behind.

Once on the ground floor, the massive room smothered in darkness, McDonald gave out assignments.

"Okay, listen up, everyone. Mark and Sara, you go check on the front door and make sure it's secure. Shawn, you take the back with me. And watch it, we don't know for sure if this place is empty," he said as he headed for the back of the building with Shawn behind him. "Oh, and see if you can find the switches to turn on the lights." He took three more steps and then stopped again, turning back to the others. "And one more thing," he said before everyone headed off. "Here, take this," he said to Mark as he handed him his panga. "Just in case."

Mark nodded as he took the heavy blade and then turned to go with Sara on their designated assignments.

They had no idea what they would find in the Stygian darkness of the commissary, but after what they had dealt with on the streets of Kryton station, they could only hope their luck would change.

*   *   *

Mark and Sara walked off to the front of the store, their eyes trying to see everywhere in the gloom of the aisles. Their shoes dripped water behind them, the ice on their footwear melting in the warmer temperatures of the commissary.

The aisles were so dark they could barely see their feet while they crept in between the rows of food like silent assassins on a mission.

While Mark walked along the rows, he marveled at all the food stored on the shelves. At least they wouldn't starve while they waited for the icebreaker ship to arrive next week.

Sara was quiet as they walked together to the front doors. Upon reaching the double doors without incident, he quickly checked to make sure the doors were secure and was very happy to find it exactly the way he'd hoped.

With a wide grin, he looked at Sara and said: "See? I told you we'd be fine."

Before she could reply to his statement, a shot rang out from the back of the commissary, quickly followed by another one.

"Damn it," Mark grunted. "Something's happening in the back. I'm gonna go see what's happening," he told her as he brandished the panga in front of him. "You stay here and wait for me. If anything looks out of the ordinary, get back to the roof."

"Okay, be careful," Sara said as Mark took off at a run. She thought it odd that he said 'if anything happens out of the ordinary'.

The past few days were exactly that, so how much weirder could it get other than walking dead people?

Shaking her head, she moved over to a nearby shelf and leaned against it while her eyes studied the darkness for signs of movement. Her arms were wrapped around her tightly, as if she could keep her fears at bay with that simple act.

Slowly, with each passing second, Mark's running steps diminished as he drew farther away from her.

Mark could hear nothing but his footsteps and his breathing as he ran through the aisles of food, retracing his steps until he was almost at the back of the store.

That was when he heard the sounds of exertion and the distinct sound of something heavy falling to the floor. Another shot rang out just as he turned the corner, but he was already too late to help.

*   *   *

McDonald and Shawn walked to the back of the store together. McDonald was on point with Shawn following in the rear.

McDonald stopped when he came upon a set of double doors that would swing both ways if necessary. Pushing the left side open with his gun, he crept into the back room with Shawn. The first thing the men noticed was how cold it was. It felt like they were outside, their breath clouding in front of them when they exhaled.

They were now in the back of the store where all the cardboard boxes would be stored until they were ready to be torn up and discarded. On their left was a pile of canned goods that needed to be properly stored and further down in the dark room they could see the back door that led out into the back alley.

And the door was open!

"Shit, the goddamn door is wide open. You had us roof hopping for nothing, Sarge," Shawn said from behind him.

"Maybe so, but that door should be locked, which means we might have trouble in here, so stay alert," McDonald ordered Shawn as he walked slowly to the door.

"Well, at least that explains why it's so damn cold in here," Shawn mused.

Upon reaching the open door, McDonald inspected it and discovered the keys were still in the lock. Someone had been attempting to unlock the door when something had happened that had left the keys and the door unattended. If he wanted a clue as to what may have occurred, then the frozen splashes of crimson coating the outside of the door was proof enough.

McDonald carefully reached out and wrapped his hand around the doorknob of the open door, expecting something to jump out him at any second. Then he pulled it shut, sliding the locking bolt home.

Looking at Shawn he breathed a soft sigh of relief. "That was easy. I was just waiting for something to try and take a bite out of me," he said.

Before Shawn could answer him, a figure materialized out of the shadows behind McDonald and lunged for his back. McDonald was still looking at Shawn, oblivious to what was happening behind him, and one second the private was just standing there, and the next Shawn had his gun aimed at his face, finger already squeezing the trigger.

Not understanding this act of betrayal, McDonald closed his eyes and waited for the bullet that would end his life. He knew he could never stop Shawn in time from shooting him, when he heard the blast of the gun, the echo sounding like a cannon had gone off in the tight confines of the back room.

But instead of feeling the impact of a bullet, he felt the displacement of air as the round flew past his head almost nicking his right earlobe.

As the gun blast ended, and he realized he was still alive, it was then that he heard the rustling sounds coming from behind him. Moving on instinct, he threw himself to the floor. Rolling onto his back, he looked up to see a zombie lying on the floor where he'd been only a moment ago.

Shawn had acted quickly and had shot the ghoul in the shoulder, causing the dead man to lose his balance when he had lunged for McDonald.

McDonald quickly got back to his feet and went to stand next to Shawn.

"Wow, for a second I thought you were going to shoot me, Private," he said as he watched the ghoul claw its way back to a standing position.

"No worries, Sarge, as a superior, you're all right. What do you want to do with that?" Shawn asked as he waved his gun in the direction of the slavering ghoul.

"Simple, we kill him, unless you want to make friends with him. But I have to tell you I knew this guy when he was alive and he was real asshole," McDonald said as he reached for his panga. When his hand grasped empty air he realized where it was and cursed.

"Shit, I gave my panga to Simmons. Oh well," he shrugged, "I guess we'll have to do this the hard way then."

At the same time McDonald finished his sentence, the ghoul came at him once again, but this time he was ready. McDonald brought up his M-16, and as casually as if he was on the gun range for target practice, he put a bullet through the man's head.

Unfortunately, the bullet went in at an odd angle and was deflected off the skull, leaving a bloody smear across the man's hairline. As the man came at them, Shawn was thrown to the side as McDonald and the ghoul began to grapple with each other. McDonald had a hand under the man's neck as he tried to keep the gnashing teeth from finding a home in his neck.

That's when Shawn walked over after picking himself up and placed his pistol against the zombie's right ear and squeezed the trigger.

Suddenly, the ghoul's head snapped to the left when the force of another bullet impacted with its head. In a matter of seconds, the dull light went out of its cold eyes and it slumped onto McDonald's chest, pinning him to the floor.

Shawn helped the trapped Sergeant extricate himself from under the body, and Shawn tossed the ghoul into the corner where a few empty boxes fell on it, partially obscuring the corpse with the exception of a limp hand and foot.

Then Mark came running into the back room waving the panga around like a wild man.

"Whoa, there, cowboy, relax, everything's fine, we took care of the problem," Shawn said to Mark while he helped McDonald to his feet.

"What happened? I heard the shots and I came to help," Mark said in gasps as he tried to catch his breath.

"No big deal, really," McDonald answered while he brushed dust and slush off his clothes. "It looks like the commissary manager was showing up for work when he must have been attacked. He left the back door open and when we came back here he jumped us. But thanks to Shawn, we took the guy down without much trouble."

Mark then noticed the body in the corner, covered by spilled boxes.

"Great," Mark said as he glanced around the room. "Do you think there's any more in here?"

McDonald shook his head. "No, I think we got lucky, the dead bastards must have continued on after they got him," he said, pointing to the corpse on the floor.

"Later on, when we know this place is locked down, I'll take the guy up to the roof and throw him off it. Shit, it'll be fun to see if I can cream any of the dead bastards below when I do it," he said with a sinister smile.

Mark looked at him and thought again how McDonald seemed to revel in the death and carnage they had all been thrown into. He was a good man to have around in a fight, but what if he got careless and got one of them killed?

Mark was so caught up in his own thoughts; he didn't realize Shawn was talking to him. "Oh what? I'm sorry, Shawn, I zoned out for a second. What did you say?"

"I said, how is it out front, is it safe?" Shawn asked.

"Yeah, it's fine, the front doors are locked up tight. Look, if you guys are okay, I'm going back to check on Sara. I don't like leaving her alone out there," Mark said as he turned to leave.

"Wait up, Simmons, I'll join you," McDonald said and then turned to Shawn. "Private, make sure there aren't any more surprises back here and then join us out front," he told him as he started to leave with Mark.

"Sure, no problem, Sarge," Shawn said as the two men walked through the swinging doors, leaving Shawn alone in the back room.

Shawn walked around the rest of the back room, checking to make sure it was locked tight. The few windows on the wall were set too high for the undead to use to gain access and there was only the one door.

He turned to leave and join the others when he paused to check his arm. As he rolled up his sleeve, he winced when pain shot through it. He thought it strange how there wasn't more blood, and when he inspected the wound it felt cold to the touch. The blue lines seemed to be growing more, too, and they now went all the way up his arm and disappeared under his jacket sleeve.

He frowned, not knowing what to do.

Should he tell his friends? What would they do? He had a flash of McDonald putting a gun to his head and blowing it clean off his shoulders. He shook the image away and rolled down his sleeve, once again wincing when the material of the sleeve touched the open wound.

No, for now he was fine. If it got too bad then he would tell the others. Once he left the back room, he would detour by the pharmacy and grab some antibiotics. That should do the trick and knock out any infection he may have picked up. Come to think of it, he'd grab a couple of bandages, too. Some hydrogen peroxide would be just the thing to make sure he stayed healthy. His entire life he'd always been a quick healer and now would be no different. He grinned when he thought about the cool scar he'd have after the wound healed.

Yeah, man, chicks digged scars. Hey, he could even tell them he got it in action, fighting in some far away place.

With his mind made up, he walked out into the now brightly lit commissary to join the others, while the fluorescent lights hummed overhead like a hive of bees were hiding in the ceiling.

CHAPTER FORTY

FREDERICKS HAD BEEN slowly making progress back to Simmons' building when he had to seek cover. The frozen dead were everywhere on the streets, and while he was fast, there was more than enough ghouls nearby to overwhelm him easily.

So he'd been hiding while he patiently waited for another chance to move.

As he sat in the shadows of a doorway, he finally saw his chance. The ghouls had wandered away from each other enough that if he moved fast enough, he could get past them and be around the corner of the street before they knew he was amongst them.

He took three quick breaths to pump himself up, then bolted for the gap in the undead crowd. He was almost through when a lady ghoul stumbled into his way.

Without even slowing down, he swung the shovel in his hands and whacked the woman on the side of the head. The sound of breaking glass filled the street as the woman's skull shattered from the impact, raining red crystals down to the churned snow beneath her feet.

Fredericks filed what had just happened away in his mind for further contemplation. It seemed the colder the temperature, the more fragile the ghoul's bodies became.

As the headless woman pitched to the side, he dashed through the gap and was around the corner before any of the others could grab him. The next street was about the same, so he ducked behind a trash can and weighed his options.

He could see Simmons' building from where he now hid, and as he watched, he saw that the door to Simmons's room was open. But when a ghoul stumbled through the doorway, he realized all was lost. If Simmons and the others were inside that room then they were undoubtedly dead...or worse.

He was trying to decide where he should go now when one of the ghouls in the street spotted him. As the dead scientist began to move towards Fredericks' hiding place, others soon took up the chase, as well.

Fredericks had to move now or he would be surrounded in moments.

He scanned his area for any more possible weapons and the only thing worth using was the trash can he'd taken refuge behind.

He dropped the shovel, picked up the trashcan and then threw it at the oncoming crowd of undead. The trash can struck the scientist in the chest, and the weight of it knocked the dead man on his butt, where his body soon slowed the other undead that now had to walk around him while the ghoul tried to regain his footing. As the man flopped around on his back like a landed flounder, Fredericks realized in different circumstances he would have found the tableaux comical.

With the ghouls separating to move around the downed scientist, Fredericks saw he had the opening he needed to escape. Picking up his shovel, he ran at the next ghoul--a dead soldier--blocking his path, and when he was in front of the man, he walked right over him. His first shoe landed on the ghoul's stomach and before the soldier could grab him; his second foot landed on the dead man's head and pushed the ghoul to the ground. Fredericks kept right on moving through the gap the ghouls had made, the other ghouls having to move around the obstructed corpse lying in the street.

He then used the shovel to knock a few bodies out of his path. Every time the shovel hit a ghoul, that part would shatter like ice crystals, frozen bone and blood falling to the street like crimson hail.

Fredericks kept on running and he soon outdistanced the frozen dead. He was starting to wonder just where the hell he should go when he spotted the commissary at the end of the street. The unusual thing was that all the lights were on. Glancing around the street and the one behind him, he saw no other building had internal lights on.

He knew the store wouldn't normally be open at this time of the morning unless there were people inside, so without hesitation, he ran for the double doors and began to pound on them. He glanced furtively over his shoulder to see the ghouls in the area had spotted him, and they were now coming his way. He began to panic and renewed his pounding on the main door of the commissary, praying out loud to every god he could think of that someone inside would hear him and let him in.

He only had seconds now as the frozen dead swarmed around him. He put his back to the doors and held up his shovel, feeble a weapon as it was against so many of the undead that were surrounding him, and prepared to make his last stand.

Though it was hard for him to admit, it looked like he wouldn't be getting out of this scrape in one piece.

And that was a shame, because now the world would be denied his brilliance.

*   *   *

Simpson watched as Fredericks ran by him on the street and something that vaguely reminded him of pleasure filled his dead heart.

At last he had found him!

As fast as his stiff legs would move, he followed Fredericks as the man fought his way down the street until he wound up at a building with lights seeping from the windows.

As Simpson watched, he saw Fredericks pounding on the main doors to no avail.

His mouth showed the slightest inflection of a smile as he watched his fellow brethren surround the little man.

It would be a shame that he wouldn't be the one to personally kill the man, but he could accept that easily if he was still able to watch the man ripped apart piece by bloody piece.

Any second now his vengeance would be fulfilled.

His dead eyes twinkled with rage as he watched Fredericks spin around and face his undead attackers. But it was hopeless. There were only moments to go before Fredericks was overwhelmed by the horde of frozen bodies.

*   *   *

Shawn walked over to join the others as they stood in the middle of the canned fruit aisle. He only caught the last bit of what Mark was saying as he came within earshot of the group.

"…and we'll still have to fight our way to the docks," he finished just as Shawn came up next to him.

"Oh, good, Shawn, you're back. I'd like to get your opinion on what we're discussing," Mark said to him.

"Sure, shoot," Shawn replied.

"Well, we were discussing how we're going to get to the docks once the ship arrives, and I pointed out about all the zombies in the streets and how tough it's going to be to make it all the way to the docks without getting attacked."

"And you want to know what I think? Is that right?" Shawn asked.

Mark just nodded and the others waited for his reply.

"Well, I think we haven't even been here long enough to take a shit. Why the hell don't we worry about it later?" He asked the three of them.

Mark frowned and was about to say something back when Sara spoke up.

"Wait a second, Mark," Sara said. "He may have a point. We'll have plenty of time to figure out a plan to get to the docks later. For now, why don't we just relax and thank our blessings we're still in one piece?"

"I hear that, and on that note I'm starving, let's get something to eat," McDonald said as he wondered off to find some breakfast.

Mark was about to protest when suddenly there was a pounding on the front door.

"Who the fuck is that?" McDonald said as he raised his rifle and moved to the front door with the others behind him.

"Don't know, could it be one of those people, you know, a zombie? How the hell did they know we were in here?" Shawn asked as he pulled his gun from its holster with his left hand.

"Well, whoever it is, they want in," Mark said. He still had McDonald's panga and held it up so as to be ready to strike if the door broke in.

As the four of them gathered around the door, they could barely hear talking. Sara put her ear on the door and closed her eyes while she listened.

"I'm pretty sure someone's praying out there," she said.

"Well, that settles it, those bastards don't talk and they sure as hell don't pray, so that means there's a live person out there. We gonna let them in or what?" Shawn asked McDonald.

"Of course we'll let them in. Now, look out and let me open the damn door," McDonald barked to the group. "Simmons, come here and trade with me," he said as he held out the M-16 for Mark to take.

"All you have to do is point it and shoot, the safety's off. And be careful, she's got a hair trigger," he said as he took his panga from Mark. He weighed the long knife in his hand, relishing the weight of it.

Then he unlocked the right hand door, and on a count of three, pulled it open.

And in fell Fredericks right onto his ass.

McDonald slammed the door shut as a swarm of ghouls converged on the spot where Fredericks had stood half a second ago, their bodies rattling the heavy doors, but not breaking them.

Fredericks was still lying on the floor, too stunned to speak. He couldn't believe he was still alive and in one piece.

Then McDonald put his hand out to help Fredericks up. The little man took it and was soon standing on wobbly legs.

"I don't know how to thank you, you saved my life," Fredericks said as he straightened his clothes. When he looked around at the faces gazing back at him, he was shocked to see who they were.

"Well, I don't believe it, Simmons? You're alive? When I saw the building you slept in last night was swarming with zombies, I just naturally assumed you were dead." He looked around at the others. "Along with the Private and Sara, of course."

"Of course," Mark snapped back. "Jesus Christ, Fredericks, you have more lives than a friggin' cat. How the hell did you find us again?" Mark asked.

Fredericks stood up straight so as to look more imposing and then regaled them with his small adventure from the research building all the way to when he was banging on the front doors of the commissary.

"And then the Sergeant opened the door and saved me from being torn apart. Thank you again, by the way," he smiled at McDonald.

"Not a problem, that's what I'm here for," McDonald said and then walked away. He'd had enough of these scientists for a while, he needed a break.

"Welcome back, Doctor," Sara smiled at Fredericks.

"Why, thank you, Dr. Edwards… I mean, Sara, it's nice to be welcomed."

"She doesn't speak for all of us," Mark mumbled unctuously under his breath, and while Fredericks and Sara began talking, Mark wandered off to explore the group's temporary home for the next week.

And he was most definitely not relishing having Fredericks around again.

As he walked away, he didn't notice Shawn was favoring his right arm while he tried to open a can of soda. And even if Mark had, he might not have given it any thought.

*   *   *

Simpson stood outside the main doors of the commissary as his undead army flowed around him. The whole purpose of his existence had just slipped out of his reach. He'd been so close to finally killing the little bastard, and then the man had just fallen into the building and the door had slammed closed.

But no worries, Frederick's was now trapped in the building, and as he directed his frozen army of the undead to surround it, he knew that sooner or later they would get in.

After all, if there was one advantage to being dead, it was that you had all the time in the world…literally.

CHAPTER FORTY-ONE

MCDONALD HAD JUST reached the roof and was closing the access door behind him when he stopped and gazed out across the nearby rooftops.

There were many more buildings burning now, dark pillars of smoke rising into the sky, but lost in the darkness. Thankfully, none of them were in the general vicinity of the commissary. At least for now.

He threw down the corpse of the manager from off his shoulders as he scanned the closest rooftops. The one from which they had jumped from was now full of the frozen dead. When some of them spotted him, they tried to attack him and only succeeded in tumbling off the edge of the roof and falling on the others in the alley below.

McDonald smiled when he saw this happen. "Dumb fucks," he said as he dragged the corpse over to the roof's edge, and without preamble, kicked it off.

The corpse fell with arms flailing and landed hard on two ghouls unfortunate enough to be in the wrong place at the moment.

The weight of the corpse flattened the two ghouls, and when McDonald looked down, he could see them twitching as they tried to extricate themselves from under the dead weight of the body. The task infinitely more complicated now that they had shattered arms and legs.

McDonald watched for another second and then went back to the access door.

Before he entered, he took one more look across the rooftops.

What was once a quiet little research station now resembled what hell would be if it actually did freeze over. He sighed heavily and with a more subdued face then when he had arrived he went back inside, leaving the frozen dead alone once again.

* * *

Outside on the adjacent rooftops, the ghouls continued to grow in number until the weight of their bodies threatened to collapse the roofs.

Down below, Simpson continued to place his undead army in particular spots. Soon he would be ready, and when he was, Fredericks would die. Along with anyone unfortunate enough to be with him.

* * *

McDonald walked down the stairs and onto the main floor of the commissary, wondering where everyone was.

Then he heard voices coming from a few aisles over, so he turned and began walking in the general direction of the voices until he spotted a side room with a glass window.

Upon entering the room, he could immediately tell it was a break room, probably for the employees. There were store related pamphlets scattered on a nearby table as well as signs on the walls telling anyone who read them about: "Your rights as an employee," and, "What you don't know about your 401K."

The others in his little group were sitting around a small round table that could fit four people on a good day.

He also noticed the smell of coffee and immediately wanted a cup.

Noticing where McDonald was looking, Mark pointed towards the counter where a small portable coffee machine was percolating away.

McDonald nodded thanks and walked over to get himself a cup.

While he poured the coffee into a mug that had the words: **World's Greatest Dad**, printed on the side of it, he listened to what the little scientist was talking about. He thought his name was Fredricos or something like that.

"So you all want to wait here until some ship will hopefully arrive and then take you away from here. Is that correct?" Fredericks asked Mark, Shawn and Sara.

"Yeah, Fredericks, that's pretty much correct," Mark mimicked back in the same tone. "If you have any better ideas, feel free to share them with the class."

"Well, for one thing, I believe that by the time you need to leave, every infected person in this station will be swarming in the streets and, my dear Dr. Simmons, you simply do not have enough firepower to make it all the way across the station. When I came here, I only had to go a few streets and I barely survived. Although I'll admit I might have faired better with a firearm."

"What about grenades?" McDonald asked as he blew on his coffee to cool it down. It was still too hot to drink.

"Shit, Sarge, are you saying you have some?" Shawn asked from across the tiny table.

McDonald nodded as he leaned against the counter the coffee pot was on. "Yup, grabbed four of them when I went back to my office to retrieve my M-16 and panga," he accentuated the last word by patting his knife where it once more rode his hip.

Frederick's brow furrowed in concentration. "You know, with those hand grenades and chemicals that are here in the store, I could whip up some devastating mini-bombs that would clear quite a path in the streets as we made our way to the docks." "Sounds good, Fredericks, why don't you get started then," Mark said as he raised himself from his chair to leave. "Sara, would you come with me, please?" Mark asked her as he held out his hand for her.

"Sure, I'll see you boys later," she smiled as she walked out of the room with Mark.

Once they were out of earshot, McDonald looked down at Shawn and smiled.

"Is he hittin' that?" he asked.

Shawn nodded affirmative. "Yeah, they've been an item from around the time we left Amusen Station. Why, were you interested?" He queried.

"Shit, of course I was interested. She's a fine looking woman and at the moment the only one available. So what the fuck do you think?"

"Well, don't look at me, you're not my type," Shawn quipped as he looked up at McDonald.

"Not in your best wet dream, Private," he sneered and then walked out of the room to leave Shawn alone.

When Shawn knew he was alone, he opened his shirt and checked his shoulder. He could see that the blue lines were spreading from his arm and were now slowly progressing across his chest. He winced when he closed his shirt and carefully rebuttoned it.

Okay, now he was starting to get worried.

Once Mark and Sara had left the break room, Mark led her down to the back of the store. Once there he sat her down on an unopened box of peas.

She looked up at him and smiled. "So, what did you want to say to me that you had to bring me all the way back here?"

Mark frowned and then said: "I wanted to talk to you about Fredericks."

"Again? Look, Mark, I thought we'd been over this before," she said.

Mark held up his hands in surrender. "I know, I know, but that was before he deserted us in the middle of the night. Doesn't that change your mind at all?"

"No, not really," she said as she folded her arms in front of her. "Dr. Fredericks was under no obligation to stay with us. Besides, we thought we were safe and that this nightmare was over. Now, I don't want to hear another word about it. Got it?" She said with a look in her eyes that would brook no argument.

"Fine," Mark sighed. "But I hope you're right, because if you're wrong, it could mean some bad shit for all of us."

"I'm not wrong. And don't swear, it's unbecoming." Then she looked around the area to make sure it was clear, and when she was satisfied it was, she winked at him. "Now that the discussion is closed, come here and give me a kiss."

Mark smiled from ear to ear. "Yes, Dr. Edwards."

The two of them kissed and held each other for a good minute before being interrupted by McDonald clearing his throat.

"Yes, Sergeant, can we help you?" Mark asked.

"Ah, yeah, I figured we could work out the sleeping arrangements and stuff in a little while. What do you think?" McDonald asked as he scratched his head embarrassed.

Mark looked at Sara and she nodded yes.

"Sure, how 'bout we meet back in the break room in fifteen minutes or so," Mark suggested.

"Okay, yeah, that sounds good, see you then," he said and then stumbled away to disappear down another aisle.

"Why I do believe we embarrassed the Sergeant," Sara said as she looked up at Mark.

"Maybe so, but gimme another kiss. We still have fifteen minutes to kill," he breathed with a lecherous grin.

She smiled with that look all women get when they know something you don't.

"Too bad you said fifteen. You should have said half an hour." Then she stood up and walked into the back storeroom. Mark watched her for go a moment, and then realizing what she meant, he quickly followed her.

If possible, his smile was now even bigger than before.

CHAPTER FORTY-TWO

SIMPSON STOOD OUTSIDE the commissary and watched the doors.

Ever since the moment he had come back from the abyss of death, he'd been slowly remembering who he was.

Somehow, his desire for vengeance on Fredericks had kept his mind from disappearing into the void.

He was Simpson…and yet he wasn't. The desires of a human being no longer mattered to him anymore. And he felt different now, like his brain was in a fog.

Nothing seemed clear to him and it took him longer to think, as if his brain wasn't working at peak efficiency anymore.

But think he could and even now he was devising a plan to gain access to the commissary.

It would take days to bring to fruition, but soon there would be enough walking dead to easily storm the main doors of the building. And when that happened, they would swarm into the commissary and kill everyone inside.

His cold heart felt a little warmer as he imagined the pain he would inflict on Fredericks.

Soon, he thought, just a few more days.

As the first night trapped in the commissary approached, the five survivors gathered in the break room for an evening meal. Everyone was eating something different and why not? They had an entire food store to themselves and plenty to choose from.

"So when exactly is this ship arriving?" Mark asked McDonald around a mouthful of canned spaghetti and meatballs. The sauce had spilled over the side of the can, partially obscuring the smiling face of a chef in a white hat.

McDonald put his can of beef stew down and thought for a second.

"Let's see, today is Tuesday, so it should be here by Friday the latest. That is, as long as there's no bad storms to slow it down."

"How often do the ships come?" Sara asked as she set down her can of peaches on the table.

"Oh, I'd say about once a month. They bring us fresh supplies and then take our trash and experimental samples back with them," McDonald said. "They do the same for you, too, ya know. Where do you think all that trash from Amusen Station gets hauled to? Here, that's where, and then it's loaded onto the ships."

"What do you think will happen when the ship arrives and there's no one there but dead people to greet it?" Shawn asked as he now ate from his own can of beef stew, the spaghetti already finished. His arm still ached, but his appetite was strong. In fact, he was craving meat like it was nobody's business.

"That'll be interesting to see, won't it?" McDonald replied. "They should probably know something's wrong as there won't be anyone to answer their radio calls. I guess we'll just have to wait and see." Then McDonald grew silent and concentrated on his food.

That's when Fredericks spoke up. "You know, gentlemen and lady, it's going to be quite a feat to fight our way to the docks, hand grenades or not," he said as he ate from a can of chili with beans.

As Mark watched him eat, he made a mental note not to sleep anywhere near the little man when he bunked down for the night.

"Well, it's not like we have a choice," Mark said. "Either we run for it or we probably die in here. Did you see how many of those *people* are outside? Before too long they'll be everywhere and it's going to take a while to clear them all out. That's if anyone even tries. They might just decide to blow this whole damn place to Hell and us with it. No way am I staying here. As soon as that ship arrives, I'm out of here, with or without you."

Fredericks just looked at him and then put another spoonful of chili in his mouth, chewing slowly, acting as if Mark had been talking about the weather. Mark had to admit he might be a prick, but the man knew how to let things roll off his back.

For the rest of the meal, they talked about miscellaneous things. McDonald told them about his last assignment and Shawn filled them in on how he had joined the Army and had wound up in Antarctica.

By the time dinner was over, everyone was pretty well talked out, so the five of them each went their separate ways to relax for the night and then sleep.

McDonald and Shawn each grabbed some magazines from the front of the store to pass the time and Fredericks went off to find some of the chemicals he'd need to make his mini-bombs.

That left Mark and Sara together.

The two of them went off into a corner of the commissary, and with a few towels and blankets found in one of the aisles, they made themselves a bed on the floor.

Mark smiled at her and said: "Well, it's not the Ritz, but it'll do in a pinch."

"It's fine, really. It sure beats sleeping in an igloo."

"Hey, don't knock the igloo; it saved your ass, didn't it?"

"Okay, I'm sorry," she said as she lay down on the blankets. She squinted up at him as the bright lights on the ceiling shined down on her. "What about the lights?" She asked.

"Oh, I'll wait until we're ready to go to sleep and then I'll turn off the ones over us. But I don't want to shut them all off in case there's trouble. McDonald agrees with me, we talked about it earlier."

"Why, do you think there's going to be trouble?" She asked with more than a little concern.

"No, of course not, I just want to be prepared, that's all," he said and then sat down next to her and gazed into her eyes. "I promise."

That seemed to placate her, and together the two of them lay down, relaxed and enjoyed each other's company.

Hours later, they drifted off to sleep in each others arms in the relative silence of the commissary. For it was far from quiet. The ghouls were still banging on the front doors, but after almost a day of the staccato never ceasing, it had become a dull background noise to be tuned out.

*   *   *

Shawn sat back and tried to relax.

His right arm was throbbing worse now and he couldn't concentrate on the magazine he was trying to read, so he decided to try and find some aspirin. He was beginning to believe the antibiotics he'd taken earlier weren't doing a damn thing to help him.

As he wandered around the aisles of the commissary, he was amazed at all the products lining the shelves. These people may be in the middle of nowhere, but they sure didn't eat that way. Rounding a corner, he walked into the medicine aisle. He smiled when he saw all the cold and flu medicine on the shelves. After a moment, he found what he needed and returned to where he'd set up camp at the front of the store. McDonald was situated on the other side of the aisle, opposite him, and he smiled to himself when he heard the man snoring.

Sitting back down on his makeshift, bed he popped four aspirins into his mouth and tried to relax again. He doubled the dose, hoping it would quiet his pain.

As he sat there thumbing through his magazine again, he suddenly felt a sharp pain in his chest. He waited, hoping it would go away, but instead it intensified.

The pain was so bad he began to see stars in his eyes, his vision then becoming blurry. He tried to get to his feet, to call someone for help, but all his breath was gone.

When the next bolt of pain shot through his chest, he ripped open his shirt to check his skin. He was horrified to see the blue veins had totally covered his chest and stomach and they now seemed to pulse with the rhythm of his beating heart.

Scared out of his wits, he tried to stand again, and this time he made it.

He stood swaying back and forth, not able to move his legs, no matter how hard he tried. And then a wave of dizziness began to overwhelm him, and in the back of his mind, he knew he was going to faint.

Then, like a light switch being turned off, he slumped to the floor and lay still, only some gentle twitching to signal he wasn't dead yet.

*   *   *

Fredericks was off in another corner of the commissary, tinkering with chemicals. He'd found ammonia, bleach, paint thinner, and a few other ingredients he would need to perfect his cocktail of destruction. He'd already decided to use one gallon water containers as reservoirs for the explosive liquid and then strap the grenades to the bottles. The resulting explosion would be at least three times as deadly as just a single grenade.

Fredericks smiled to himself as he mixed the deadly cocktail. He liked making weapons of destruction. It was times like this when he wished he had been born a generation earlier and it had been him who had created the atom bomb.

As he worked well into the night, his delusions of grandeur floated through his head.

He thought of the walking dead even now outside their building and smiled even wider. Could it have been him that created them? It couldn't be more than a coincidence that the outbreak happened hours after his rogue experiment at Amusen station. Could it?

And if it was he that was responsible for creating an unstoppable killing force, than he would go down in military history.

The military would be lining up to learn his secrets. He'd be rich, famous, and he would finally receive the respect of his colleagues.

All these thoughts floated through his mind long into the night until, he too, finally lay down and slept through his first night in the commissary.

Meanwhile, outside the commissary, the frozen dead continued to gather, eager to enter the building and feed on the prey within. They were waiting for something to happen; only they didn't know what it was just yet.

CHAPTER FORTY-THREE

MARK OPENED HIS eyes and stretched, blinking the sleep from his eyes.

Although it was early Wednesday morning, time was relative in a world where the sun didn't rise and set each day. He glanced at Sara, still sleeping soundly next to him, and felt a wave of love for this woman he had grown to know so much more in such a short time span. An errant hair had fallen in front of her face and he reached over and gently brushed it away. She stirred for a moment and with a slight sigh, grew still again.

He decided he might as well get up, use the bathroom and see if any of the others were awake.

He rose from his makeshift bed and wandered down the lonely aisles. As he passed a display for fruit cocktail, he thought to himself they would make a great breakfast. He grabbed three cans in case one of the others might be interested, too, and then walked off to the break room where he planned on dropping them off before going to the bathroom.

Upon arriving at the room, he was greeted by McDonald who was sitting at the small table in the middle of the room.

"Morning, Simmons, want a cup of joe?" He asked.

Mark just put up his finger in a "wait a second" expression and said: "Hold that thought Sergeant," and then he dropped the cans on the counter and hurried off to the bathroom before his bladder exploded.

A few minutes later, he returned to the room feeling just a little lighter. This time he smiled at McDonald and said: "All right then, you were saying?"

"I was saying," McDonald repeated. "Would you like some coffee? I just brewed it."

"Yeah, thanks, that'd be great," Mark said as he walked over and poured himself a cup.

"Anyone else up yet?" He asked as he walked over and sat down at the table with McDonald.

"I couldn't tell ya. When I woke up, I just wandered in here. You know, there's not that much to do around here. We don't all have a pretty woman to keep us company," he said as he took a sip of coffee.

Mark was just about to ask him what the hell he meant by that when Sara walked into the room. So, he decided to change the subject. He'd bring it up later with McDonald when they were alone.

"Morning, Sara, coffee's hot," Mark said to her.

She stretched in the doorway like a cat after a long nap which she then followed with a yawn. "Thanks, that'd be great," she said as she glided over to the coffee pot. Once she poured herself a cup, she too, sat down.

"I figured you would've stayed asleep a little longer," Mark said as he glanced at her. "How come you're up?"

"I'm up because I could hear Fredericks banging away on something. So I decided to just give in and get up, also. Where's Shawn?" She asked.

"Probably still sleeping," McDonald answered. "I'll give him another hour and then I'll get him up. I want him to help me make sure this place is locked down tight."

Sara nodded at his reply and then concentrated on her coffee, blowing it gently to try and cool it down.

After a few minutes had passed with idle chit-chat, McDonald began feeling like a third wheel so he excused himself. He walked off to find a place to do his morning exercises. On his way, he grabbed a couple of large cans of canned tomatoes, figuring he could use them as weights. His footsteps soon faded away as he headed to the back of the commissary.

Mark and Sara continued to talk about things two people who had become one couple would always share with each other. They shared where each was from and who their parents were. Who had brothers and sisters and who had a favorite pet named 'Booboo'; it was Sara.

They talked long into the morning until McDonald's head appeared in the doorway.

"Hey, guys, have you seen Shawn?"

Mark shook his head back and forth. "Why no, we just assumed he'd gotten up and was with you. You mean he's still sleeping?"

"Must be, because he hasn't reported to me," McDonald grimaced. "I'm gonna go find him and kick his ass out of bed." And then his head disappeared as he went off to give Shawn that kick in the ass.

When he had reached where Shawn had slept for the night, he walked over quietly, wanting to yell the private out of bed, and was ready to wake his ass up in style when he noticed the position Shawn was sleeping in. His body was twisted with his arm at an odd angle underneath him. McDonald kneeled down and checked his pulse. It was there, only slower than it should be for a healthy young man. Gently, he rolled Shawn onto his back and then jumped back when he saw the condition he was in.

Shawn's skin was ice cold and he had dark-blue lines running up and down his face and neck. McDonald stood up and decided this was way over his head and ran off to find the others.

Appearing in the doorway Mark noticed this time McDonald looked a little frazzled.

"Guys, come quick, there's something wrong with Shawn!" Then his head disappeared as he charged off to find Fredericks. It was easy to find him. All McDonald had to do is follow the noise, which was so loud it drowned out the banging of the ghouls on the front door.

Fredericks had set himself a poor man's chemistry set. He'd taken bottles of food and cleaning supplies and had fashioned them into a makeshift laboratory. Complete with soda bottles for test tubes.

McDonald hesitated for a moment as he took in what this crazy bastard had done, but then he remembered why he had come and called out to Fredericks.

"Hey, Doc, there's something wrong with the Private. Would you come and see if you can help?" He asked Fredericks.

Fredericks looked up from his work. "Well, I don't know what you think I can do. After all, I'm not a medical doctor," he said.

"Yeah, well, you still know a shitload more than I do, so drop what you're doing and come on." McDonald's tone was hard, and Fredericks could tell the big Sergeant wasn't going to take no for an answer.

Fredericks shrugged and followed McDonald to where Shawn was. When they arrived, Mark and Sara were already there and were kneeling down by the private's side. Sara had Shawn's face in her hands as she pushed his hair away from his forehead.

"Oh my God, he's so cold," she exclaimed.

When Fredericks moved around the others, seeing Shawn's face and neck for the first time, and then noticing the blue lines crisscrossing his flesh, he was shocked, although not so shocked he wasn't able to hide his astonishment from the others. Leaning down, he examined Shawn and nodded when he stepped back.

"He's infected," he said flatly.

"Infected? What the hell do you mean infected? How could that have happened?" Mark asked.

Fredericks chose his words carefully so as not to give too much away. The blue lines crossing Shawn's face were incredibly similar to one of his past, failed experiments. That settled it for Fredericks. Somehow, his hypothermia serum had mutated into a killer virus that brought the dead to life, and if a victim was bitten, it would infect the living, as well.

Despite knowing this, he kept the information to himself. He doubted his new companions would take too kindly to knowing the truth and how he was involved.

"I'd say that whatever biological agent has infected those poor people outside has the ability to invade a live specimen also. In time, the poor Private will become like those outside," Fredericks explained.

"Shit, Doc, are you serious? Are you telling me he's gonna turn into one of those dead fuckers?" McDonald asked as he pointed at the doors, and to the further extent, outside in the street.

"Yes, Sergeant, I'm afraid so. All we can do is keep him comfortable until he finally succumbs."

"Oh God, it can't be true, there must be something you can do for him," Sara pleaded as she cradled Shawn in her arms, tears beginning to roll down her cheeks.

"I wish there was, my dear, I truly do. Now if you'll excuse me, there's nothing else I can do here and I have a lot of work to do." Then Fredericks walked away back down the aisle without a backwards look.

Mark watched him go. "What a coldhearted bastard that guy is," he spit as he kneeled down next to Sara. "Come on, honey, there's nothing we can do for him. As much of an asshole as Fredericks is, I can't fault what he said. I'll make sure Shawn is comfortable. I'll stay with him for now. You go and come back in a while and take over for me."

She wiped away the tears and nodded. Then she gently put Shawn's head down on the blanket and quietly walked away.

Mark looked up at McDonald who was towering over him "Will you help me get him into a more normal looking position? He can't be that comfortable like he is."

"Sure, of course," McDonald said while he bent down and grabbed the right side of Shawn.

Together, the two men pulled him up and fixed his clothes, followed by placing a small blanket over him.

"Christ, he feels like ice," Mark said after they had Shawn positioned where they wanted him. The entire time Shawn hadn't opened his eyes.

"Yeah, I know, it's weird," McDonald said and then turned to look at Mark.

"Hey, you know what we're gonna have to do sooner or later, don't you?" He asked in a flat tone, his eyes hard.

"Yeah, I was thinking the same thing, though I don't want to think about it. But listen, when it happens, let me do it. He was my friend and I owe it to him. While we fought our way here, he saved my ass a few times," Mark stated as he looked down at Shawn's still form. The man's chest rose and fell slightly, almost nonexistent, as if he was dead already

McDonald nodded and then retrieved Shawn's gun where it lay on the bedroll. "Here, you take this. He doesn't need it anymore," he said while he handed the weapon to Mark. "You do know how to use it, right?"

Mark nodded he did, took it from him, and put it through his belt.

"Thanks, I guess it's got to go to someone, right?"

McDonald gently slapped Mark on the back.

"Yeah, guess so. I'll see you later." Then he stood up and went off to check the commissary and make sure it was still secure.

Mark sat down and watched his friend. Shawn's skin was turning a light shade of blue, his flesh color draining away. Mark put his head between his hands and sighed. He was going to lose another friend to all this damn madness.

And when the time came that Shawn turned into one of the frozen dead, Mark knew he was going to have to put a bullet in his head, too.

CHAPTER FORTY-FOUR

SARA WALKED AWAY from Shawn and the others, the weight in her heart unbearable. She decided she needed some air, so she climbed up the stairs to the attic and made her way to the roof access door.

Stepping out onto the snow-covered roof, the cold air felt good on her face and the tears on her cheeks froze in an instant. As she looked around, she could see that many of the other buildings were in flames, the yellow and orange tendrils of the fires pushing back the darkness. And she was beyond horrified to see all the ghouls milling about on the adjacent rooftops.

She walked over to the edge and looked down into the alley below. By the time she reached thirty, she' lost count of the undead as the undulating mass of bodies kept shifting and moving.

She walked over to the front of the commissary and gazed down. She was shocked to see how many bodies were there. As she tried to count them, she got lost somewhere in the early seventies. She continued around the building and found it to be the same there, as well.

"Oh my God," she whispered to herself. It was like every ghoul at the station was congregating outside. But why? What were they waiting for? Were they smart enough to figure out a way to get in? So far, all they'd done is impotently bang on the front doors.

She decided to go back down and inform the others of what she'd seen. They only had to make it two more days and the icebreaker ship would arrive and get them out of here.

Just two more days, she thought, as she stared at the mass of undead bodies on the neighboring rooftops. With the flames of the burning buildings setting the darkness ablaze, she wondered if they would truly make it.

*   *   *

McDonald was making his rounds of the commissary, checking to make sure everything was secure, which luckily for all of them, it was, when he saw Sara come racing down the stairs from the attic. She was moving so fast she literally fell into his arms.

Even though the moment was quick, McDonald was very aware of how she felt and how soft her breasts were when they pressed against him.

"Whoa, there, little lady, what's the rush? Are you okay?" He asked as he set her back down in front of him.

"Yes, I'm fine," she breathed as she caught her breath from her dash down the stairs. "It's just that I went on the roof and I saw some pretty weird stuff up there, and I wanted to tell you and Mark about it."

"Oh, okay, so let's go see him and you can tell us both together. Ladies first," he said as he held out his hand in deference.

She nodded and proceeded down the aisle with McDonald following close behind. As he walked behind her, he admired the way her buttocks swung from side to side. She turned to see if he was following her and he quickly averted his gaze, raising his eyes to her face. He flashed her his best smile. She smiled back half-heartedly and continued on until they reached Mark and Shawn.

"Wow, that was fast. I thought you would've taken a little more time," Mark said as he stood up from the chair he'd found in another aisle and had carried over to use in his vigil over Shawn.

"No, it's not that, Mark. I went up on the roof and I saw some things you and the Sergeant here should know about," she said anxiously.

And then she filled them in on what she had seen and how many ghouls were massing outside the commissary's doors.

"Shit, that's not good," McDonald said as he looked down at Shawn. "I was up there earlier and I saw them, too, but not that many."

"No, it's not good, but that still doesn't change a thing. In two days, when that ship arrives, we're out of here. Hey, Sarge, will you check on Fredericks and see if you can get a timetable on when he'll be done with the explosives?"

"Sure, no problem," he said and then headed off to see Fredericks.

Mark looked at Sara and saw how shook up she was, so he took her by the shoulders and looked into her eyes. "Don't worry, Sara. Didn't I say I wouldn't let anything happen to you?"

She nodded as she gazed into his eyes.

"And so far I've kept that promise, right?"

She nodded again.

"All right then, relax, we'll get through this, somehow. I promise."

Then Shawn began to moan and when they turned and glanced down at him, his eyes were open.

The two of them quickly got to their knees and helped Shawn to sit up.

"Oh, my head. What happened?" Shawn asked, his voice barely a whisper.

"You passed out from what we guessed," Mark said. "Do you want anything? Water, food, maybe?"

Shawn shook his head no. "No, I'm fine, Mark. What's wrong with me? I feel so cold," he said and then began coughing, a low phlegm cough that racked his body and took his breath away. When the coughing attack had subsided, Sara was the one to answer him.

"Dr. Fredericks said you'd been infected by one of those people outside. He said you're going to turn into one of them. Oh, Shawn, I'm so sorry, I don't know what to do," she said as the tears began to roll down her cheeks.

Shawn tried to smile. "Hey, don't worry 'bout it. It's not your fault. It's a miracle I made it this far," he said, trying to console her.

Mark bent closer and looked at him seriously. "Shawn, do you know how you got infected?" He asked softly. "Maybe if we knew we might be able to do something about it, no matter what that asshole Fredericks said."

"Yeah, I think I do," he said as he slowly raised his right arm. "Roll up my sleeve, will you, Mark? I don't seem to have the energy."

Mark nodded and then proceeded to raise the sleeve and gasped when he saw the wound on Shawn's arm.

"Dammit, man, when the hell did this happen? Why didn't you tell me? Maybe we could have done something about it," Mark hissed.

Shawn tried to chuckle. "Yeah, like what? I don't see any hospitals around here, do you? Look, there's nothing that anyone could have done and you know it. Just promise me one thing, will you?" Shawn asked.

"Anything, buddy," Mark said.

"Just promise me that if I come back like one of those dead bastards that you won't let me stay that way. That you'll take me down."

Mark swallowed a knot in his throat as he tried to keep it together. Then he looked at Shawn with tears in his eyes.

"I promise, buddy."

"Good, Mark, that's real good. Look, guys, I'm tired, I think I'm gonna take a nap for a while." Then he closed his eyes and went back to sleep again. Mark stood up and wiped his eyes with his shirtsleeve and then turned to Sara.

"Can you watch him for a while? I need to be alone," he said.

"Sure, Mark, go on. I understand. Take all the time that you need. I'll call you if anything changes," she said softly from the floor next to Shawn.

Mark nodded thanks and walked away to be alone and try to take in all the shit that had happened this morning and before. All of it came swimming up and hit him like a freight train.

And in a corner of the commissary, where he knew none of the others would be able to see or hear him, he slid to the floor and wept like he had when he was five and had skinned his knee for the first time, the stinging cut on his leg a frightening sensation.

And when he'd let it all out, he wiped his eyes and stood up again. He felt slightly embarrassed for crying like a little girl, but also feeling better; some of the emotional burden he'd been carrying now off his back.

Squaring his shoulders and making sure his face was clear of tears, he set his jaw firmly and headed back to the front of the commissary to be with Sara and Shawn.

* * *

The entire time he had been alone, the continuous cacophony of pounding continued unabated, the frozen dead never tiring, never slowing in their tenacity to gain entry to the building and the trapped humans within

CHAPTER FORTY-FIVE

MCDONALD STRODE DOWN the long aisle, following the sounds of Fredericks' tinkering. While he walked, he thought about Sara. He was really beginning to take a fancy to her, but how could he steal her away from Mark? What did that wuss of a scientist have that a real soldier like him didn't?

He resolved that the next time he was alone with her, he would at least make a play for her; after all, what did he have to lose?

When he reached the end of the aisle, Fredericks came into view. He was working behind his makeshift lab table and bubbles and smoke could be seen coming off of some of the glass bottles he was using as beakers.

"Hey, Dr. Frankenstein!" He called out as he approached from behind the little man. "Mark and I were wondering how much longer until you'll have the explosives ready?"

Fredericks didn't appear to notice McDonald, so after a few heartbeats had passed with no reply, McDonald yelled out again, only louder this time.

"Hello! Wake the fuck up, Doc!"

That did it and Fredericks snapped out of whatever world he'd been immersed in. He glanced up at McDonald over his shoulder.

"What? Oh, Sgt. McDonald, to what do I owe the pleasure?" McDonald washed his hands over his face in frustration.

"I said, how long until the boom-boom juice is done?"

"Oh, I'd say it shall be done later today, why?" Fredericks inquired.

"Well, I know I want to try it out, so you come get me when its done and we'll go up on the roof and blow up a few of those dead bastards. Got it?"

Fredericks nodded, that yes, he did indeed understand.

Sgt. McDonald didn't seem like a man who would put up with Fredericks' idiosyncrasies, so he tried to stay as agreeable as possible with the gruff soldier.

"Good, I'll see you later, Doc. Remember, the second you're done, come find me." And then he turned and walked away, leaving Fredericks to fall back into his world where he was God and all others bowed before his brilliance.

McDonald walked back to check on Shawn and to fill Mark in on the information he'd just received from Fredericks. As he neared Shawn's bedroll, he slowed down to a crawl and then stopped behind the last shelf before he would walk out into the open.

From where he was, he now had a bird's eye view of Mark and Sara through an opening where some cereal boxes had been moved. He saw they were in a heated discussion, but then she seemed to relax, her shoulders slumping in defeat. McDonald watched Mark put his arms around her, and moments later they were in a lover's embrace.

As they kissed, McDonald thought it looked more tender than passionate. While he watched them, he admired the curves of Sara's body, and especially the way her hips flared out just so.

Then the trance was broken as the two disengaged themselves from each other and kneeled down to talk to Shawn.

That's when McDonald decided to make an entrance. As he walked over to the three of them, he could see Shawn's eyes were open and he put on a smile for the young man's benefit.

"Well, look who's up. You need to get well, Private, we have work to do," he said jovially as he kneeled next to Mark and Sara.

"I'll try my best, Sarge," Shawn rasped. His voice sounded like he'd swallowed sandpaper.

"Sure you will," McDonald said. Then he turned to Mark. "Hey, Mark, can I talk to you for a minute?"

"Yeah, sure," he said. The two of them walked over to the side of an aisle where McDonald filled him in on what Fredericks had told him.

"That's good," Mark said. "And you want to try some of it outside?" He asked him incredulously.

"Yup," McDonald said. "As soon as he's done, I figure I'll do a little experiment of my own."

"I just hope you don't blow us up, too, when you do it."

With a gleam in his eyes, McDonald grinned widely. "Relax, I'm a professional."

With a chuckle he walked away on some errand.

Mark watched him walk away and frowned. "Yeah, that's what I'm afraid of."

When Mark walked back to Shawn, he found the private was asleep again. He sat down on the floor next to Sara and cupped her left hand in his. He didn't say anything as there was no need.

The two of them stayed with Shawn for the rest of the day, only leaving for bathroom breaks and to grab something to eat. Only ten feet away, the front door continued to shake as the ghouls pounded on it, but to no avail.

The waiting was hard as they sat there and watched Shawn slowly growing worse. One time during their vigil, Shawn became spasmodic and it had taken both of them to hold him down so he wouldn't hurt himself.

After the episode, he didn't regain consciousness.

Later that day, McDonald popped up to tell Mark the explosives were done and that he should come out and give him a hand.

Mark looked to Sara who nodded and told him to go.

He stood up with a groan, his legs not happy about being moved after being in the same position for so long, and after a gentle squeeze of her shoulder as a farewell, he left with McDonald to go blow something up. He left Shawn's gun with her, too, just in case there was trouble.

Sara sat very still while she gazed down at Shawn's still face. She was all alone now with nothing but her thoughts to keep her company.

And the gun in her hand.

Then she cried some more, a few tears slipping off her cheeks to land on the gun in her lap, the ceiling lights of the commissary catching the wet barrel and reflecting off it like a thousand small stars.

CHAPTER FORTY-SIX

MARK FOLLOWED MCDONALD through the aisles of the commissary until at last they came upon Fredericks.

When Fredericks saw them, he stopped what he was doing and grinned proudly.

"Ah, at last you're here. Come here, please, I have a lot to show you," he said as he waved them over excitedly to a table he was standing in front of, blocking the contents with his body.

As the two men moved closer, their nostrils were assaulted by the acidic smells that seemed to hover around Fredericks. What was surprising was how Fredericks didn't seem to notice the odors at all.

"What's up, Doc?" McDonald asked and then glanced over at Mark.

"I always wanted to say that," he chuckled.

Mark just looked at him and wondered how this man had managed to reach the rank of sergeant.

Then the two men saw what Fredericks was referring to. On the table were four bleach bottles, and each had a grenade attached to it with duct tape Fredericks had found on one of the shelves in the small hardware section. Other than that, the white bottles looked pretty unimposing.

"That's it?" Mark snapped at him. "This is what you've been doing for over a day now? Attaching grenades to bleach bottles?"

"On the contrary, my dear Dr. Simmons, it's what is in the bottles that constituted the hours of labor. There is anything but bleach in those bottles, I assure you," Fredericks said as he picked a bottle up for the two men to examine more closely.

"Why, what's in them?" McDonald asked as he took the bottle from Fredericks.

"Let's just say there are more additives in that bottle than I have time to list. So listing them to you would be counterproductive," Fredericks told him as he walked around the table. "I propose you test one of the bombs so we can see how effective it is and whether or not I have measured the ingredients in the correct amount. With these primitive instruments I've been forced to use, it may not work as well as I would hope. Surely there is something that needs to be blown up around here, Sergeant?"

McDonald got that weird, sinister smile again as he looked at the bomb and then at Fredericks.

"That won't be too much of a problem, Doc. I think I can find a use for it," he said as he walked away.

Simmons turned to follow when Fredericks put a hand on his shoulder to halt him.

"Dr. Simmons, wait a moment will you, please?"

Mark turned and waited for whatever the man had to say.

"I was just wondering how, Private…I mean, Shawn is doing? I heard what you said as I walked away earlier, and you know, it's just not true. I truly do care how he is and if he's suffering."

"Well, Fredericks, then you're in luck, because he is suffering and he's dying, but hey, don't worry 'bout it, I'll pass on your 'get well card' to him if he ever wakes up."

Then Mark turned and walked away, leaving Fredericks standing open-mouthed from Mark's callous treatment of him when he was actually trying to reach out to a fellow human being.

After a minute or so had passed, he closed his mouth and returned to work. Ah well, he should have known better in the first place. That was why he had remained alone for so long. Human interaction was just so damn tedious. And far too much work for him to want to spend the time to get it right.

No, better to stay alone, where he could work on his experiments in peace, without the annoying distractions of humanity to get in the way.

Mark caught up with McDonald just before he was about to climb up the stairs leading to the attic and then the roof.

"Hey, Sarge, just what exactly are you planning on doing with that thing?" Mark asked him as he followed him up the stairs.

"Do with it? Shit, I'm gonna blow me up some fuckin' zombies, that's what," he said as he reached the roof access door and stepped outside.

Mark followed him, and after he got over the bitter cold blasting his exposed, hands, face and neck, he was shocked to see all the frozen dead that were on the other roof tops. There must have been at least thirty or more. It was hard to tell as the bodies were always moving around and getting intertwined.

As Mark watched them shuffling about like old men, he wondered if their feet hurt. He knew his would if he did as much walking as an average ghoul seemed to do.

He saw McDonald walk over to the edge of the rooftop and kneel down with the bomb. Then he glanced over at Mark. "You ready!" He yelled.

"Sure, go for it!" Mark called back.

With a curt nod, McDonald pulled the pin on the grenade and tossed the whole contraption onto the adjacent roof. The bottle rolled for a moment and then stopped when it hit a ghoul's ankles. The dead man wore a set of hospital scrubs and resembled an orderly in every way.

The dead orderly stopped moving and looked down at the bomb, then bent over and picked it up, wondering if it was food. Not being intelligent enough to understand what he was holding, the orderly just stood still with the bomb in his hands…for another three seconds.

Then the night sky lit up as the grenade exploded, igniting the contents inside the bleach bottle. The orderly was vaporized in a nanosecond as the fireball the bomb created spread out across the rooftop, consuming everything in its path. The shock wave was enough to send McDonald flying onto his back and he landed in the snow-covered gravel on the roof, blinking up at the dark sky. Mark was thrown backward into the roof stairwell, as he was caught completely off guard by the massive explosion. Luckily, he was able to grab onto the small railing on the inside of the door and prevent himself from falling down the stairs, where he would have probably cracked his head open like a ripe melon.

His eardrums instantly shut down from the volume of noise they were receiving. Through the dull muffled sounds, he could hear the patter of small things hitting the roof of the enclosure he was in. He immediately thought of what hail sounded like when it hit the roof of a car.

When he pulled himself back up and gazed out onto the rooftop, his jaw dropped at the sight before him. The roof was now covered in what appeared to be bloody body parts, the crimson fluid seeping into the snow and staining it a bright scarlet. As he stumbled back outside, he accidentally kicked half of a head that had wound up near the doorway.

Everywhere through the billowing smoke, he could see bits and pieces of what were once human beings. A few times, as he walked around the roof (or more like shambled, like he had died and come back as a zombie himself), small body parts bounced off his head or shoulders while they rained down from the sky. Then like God had turned off a switch, it ceased and the rooftop seemed to give off an almost preternatural quiet. Or maybe that was just his shocked eardrums not working yet. He was now able to really look at the devastation Fredericks' concoction had wrought, thanks to the thick pall of smoke that was slowly being whisked away by the gentle wind blowing across the rooftops.

His roof looked more like the aftermath of a bloody battle than anything else, and when he gazed across the divide between the two buildings, he was even more shocked at what he saw.

Where before there were at least thirty ghouls roaming around on the adjacent rooftop, now there were none. They were totally destroyed, and when Mark walked out further onto the roof, he could see the actual roof on the building next to him was obliterated. There was nothing left but a hole with small fires burning on the fractured edges.

"Holy shit, what the hell did Fredericks put in there?" Mark gasped as he moved next to McDonald to help the soldier up. McDonald's face was bright red, like he'd been out in the sun for far too long. Mark had to hold him up or the man probably would have fallen over.

"Hey, Sarge, you all right?" Mark asked as he looked into his glazed eyes, wondering if maybe the man had a concussion. Then

McDonald's eyes cleared and he stepped away from Mark, pulling his arm free. The he inspected his handiwork. From the smile on his face, Mark could tell he was pleased.

"Wow, would you look at that? Goddammit, if I'd known what the Doc could do with a few chemicals, I would've made damn sure to grab as many grenades as I could when I was at my office," he said as he moved over to the edge of the rooftop. As he walked, he sometimes had to sidestep one of the human body parts now littering the roof.

"Well, come on, Mark," he said as he turned to look at the stunned man. "Let's go tell the Doc the bombs are a success. Shit, I just wish we had more than three left, though." He kicked a severed head out of his way like it was just an empty soda can, the head rolling to the edge of the roof where it dropped from sight to fall into the alley below.

Then he stepped inside the roof access door and began to climb back down. Mark stayed on the roof for another moment, surveying the carnage around him. Then he looked at the other nearby rooftops. The ghouls on the other rooftops seemed more agitated now. As if they knew what had just happened to their brethren. The moaning and dry rasping of their voices was really freaking him out, not to mention he was freezing cold, so he turned and headed back down the stairs behind McDonald.

Outside on the neighboring rooftops, the moaning and wailing continued as the undead seemed to mourn their lost comrades. And then, one at a time, they began to descend to the frozen ground below. In minutes the rooftops were empty again, and there was nothing but the smudged footsteps left in the snow-covered rooftops to show they had been there at all.

* * *

Simpson stood in the street in front of the commissary as body parts rained down around him. He'd heard the explosion through his frozen eardrums and looked up in time to see the flame and smoke as the roof exploded upward in a glorious fireball.

He screamed to the night sky in frustration. There were no more live bodies in the station to infect. What he had here with him now was it. Every time one was destroyed, there would be no immediate replacement. But he still had more than enough to do what needed to be done.

He knew soon something would happen.
It had to.

CHAPTER FORTY-SEVEN

ONCE MARK AND McDonald were on the ground floor of the commissary again, they split up. McDonald went to see Fredericks so he could tell him the good news and Mark went to check on Shawn and Sara.

With his ears still ringing from the explosion, he walked down the aisles until Shawn and Sara were in sight. Sara was sitting in the chair he'd found earlier with her elbows propped on her knees and her head cupped in her hands. Mark thought she resembled a little girl of eight who was sitting on the curb waiting for her daddy to come home from work.

When she heard his footsteps, she looked up and ran to him.

"Oh, thank God, I heard the explosion. Is the Sergeant all right, are you okay?" Her face was creased with worry lines.

Mark took her hands in his and smiled softly to her "Relax, Sara, everything's fine. Although I have to admit that the explosion impressed the hell out of me. You should have seen it, Sara. The entire roof of the other building was blown away." He snapped his fingers to illustrate his point better. "Just like that. One second it was there, and then *boom*, it was gone. I think if we set those off on our way to the docks we should be able to clear a path and get through easily."

He looked down at Shawn who was lying quietly.

"Any change, did he wake up again?" He asked.

She shook her head no. "He hasn't changed at all. If I had to guess, I'd say he was in a coma."

Mark sighed. "Poor kid, listen, I'm starving, I'm gonna grab something to eat. You want anything?" He asked as he turned to walk away.

"Yes, please, would you grab me a juice or something?" She called to him as he walked down the aisle.

"Sure, no problem, I'll be back in a few minutes," he said with a wave of his hand in a parting gesture. Then he was gone as he turned a corner in the aisle.

Sara turned and moved back to her chair, glancing at Shawn while she sat.

He definitely didn't look well. His skin was a darker shade of blue now, and his breathing was shallower than before. When she felt his forehead, it was like touching ice, his skin was so incredibly cold. She leaned over and pulled the blanket up a little farther around his shoulders and sighed deeply.

The banging sounds from the other side of the front doors grew in intensity and made her jump in her seat, as she turned to look. She half expected the door to come flying open and hordes of zombies to come flooding in. But thankfully, the doors were fine. It was just her imagination getting the better of her again.

She leaned back in her chair and continued her silent vigil over Shawn.

McDonald had just left Fredericks after filling him in on the good news about the bombs and had decided to seek out Mark and run a few strategy ideas by him. He liked the guy a little bit, deciding for an egghead he was all right.

As he rounded an aisle that would bring him to Shawn, figuring that was where Mark would be, he noticed Sara sitting alone, so he decided now would be as good a time as any to make his move with her and see where it led.

He strode over to her and put on a wide smile, trying his best to look charming.

"Hey, Sara, how're you doing?" He asked as he walked to within a few feet of her.

She looked up and smiled wanly at him.

"Oh, hi, Sergeant, okay I guess. It's good to see you're all right. I heard about the explosion from Mark. I felt it in through the floor and I was so worried."

"Yeah, thanks, it was pretty big," he said as he walked around her chair and stood behind her.

"How's the Private doing?" He asked softly.

"About the same," she said as she looked down at Shawn.

"Listen, I've been thinking that maybe you and I could get together tonight. You know, to talk and *stuff*," he said smoothly as he gently put his hands on her shoulders and began massaging her.

For a moment she remained immobile, her body inert, but then she jumped to her feet and spun around to face him.

"Whoa there, Sergeant, if you're suggesting what I think you are, then I'm sorry, but I'm with Mark. Surely you must have known that," she stated as she backed away from him, wanting a little distance between the two of them.

McDonald casually walked around the chair and over to her.

"I've noticed you together, yeah, but I didn't think it was anything serious."

He then moved closer still, causing her to back away until she came up against one of the shelving units that created the aisles. Before she could stop him, he placed both his arms on either side of her, trapping her within and stared straight into her eyes.

"I think I could make you very happy if you'd give me a chance," he said as he leaned in to try and steal a kiss. "I haven't had any complaints   yet."
Sara turned her head away from his lips as she tried to avoid his advances.

"Sergeant, please, don't do this," she begged as he pushed his body against hers. He was now holding her arms in his hard embrace and she was trapped!

He breathed in her ear as he kissed her neck. "Relax, baby, I promise you'll like it." She gasped when one of his hands began to grope her breasts.

"What the fuck is going on here?" Mark barked as he walked down the center aisle towards the two of them. He had two bottles of grape juice with him, one in each hand.

McDonald stepped back and Sara bolted away from him, running to stand next to Mark. Tears filled her eyes and her hands shook from fear.

"Thank God, Mark! He attacked me and wouldn't let me go," she said as her voice shook. "If you hadn't shown up when you did I…" She trailed off, not wanting to think of the alternative.

Mark glared at McDonald with hate in his eyes. "Is this true, Sergeant?" Though he asked, he was confident he already knew the answer.

McDonald held out his hands like what had happened was no big deal.

"Hey, relax, Mark, we're all friends here and I just thought there was more than enough of her to go around. I mean, shit, man, I have needs too," he grinned in the same way as before, the one that Mark found unsettling.

"Well, you can forget it. She's with me and you better stay the fuck away from her," Mark threatened, holding Sara closer.

Now that got McDonald's testosterone kicking into high gear.

"Oh, really? And what the fuck are you gonna do about it if I don't?" He yelled as he walked over and stopped directly in front of Mark's face, his eyes now flaring with anger.

"I'll knock you on your ass, that's what," Mark said. He was feeling a little intimidated by the burly soldier who was taller and stronger than him, but he wasn't backing down.

That's when McDonald threw a punch that connected with Mark's jaw and sent him flying. McDonald didn't stop then, but went after Mark.

"They always think they're so tough," McDonald sneered to himself. "Well, I'll just have to explain the rules of survival to him. That only the strong survive." He turned to Sara who was staring in shock at the two men. "Don't you move, baby, we have some unfinished business to attend to when I'm finished with your boyfriend."

When McDonald was right on top of him, Mark kicked out his right leg and connected with the soldier's stomach, the man not expecting Mark to go on the attack. McDonald bent over and staggered away as he tried to catch his breath. That gave Mark a chance to get off the floor so he could meet his foe head on.

As he regained his footing and rubbed his jaw with his left hand, he scowled at McDonald.

"That was a pretty cheap shot you took, Sarge. Let's have a go now that I'm ready."

McDonald grinned, and then before Mark could dodge out of the way, the soldier charged into him, wrapping his muscular arms around

Mark's waist. The two men went crashing into a display of potato chips as they struggled with each other, trading blows back and forth.

McDonald might have been the larger opponent, but Mark was faster and he was fighting for more than just a quick lay, he was fighting to protect the woman he loved.

While the two men scuffled, Sara was transfixed by the display of violence in front of her, so no one noticed when Shawn's eyes snapped open as he lay on his bedroll.

Within the past hour, Shawn had slowly been falling deeper towards death, and while the two men were fighting off to the side, Shawn had finally given up the fight and passed on. But he didn't remain that way for long as the chemical cocktail created by Fredericks jumpstarted his brain, reviving him once again.

While his dead eyes scanned his surroundings, he slowly stood up on unsteady legs. Once he was standing, he noticed the steady pounding coming from the front doors, and like a baby being attracted to something shiny, he followed the noise until he was heading in the right direction.

Slowly at first, but in a matter of seconds with more alacrity, he stumbled to the doors. His legs were difficult to move as they were frozen and bent in death, but with each step forward, it became easier as he adapted to his new body…his dead body.

In a matter of seconds, he was standing in front of the double doors, and without fully understanding what he was doing, he reached out his hands and pushed on the cross bars that went across the middle of the doors.

The bars moved downward, unlocking them with a soft click.

Shawn stopped then, as if he was waiting for something, and then the doors were thrown open and the swarm of frozen dead that had been milling around outside began to force their way in, knocking Shawn to the floor and crushing him beneath their stomping feet.

Within moments, the doorway was packed with bodies as the ghouls jostled each other for position while they fought their way inside the commissary. They knew there was meat in this building, and they were hungry.

When Sara turned and saw the ghouls pouring into the commissary, she screamed, long and loud.

Mark and McDonald heard her scream and stopped fighting to look over at her, and then they jumped to their feet, their squabble forgotten when they saw they had more important matters to attend to…like staying alive!

"What the hell!" McDonald yelled as he saw the horde of undead flooding into the building. "Shit, we need to go right fucking now!" he was already backing away from the front of the commissary.

"Sara, come here, quick, we've got to go now before we're overwhelmed!" Mark screamed at her as he reached her and began pulling her along behind him.

The three survivors ran to the break room to gather their weapons, and once finished, they headed to the rear of the commissary so they could get to Fredericks and the bombs he'd made. At the moment, those bombs might be their only way of escaping the crowd of undead, and they all knew it.

As they dashed down the aisles, they could hear the crashing of the ghouls as they tipped over carts and racks filled with displays of food. Their moaning echoed off the commissary's walls, making the place feel like a low-budget haunted house.

Rounding the corner of an aisle, they stopped when they saw Fredericks. The little man glanced up from what he was doing to stare curiously at the three people in front of him, and when he saw the cuts and bruises on Mark's and McDonald's faces, he was even more intrigued.

Before he could even get his first question out, Mark held up his hand.

"No time, Fredericks, the zombies have gotten in here and I'd say we have about a minute before we're overwhelmed! We have to go, now!"

"But my experiments, I can't just leave," Fredericks said as if that made all the sense in the world.

"Listen, you crazy fuck, stay if you want to, but I'm out of here," McDonald said as he picked up two homemade mini-bombs in each hand and then ran off down another aisle.

Mark watched him go and then bent over to retrieve the last mini-bomb off the table. There was a knapsack nearby, so Mark placed the bomb inside it and quickly secured the straps.

"Look, Fredericks, you can do whatever the hell you want, but those things are coming right now, so I'd suggest you start running," Mark said as he turned to leave with Sara.

"Good luck, Dr. Fredericks," Sara called as they turned a corner and were lost from sight.

Fredericks frowned deeply. Every time he was making progress, fate found a way to crush him. He sighed wearily, and then began grabbing what he needed in his abandonment of the commissary.

McDonald headed directly for the back door of the commissary, hoping he could sneak out that way. Plowing through the swinging double doors leading to the back room, he could hear the shuffling footsteps of the ghouls behind him. It reminded him of a crowd of people who had arrived for an early bird sale, their slapping footwear echoing off the walls.

Upon reaching the back door, he slid the slide bolt and unlocked it, then pushed it open only to jump away when a blue hand missing three fingers shot through the opening and tried to grab his face. A heartbeat later, three more limbs forced their way through the opening and tried to gain access into the room, as well.

He was able to catch a quick glimpse through the gap in the door and he frowned when he saw the alley was full of ghouls.

He tried to close the door again, but the damn arms had gotten stuck and he knew he didn't have the time to deal with them. Releasing the door, he ran back through the storeroom and into the commissary, only to be stopped short.

The long aisles were wall to wall with walking corpses, so he headed to another aisle, and found the same thing there, as well.

He turned at the sound of crashing behind him, the sound coming from the back room and he let out a curse as the zombies began to push through the swinging double doors after getting the outside door fully open.

He was trapped!

Holding the two bombs tighter against his chest, he ran across the aisles, hoping one of them wouldn't be as full of walking corpses as the others so he could try to make his way through safely.

Reaching the end of the aisles, he found that his luck had run out. There were no avenues of escape. He put the bombs on the floor in between his boots and drew his M-16 from where it had been strapped to his shoulder. As the ghouls shuffled closer to him, he began to shoot any who came closest to attacking him. For the moment he was just trying to keep them at bay. He knew it was a futile gesture, however, because for every one he shot, two more would take their place and he quickly realized he was in a no win situation.

One ghoul came up on his side and sank its teeth into his shoulder. With a roar of pain, he threw it off him and shot it in the head. The skull blew apart, blood and bone matter splattering everywhere, and the body slumped to the floor, for the moment at least slowing some of the others down who now had to step over the prone corpse.

With his shirt slowly turning bright red from his shoulder wound, he backed up until he was crammed into a corner, pushing the bombs with his boots like he was pushing a soccer ball. His rifle bucked in his hand as he continued to mow down the opposing ghouls within reach. But then it happened, as he knew it eventually would. He ran out of bullets and there was no time to reload.

Flipping the gun around like a spear, he threw it at the closest threat. The front of the rifle went straight in a ghoul's eye socket and then stuck there. The ghoul's head sagged with the weight of the weapon, but still continued to move forward, its hands now firmly grasping the barrel of the rifle.

McDonald screamed in frustration at his situation as he desperately looked around for an avenue of escape. He only had seconds before the other ghouls would be on him, and he was all out of options.

The he looked down at the bombs at his feet, picked one up, and grinned widely with that same grin that made Mark nervous.

"All right, you fuckers, come on! You want a piece of me!" He yelled as the zombies began to surround him. Their hands reached out and grabbed his arms and pulled him into their midst.

He smiled and let it happen, patiently waiting as more and more tried to gain access to his body.

When he felt teeth ripping into his flesh, he clamped his jaw closed and stayed quiet, silently enduring the pain. But as more and more teeth began to devour him, he couldn't hold it anymore and he began screaming, his voice echoing off the walls of the commissary.

Finally, when he thought he couldn't take it anymore, and he felt himself beginning to black out from blood loss and pain, he pulled the pin on the grenade of the mini-bomb still cradled in his arms like a mother would a newborn baby.

The bleach bottle was now dripping red with his splattered blood and there were only a few spots of white plastic still peeking through.

He shrieked up at the ceiling as the darkness flooded over him, and with his last gasp of breath, he yelled with everything he had left in his body to the surrounding dead.

"See you fuckers in Hell!"

Then the fuse on the grenade ran out and the explosion ripped through the crowd of zombies. The inferno consumed everything in its path and blew out the back wall of the commissary. Cans of food and shelving units were thrown across the store as the devastating effect of the blast continued.

A second explosion rode a heartbeat later on the coat tails of the first one as the second bomb McDonald had left on the floor at his feet was consumed in the explosion also. A crater the size of an Olympic sized swimming pool was left behind by the second blast and ghouls that weren't vaporized found themselves tumbling into the hole and landing in the bottom with missing limbs that had snapped off on their downward journey.

More than half of the commissary was nothing more than a gaping hole in the icy ground.

When the smoke began to clear, helped by the frigid wind now blowing in through the gaping hole in the wall, there was nothing left of Sgt. McDonald.

He had been at the epicenter of the blast, so his body had been instantly vaporized.

The surviving ghouls who had been on the outskirts of the blasts, turned away to look for prey elsewhere in the commissary, their dead minds barely caring that half their numbers were now nothing but shattered body parts of blood and gore.

Chapter Forty-eight

MARK DASHED DOWN the aisle with Sara at his back. He didn't quite know where to go and because of all the chaos surrounding him, he didn't have anytime to think.

Before he could stop himself or Sara, they rounded the end of the aisle and ran smack dab into a group of ghouls.

Mark plowed into the first one and took the dead man completely by surprise, and thinking fast, he pulled out Shawn's pistol and shot the second ghoul, a woman, in the head before she could so much as turn his way. The bullet struck the woman's head just a little off center of the nose, sending half her skull spilling to the floor amid bits of frozen brain matter.

He kicked the third ghoul in the groin, but the action did little to slow the attacker down. That's when another one came up behind him, and was about to take a bite out of his shoulder, when the body suddenly dropped to the floor with a dull thump.

Mark looked over his shoulder to see Sara holding a bunch of small cans in her arms. She had used one like a rock and had beaned the ghoul on the head.

As he watched her, she let fly another can that smacked a ghoul on the nose, flattening the cartilage against its face. She threw another one at a ghoul with its hands up, and as the can flew through the air, it broke off three fingers of the zombie's hand on its flight path to its forehead.

Mark smiled at her ingenuity, then put a bullet in a slow moving ghoul on his right. The bullet struck its chest, and other than the corpse twisting its body slightly from the impact, it continued forward.

Mark moved closer to her until they were standing back to back.

"We need to get the hell out of here, right now!" He yelled at her.

"Fine, but where do we go?" She hollered back as she hit another ghoul on the head with a can of beans.

From across the commissary, they could hear McDonald's M-16 singing a song of death as he fought for his life. Then the shooting stopped and it seemed to grow quiet except for the sounds of the ghouls.

Suddenly the world was turned upside down as a tremendous explosion ripped across the commissary.

Mark and Sara, along with the ghouls, were thrown off their feet amid flying cans of food and display shelves.

For what seemed like forever, Mark felt like a plastic bag caught in an updraft, as his body tumbled across the floor from the shockwave of the blast.

Moments later, or what seemed like hours to Mark, he slowly came awake. He was buried under debris and bodies.

As he pushed his way to the top of the rubble, he pulled his hand back as a bifurcated ghoul tried to take a bite out of his hand. The ghoul tried to crawl to him, but was having trouble due to the fact that the only thing holding the upper and lower halves of its body together was its clothes. While it crawled across the rubble, bits and pieces were falling out of its untucked shirt.

He scanned the area around him and spotted a dented vegetable can within reach, so he grabbed it and jammed it into the ghoul's mouth. He could feel and hear teeth breaking as he forced the can in as far as it would go. The ghoul tried to extract it with its one good hand, but the can was lodged too tight.

With the threat neutralized for the moment, he continued onward to the top of the rubble in search of Sara. He was growing very cold, the temperature below freezing. Whatever had happened, the building was now open to the outside air.

When he made it to the top of his pile of debris, he stood up on shaky legs and scanned his surroundings. Pictures of the Holocaust came to mind as he surveyed the carnage before him. The power was out and only the fires burning throughout the devastated building gave him illumination to see by, but it was sufficient.

Everywhere he looked, there were broken bodies and exploded cans of food. As he started to walk on the treacherous rubble, he could smell ketchup and other foods that had burst from their containers during the explosion.

He looked down by his feet, thinking how much blood was on the floor and then felt silly when he realized it had been a display for ketchup he was looking at. Over fifty burst bottles were scattered on the floor surrounding him.

Within a matter of seconds, he spotted Sara's blond hair and white lab coat. As he ran over to her, slipping in the mess of food and gore, he saw that she was face down in the rubble and didn't appear to be moving.

With his heart in his throat, he made his way to her and carefully turned her over. His mind played a movie reel in his head of how he would turn her over and find her throat torn out or something jagged sticking out of one of her eyes. But as he turned her over, he breathed a sigh of relief when he saw she appeared to be okay.

He carefully picked her up and began to stumble across the shattered remains of what was once the canned vegetables aisle, his footing treacherous and unstable with each footstep he made.

Making it to stable ground once again, he gently laid her down and checked her pulse. Her heartbeat was strong and regular. She had a view bruises on her face, but appeared to be fine. Damn, she was one lucky woman, and so was he, for if he had lost her….well, he didn't want to dwell on *what ifs*.

It was while he was scanning the area around them for danger that she stirred. Looking down to her, he was pleased to see her eyes were open and were now in focus. He smiled at her as she raised her hand to her head.

"Oh, wow, what happened?" She asked groggily.

"If I had to guess, I'd say McDonald used one of Fredericks' mini-bombs," he said as he watched her. "The crazy bastard."

She tried to stand up so Mark reached down and helped her to her feet, swaying slightly like one of those hula girls you see on car dashboards. After a few seconds, she slowly regained her equilibrium and stood straight and tall.

"Oh my God, Mark, your head, you're bleeding," she said as she looked at him.

Mark reached up to his forehead and found there was a shallow gash on the top of his scalp, where his hairline met his forehead.

"I'm fine, Sara, really, it's only a scratch," he said, not wanting her to worry.

She nodded, still dazed form her ordeal and stumbled a few feet away from him, for the first time really looking at her surroundings.

"Oh my God, what the hell happened here?" She gasped in astonishment as she turned around in a circle. The shadows from the fires danced on her body as she moved around in shock.

Mark remained quiet, believing the question to be rhetorical. Then he slid up beside her and gently took her arm.

"Come on, we're not out of danger yet," he said as he pointed to where ghouls were even now climbing over the rubble to try and reach them.

Only this time the undead were a little worse for wear. Most of them were missing at least one limb as they dragged their bodies towards them. There were a few that had been severed from the chest down. They used their hands to drag themselves along while their insides slowly dripped out behind them, leaving a bloody trail of frozen gore in their wake. One poor dead bastard had his intestines caught on a shelving unit and as he crawled across the rubble, his intestines slowly unwound behind him like he was leaving a bloody rope to find his way back when he was through.

The smoke was starting to diminish as the wind flowed into the building, and as

Mark and Sara moved off again, Mark was finally able to see the back wall of the commissary.

He stopped and pointed over in the direction of the now demolished wall.

"Look, that explosion took out a piece of the back wall. That's our way out of here," he said as he pulled her in that direction, his breath appearing in front of him each time he exhaled. He was cold, true, but was still able to function, but he knew he would need to get to warmth soon or risk exposure.

Sara nodded in agreement and together they climbed over toppled store shelves and shattered bodies of the dead. Halfway there, Sara screamed when a hand reached out from under the rubble and attached itself to her right ankle. Mark reached for his gun and then swore when he realized he'd lost it when he'd gone flying across the floor from the initial blast.

Scanning the wreckage, he found a piece of a broken shelving. Retrieving the piece of metal, he slammed it down on the hand and severed the limb at the wrist. The hand continued to twitch while he kneeled down and pried the hand off her ankle. Then the two continued on, now more wary of what could be hiding underneath them.

Upon reaching the crater-sized hole in the floor, they both stopped and surveyed the damage. Gazing down into the crater, they could see the writhing bodies of ghouls that had fallen into the hole after the main blast. If Mark or Sara was unlucky enough to fall down there, they would instantly be ripped to bloody pieces by the horde of corpses waiting below.

Mark looked over his shoulder and frowned when he saw at least twenty ghouls making their way in the direction of the crater.

"Come on, this way," he told her as he took her hand and led them to the edge of the crater. Their only chance was for them to carefully pick their way across the fractured edge of the hole and try to reach the other side. The only problem was, the crater extended to both sides of the commissary and only stopped when it came up against the other four walls of the building.

There was barely twelve inches of passable footing they could use to traverse the edge and reach the other side. And on top of all that, there were multiple places where the edges continued to burn due to the heat of the explosion.

Mark looked at Sara. "You ready for this?"

She frowned at him. "What do you think?"

"I think it's our only chance," he said as he put his left foot on the edge of the crater and began to shuffle out like a man who had climbed outside a high rise to commit suicide.

Sara followed on his heels and the two of them carefully side-walked onto the jagged ledge.

As they slowly made progress, the ghouls below them attempted to climb up and grab their feet, but luckily they were much too low to do more than distract them.

Mark came upon an area that was still burning nicely and he tried to use his foot to kick enough debris on the flames to smother them, but try as he might, it was doing little to solve the problem. When he ran out of material to kick on the flames, he turned and looked at Sara.

"The damn fires won't go out. I just need to get it to die down a little more and then I think we could get over it. So don't laugh at what I'm about to do, 'cause frankly, I'm all out of ideas."

"Ah, okay, do what you have to," Sara said, a little perplexed at what Mark was talking about.

Mark unzipped his fly and began to pee on the fire. He hadn't gone in a while and that can of grape juice he'd drank earlier before catching McDonald harassing Sara really wanted to come out. He waved his penis like a nine-year-old kid pretending he was a fireman trying to put a fire out, and when his stream of urine finally petered out, the fire had become a little smaller. As he zipped up his pants, he grinned at Sara, fully satisfied with the outcome.

"Well, what do you know, it worked," he said and then continued on over the dwindling flame.

Sara just smiled and shook her head, unable to believe what he'd just done, but at the same time grateful.

They continued on and soon were about halfway across. Mark's spirits were high as they made their way across the ledge until his foot came down on a weak spot that collapsed from his weight and he began to fall. Like a man who had walked out onto thin ice that then broke beneath him, he went straight down. His hands automatically reached out for something to grab and stop his plummet to the ghouls below.

Just before his body had fallen all the way into the crumbling opening, his hand caught a piece of broken rebar jutting out from the exposed sub-floor. Sara screamed and tried to bend down and grab his other hand, but there wasn't enough room for her to maneuver without losing her own delicate balance on the edge of the crater.

As Mark hung from the ledge, the ghouls below him tried to reach his feet and pull him down. Their grasping hands were only inches from his swinging shoes as he tried to pull himself back up. His tried to climb the frozen wall, but just kept slipping on the ice that coated it. And to make matters worse, his hands were growing numb from the cold and ice beginning to form over everything.

He knew he shouldn't panic, that he needed to remain calm, but he could still feel a part of him that was slowly losing his grip and just wanted to scream for help.

Sara was talking to him, telling him to hang on and they'll think of something.

That's when a ghoul who was taller than the others reached up and grabbed his left shoe. He shrieked as he felt himself being pulled down and then his shoe slipped off his foot and he was free again. That burst of fear and adrenalin gave him the extra energy to pull himself up a little more and get his arm over the edge. Then he yelled when he felt himself slipping again, but then he felt Sara's hand grasp his and with her help he was able to pull himself back up onto the precarious ledge.

As his butt settled onto the ledge, he leaned back against the wall and sighed with gratitude.

"Oh God, Sara, thank you, you saved my life," he panted as she stood next to him.

"Of course I did. What did you think I was going to do, let you fall?" She asked as she reassuringly placed her hand on his shoulder. He reached up and covered her hand with his.

"Still, thank you," he said slowly as his breathing became steady. Below him, in the crater the ghouls howled their frustration at losing their meal.

When Mark had recovered enough for them to move on, he carefully stood up and they continued on to the other side of the crater. Just before they were ready to step back onto solid ground, he stopped her and pointed at the hole in the wall.

Milling around the hole, like a bunch of stray dogs looking for scraps of meat, were seven or eight more ghouls.

Mark glanced to Sara and nodded at the ghouls.

"I think we can take them and once we're past them, we can get the hell out of here. What do you think?"

She set her jaw as she looked at the only thing between her and freedom.

"I say, let's get the bastards," she said as she looked him straight in the face.

"Okay, that's good to hear. So we hit them hard and fast. Don't stop no matter what, just push each one aside and then continue on to the next one. Remember, we want to get by them, not kill them. Got it?" He asked her, making sure she knew the objective.

She nodded and then gave him a gentle shove so he would resume moving again.

As soon as the two of them stepped off the ledge and onto frozen ground again, the ghouls turned and began moving towards them. Both Mark and Sara bent down and retrieved a piece of rebar for a weapon, the cold metal stinging their hands.

Then Mark looked at Sara one more time and nodded.

"Okay," he said. "Let's do this."

With a yell to get them psyched up, they charged the frozen dead, and hopefully, the freedom waiting on the other side.

Chapter Forty-nine

Fredericks scrambled to gather his belongings and make his escape from the commissary.

The others had left only moments ago and he could hear McDonald's M-16 shooting up a storm from across the commissary.

He was just about to run for it when he looked up to find himself trapped by a wave of undead. Cursing himself for not listening to Simmons and leaving when the others did, he now found himself in a compromising situation.

For the moment, he seemed to be safe, as the ghouls didn't seem to understand how to get at him while he was behind his homemade lab table. So he used that to his advantage.

Quickly gathering as many bottles of chemicals as he could place his hands around, he then scurried to the far end of the table and tossed a beaker full of caustic chemicals at the first ghoul in line.

The glass shattered when it struck the ghoul's forehead and the liquid covered the ghoul's face, dripping into its eyes. Now distracted and blind, the ghoul covered its face with its frozen hands, not understanding why its eyesight was gone.

When the ghoul took its hands away from the pale blue face, Fredericks could see the chemicals had eaten the eyeballs from the sockets, leaving nothing but raw, oozing holes.

Continuing on, he tossed another beaker into the next undead face.

He did this to ghoul after ghoul until he ran out of beakers. Behind him, ghouls stumbled around and grappled with each other in their blind panic, not comprehending why they could no longer see.

Fredericks bobbed and weaved his way through the ghouls as he made his way to the roof stairwell. He didn't necessarily want to go there, but his options were severely limited and it was the closest egress available.

Just before he made it to the stairwell, a ghoul came at him from his blind side and wrapped stiff arms around him. He was just about to try and fend the corpse off when the world seemed to explode, and he and the ghoul were tossed into the air to then tumble across the floor as cans of food and shelving units flew around him.

As he was tumbling, he screamed when his shoulder struck something sharp. Then blackness descended as his head struck the floor, and he fell into unconsciousness.

When his eyes opened minutes later, he realized he couldn't move, but after gently shifting his body, he found that the weight on top of him was minimal. Slowly, his head throbbing from the blow he'd received, he crawled from underneath the rubble covering him; what had happened to him still a mystery.

He looked around at the commissary and immediately put two and two together, the mystery solved. That idiot McDonald had set off a mini-bomb inside the building. And as he pulled himself to his feet, he cursed himself for giving that no good warmonger his babies. God what a waste.

He surveyed his situation as he wandered around the smoke and rubble filled building. His vision was drastically impaired due to the power outage, but there was still sufficient light to see by from the fires still burning here and there in the wreckage.

His foot came down on a hand and he turned to see it still connected to the arm it belonged to. The ghoul crawled over to Fredericks and tried to bite his leg, so he stepped back and kicked the ghoul in the face as hard as he could.

The ghoul's jaw shattered from the blow and teeth trickled to the floor. Fredericks kicked the face one more time, this time rocking the head back so hard the neck snapped. The head hung loose like a piece of spaghetti as Fredericks stepped over the now harmless corpse and continued on.

Another ghoul was just regaining its footing as Fredericks approached it and he reached down and picked up a sizable chunk of cement from the rubble strewn floor. Then he walked up and slammed the block of cement onto the top of the ghoul's skull. The weight of the stone pushed the ghoul to the floor again where its head was crushed beneath the weight of the stone. As he walked away, he noticed a red sludge was leaking out from underneath the stone and onto the floor. He smiled as he continued on, pleased with the results.

In a matter of seconds, he had found where the stairwell should be, but now it was nothing but twisted wreckage. When he looked up into the void above him, he was able to see about ten feet above him where the stairwell continued intact.

Looking around the immediate area, he spotted a bunch of overturned boxes full of canned goods. Quickly, he began piling them one on top of the other until he had a crude staircase fabricated.

Within minutes he'd piled the boxes just about high enough for him to reach the bottom stair when he turned to see that more ghouls had gathered themselves together and were now approaching him. In the flickering firelight he had to admit they looked more menacing than when the lights were on, and he quickly sprinted up his makeshift stairs and stood at the top. The bottom stair was still just out of reach when the first ghoul began to climb up the boxes in an attempt to reach him.

Desperate now, he tried the only thing at his disposal. He took the last box and stood it up the long way on the last makeshift step and then as quick as he could, he hopped onto it and jumped for all he was worth to the bottom metal step of the fractured stairwell.

His right hand just barely got three fingers on the step when the box he'd leapt from tumbled away, crushing a ghoul below. And he had only seconds before the ghoul behind him on the box stairs was at the top, with him left dangling like a fish on a hook.

He pulled himself up slowly and was able to get his other hand on the step as well. With his arms screaming from the physical exertion, he let out a shriek of pain and managed to pull himself up enough to get his knee over the edge of the step. Then he quickly pulled his other leg up just as the ghoul reached out to grab him.

Instead of the ghoul reaching out and wrapping a frozen hand around Fredericks' leg, however, the ghoul lost its balance and fell head first back to the floor. When its body impacted with the concrete floor, there was a sickening thud as its neck cracked and its body slumped over. Then its arms broke off and lay next to the body like a toy doll a child had broken into pieces and then left in the dirt.

After catching his breath, Fredericks slowly pulled himself to a sitting position on the lower stair. His arms were so strained he believed he wouldn't have been able to pick up a pencil if his life depended on it.

Not knowing what else to do, and not having so much as a coat to keep him warm, he ascended the stairs to the roof.

Once outside, he surveyed the damage to the nearby destroyed roof and the surrounding buildings, content for the moment that they were empty of any of the undead. He barely glanced at the carnage of severed and decimated body parts littering the commissary's rooftop from the recent explosion of the neighboring building.

Walking over to the edge of the roof, careful not to slip in the ice and snow, he wrapped his arms around himself for warmth and gazed down into the alley below. He only spotted about six ghouls wandering around and assumed it was because their brethren were inside the commissary.

Glancing to the adjacent roof, he already knew what he had to do to escape his predicament. He had to jump back across so he could walk down the fire escape.

But first he just wanted to take five minutes to rest.

As he went to lie down on the cold roof, he could feel the wind blowing against his exposed flesh and he began to shiver.

But still he closed his eyes and relaxed for just a few minutes.

CHAPTER FIFTY

WANTING TO PROTECT Sara as much as possible, Mark was first into the fray as the ghouls surrounded the two of them. Pulling back his arm, he swung the rebar as hard as he could at the first ghoul. The metal rod sank into the ghoul's forehead and he had to pull as hard as he could to remove it. When he'd freed it, the ghoul now had a one inch groove embedded into the front of its skull. But the walking corpse continued to stumble forward, so Mark decided to try a different tactic. Kneeling down on the snow and ice, he whacked the rebar at the ghoul's right knee. The joint instantly shattered from the force of the blow, causing the ghoul to lose its balance and topple over.

"Sara, whack 'em in the legs!" He yelled as he ducked under another's outreached hands and then swooped underneath it to shatter its knees, as well.

Sara saw what he meant and, she too, began to break their knee caps, the frozen limbs shattering like old wood.

When they had finished off the last ghoul that posed a threat to them, they continued down the alleyway and into the street where there were sporadic groups of the frozen dead wandering around.

The second Mark and Sara appeared on the street, the ghouls turned and moved towards them. If Mark had been carrying a gun, he probably could have made short work of the threatening walkers, but as it was there were still too many to fight off.

So he grabbed Sara's hand and dashed down the street in the opposite direction of the corpses and hoped they could find a way to get to the docks and hole up for another day until the icebreaker arrived.

*　　*　　*

Fredericks stirred on the rooftop. It had only been a matter of minutes since he'd lain down to rest, but he knew if he didn't get up right now, he would probably die.

Even though his body screamed for him to just lie down, relax, and let the warmness of sleep take him, he knew that was just the first stages of hypothermia setting in.

With a force of will that had driven him for so long in his scientific endeavors, he now applied that same will to raising himself to his feet. Once he was standing again and his blood began to flow a little more, he felt slightly better and so took advantage of his well being and shuffled to the edge of the roof.

He looked down to see a few ghouls wandering around in the alley below and decided it was now or never.

Backing up more than halfway to the middle of the roof, wanting to give himself some much needed distance, he ran as fast as he could towards the edge and leaped across the gap, landing in a heap of arms and legs on the other rooftop.

Picking himself up, now covered in snow and ice, he stood on unsteady legs and made his way to the fire escape.

He scanned the alley below, he breathed a sigh of relief to see no one in sight, either living or dead, so he continued down the metal stairs until his feet were once again on the icy ground. Then, as quietly as he could manage given his present state of exhaustion, he snuck up the alleyway and peeked out onto the street.

That's when Mark and Sara went flying past him, and when Fredericks switched his gaze to where the running couple was coming from, he saw ten ghouls hot on their trail. Stepping out into the street, he took off after the two scientists. He lost them for a minute, but when he turned a corner they came back into his field of vision. That's when Mark turned to check his back trail and nearly tripped over his feet when he saw Fredericks following them.

The street in front of Mark and Sara was free of ghouls for the moment, so they both slowed down and allowed Fredericks to catch up to them.

"I don't believe it. You made it out of there alive?" Mark breathed heavily as he watched Fredericks run up to them. He rubbed his hands together and shoved them under his armpits, trying to keep them warm.

"Why, Simmons, did you doubt my will to survive?" Fredericks asked him as he sucked in the frigid air. The run had helped him warm up some, and his blood was now pumping more freely, spreading warmth throughout his body. But he knew he needed to find a coat and fast or he would soon be right back where he was only moments before. And then he smiled, the solution to his problem becoming apparent to him.

As the three of them continued down the street to try and stay in front of the chasing ghouls, Fredericks spotted what looked like another survivor stumbling towards them down the middle of the street.

But as the man came closer, it was easy to tell he was definitely a zombie, the staggering gait a dead giveaway, not to mention the pale blue complexion. The man's mouth hung open and he had that vacant stare all the undead seemed to share. But the thing that pleased Fredericks was the nice big parka the man was wearing. Fredericks surmised the man must have been outside when he was attacked and lucky for him that he was.

Turning to Mark, he looked at the piece of rebar in his hands.

"Simmons, may I borrow that for a moment?" He asked with a smile cutting across his face.

Mark just nodded and handed the metal rod to him, wondering what the hell Fredericks was up to. He looked at Sara, but she just shrugged, as if to say 'why not?'

Fredericks hefted the rebar in his hand and calmly walked towards the dead man.

When the man was in striking range, Fredericks dodged out of his reach and then swooped in and cracked the man over the head. The man staggered from the blow but Fredericks didn't let up. As fast as he could, he spun the metal rod around and struck the dead man across the temple. The end of the rod disappeared into the skin of the ghoul's forehead, but still the man tried to move. Fredericks pulled the rod out and grimaced, not understanding why this man was being so difficult.

That's when Fredericks turned the rod around yet again and used it like a spear, which he then jabbed into the dead man's eye. With all of his waning strength, he forced the rod deep into the eye socket.

The dead man was forced onto his back by Fredericks and as he sprawled out with his arms spread wide, Fredericks twisted the rod inside the socket and silenced the ghoul permanently.

While Mark and Sara approached him, Fredericks began to strip the corpse of its clothes, especially the jacket.

"Just what the hell do think you're doing, Fredericks?" Mark barked as he stood behind him.

"I would think that would be obvious, Dr. Simmons. If I don't get into some warm clothes soon, I will surely die from exposure," he said as he shrugged himself into the dead man's coat and zipped it up.

Immediately, he felt better now that his body was somewhat protected from the environment, and when he looked over Mark's shoulder, he turned to the two of them.

"I think we should be moving on," he said as he pointed back down the street. The undead had been slowly making progress and would soon be on them if they didn't move soon.

Mark turned and saw what he was pointing at and frowned.

"Shit, those bastards just don't give up, do they?"

"Come on, Mark, let's go," Sara said as she pulled on his arm.

He gave in to her easily, and the three of them began jogging down the street again, warily staying in the middle of the snow covered road so as to have as much warning as possible if something were to jump out at them.

But it seemed most of the ghouls had congregated near the commissary, so their path was clear.

The three survivors kept moving until the docks came into view, and then as fast as they could, they made a run for it. Hopefully there would be somewhere in the dock area where they could hide out for one more day.

There had to be somewhere they could keep the undead at bay until help arrived.

There just had to be.

Chapter Fifty-one

As THE THREE survivors dashed for the docks, shadowy figures appeared out of alleyways and doorways. Not all the ghouls had been at the commissary. Some had stayed where they were after they had been killed and then revived as the frozen dead.

But now, as the three remaining humans ran down the streets, the zombies stirred and came out of hiding to walk in the direction the three were going.

Slowly at first, as the frozen limbs weren't used to motion. But soon, they moved faster, and as more of them came into the streets, they followed a direct path to the docks.

They were hungry and they knew where food was.

Simpson shambled along the streets, as well. He was dragging his left leg behind him in a sort of shuffle hop. His leg had been shattered during the explosion and it was only dumb luck that had kept him from being destroyed like so many of his brethren. He didn't really have a destination in mind. He just followed the other ghouls as they slogged down the street. It felt good to be around others like himself.

In the back of his frozen, fuzzy brain, he was frustrated at not finding Fredericks. He'd assumed the man had been killed in the explosion, and his vengeance had been taken from him.

Dying in a fiery blast was a death far too easy for his betrayer.

So he continued walking, not realizing he was slowly being taken to the docks, and a final meeting with the man who left him for dead; and the sole driving force behind his burning need for vengeance.

*　　*　　*

The docks came into view and the three survivors stopped for a moment to catch their breath. Their heavy breathing was the only sound other than the wind, the street deathly quiet

Mark looked behind him and could see the crowd of ghouls still shambling after them, but he figured they had a good fifteen minutes to find a place to barricade themselves in before the first one reached them.

He surveyed the area around him, trying to figure out where they could go when Fredericks slapped him on the shoulder to get his attention and then pointed to a small building about a hundred feet away. On closer inspection, it was more of a large shack than an actual building.

"What about there? It looks pretty solid and we can see the ship when it comes in," Fredericks suggested.

"We don't really have a lot of options, Mark," Sara said as she glanced back at the approaching zombies.

Mark gave it another second of thought, but couldn't think of anything better.

"You're right, come on, let's move. We don't have a lot of time," he said and took off at a run to the small structure.

When they arrived at the building, they could see it wasn't in great shape. It appeared to be more of a temporary structure than a permanent one.

Scattered around the outside of the building were various tools, pieces of wood and odd shapes of metal. It was as if the building had been under construction and the workers had gone home for the day, although Mark knew that probably wasn't the case.

The building was about ten by ten and was probably going to be a place where supplies could be stored before or after the ships would come in.

There were four windows on the building, one on each wall, smack dab in the middle.

Mark did a quick survey and realized what they needed to do.

"Okay, guys, we need to board up these windows so those bastards can't get in there with us, so each of you grab that wood and take it inside. I'll grab the tools we'll need." He glanced over his shoulder to see the ghouls much closer than before. "And hurry, we don't have much time," he added as he scrambled to grab a hammer, nails and screws, anything that could attach the wood to the windows.

His hands were turning red from exposure, and they were hard to use now, the digits not wanting to bend, but he ignored it, knowing frostbite was the least of his worries. His ears already showed advanced stages of frostbite, but as he hadn't seen a mirror, he didn't know this yet. All he knew was his ears had gone numb more than ten minutes ago.

Fredericks and Sara picked up all the wood and sheet metal they could hold and carried it into the building. Once inside, the building was cold and dark. The room was basically empty with only a few empty pallets to clutter up the floor.

Moving quickly, they entered through the only door and tossed the wood and miscellaneous items on the ground. Mark unslung his back-pack with the last bomb in it and placed it in a corner where it would be out of the way. Then the three of them began barricading them-selves inside the small structure.

The work went quickly as they secured boards and pieces of sheet metal to the windows. Mark took a large four by four piece of wood and jammed it under the doorknob of the door, hoping it would do the job of keeping the door closed.

At least now the door was secure and not a moment to soon be-cause just as he kicked the wood into place, the door rocked on its hinges as the first of the ghouls began pounding on it.

Suddenly frozen hands squeezed their way through the holes in the wood after shattering the glass in the windows. The walking dead had arrived en masse and wanted the humans inside the small building,

Sara grabbed a two by four and whacked one of the hands with it. The hand snapped off like an icicle and the jagged stump pulled back.

She ran around to the other windows and did the same thing to each one until there were about ten hands twitching on the floor.

In disgust at the severed limbs, Mark stepped on them, crushing the hands to pulp until they stopped squirming.

"Was that really necessary?" Fredericks asked from a corner of the room.

"No, but it made me feel better," Mark said as he whacked another hand with a hammer he'd found and proceeded in breaking off two fingers until the hand pulled back.

This went on for hours, the three survivors managing to keep the ghouls at bay. The undead couldn't get in, but then the three humans couldn't get out.

So even when the icebreaker ship arrived, how would they escape the building to reach it? But these questions were irrelevant for the moment, because for now they were just trying to stay alive.

It was late Wednesday night when the ghouls finally quieted down a little and gave the three of them a much needed respite. They had been fighting the frozen corpses for hours and were exhausted, but had little choice if they wanted to survive.

Sara found a lunchbox that had been left by one of the workers. It was basically empty with only a half eaten, frozen apple and a half frozen bottle of soda inside.

But to the three of them, it was like a four star meal. Mark divided the apple with a saw he'd found and they each had a few sips of the soda until it was gone. Mark had used his body heat to melt the soda enough to drink it, the bottle freezing as he stuck it under his arm inside his clothing. He was surprised he had any heat to give? He was freezing without a jacket and as he stared at Fredericks in his nice warm parka, he wanted to strangle the man with his numb hands. Thankfully Sara stayed close to him, hugging him and keeping him warm. She at least had her lab coat on, but, she too, hadn't managed to get her coat when they had escaped from the commissary.

And then Sara had found something worth more than all the gold in the world. A small heat lamp with a half bowl of kerosene was hiding under some wood in one of the corners of the room. It used a spark to ignite the fuel, and in no time they had a small amount of warmth to fight off the sub-zero temperatures. They gathered around the small lamp, rubbing their hands together and feeling infinitely better. The small bit of food they'd eaten did nothing to appease their appetites, and in fact just made their hunger seem worse as their stomachs now wanted more.

But nothing could be done about it, so they hunched down on the floor and fended off the ghouls whenever they attempted to gain access.

As the hours went by, they took turns on watch. One would stay awake while the other two slept. It was a restless sleep, though, because every time the undead would try to break in, they would all have to pitch in and fend them off.

This continued all the way into Thursday morning as the three of them fell into a kind of ritual. Once again Mark marveled at how the human mind could adapt to anything if it was given enough time to adjust.

So they continued fighting off the ghouls and grabbing sleep when they could, and slowly Thursday crawled by until they had made it to Thursday night.

They were all exhausted by now and were mostly moving on autopilot, and as their minds grew duller from lack of food and proper sleep, they increased their chances of making mistakes.

But still they carried on.

It was either that or they die.

Or worse, become one of the frozen dead.

*   *   *

Outside the walls of the small building, the walking dead continued to beat on the doors, walls and windows, never needing to stop for food or sleep. Unknown to them, they were slowly wearing down the occupants.

On the back wall of the structure, the ghouls had been slowly loosening a few wood panels that were blocking the window. The process had been slow so that the people inside had no idea it was occurring. And now all it would take would be one good push and the entire barricade would fall in.

Only the ghouls didn't realize what they had accomplished.

In the front of the building, Simpson pushed his way through the undead corpses until he was standing at one of the boarded windows. He was able to look inside the small room through the slats in the wood, and though the room was shrouded in darkness and shadows, tiny spear points of light penetrated through the cracks in the boards covering the windows, the bright lights of the docks cascading over everything.

And then the moon came out from behind the clouds, adding to the luminance, the light playing over the faces of the trapped people inside the building. And when the moonlight crossed Fredericks face, Simpson thought he would die yet again.

Fredericks was alive and within his grasp!

He roared to the darkness in triumph and the surrounding ghouls tried to mimic him, their throats howling in grunts and garbles.

Inside the small building, the three survivors heard the screams and guttural grunts coming from outside as the banging continued anew.

Sara curled up tighter in Mark's arms, and Fredericks wrapped his arms a little tighter around himself, the three weary humans cringing in the darkness.

The clouds opened up, releasing their payload, and the night sky began to blur as thousands of tiny ice crystals floated to earth.

And as it began to snow, the fluffy white crystals began to cover the docks and surrounding buildings of Kryton station with a crisp, clean carpet of white, which quickly buried the blood and gore of the past day, as if by hiding it, God himself was pretending it had never happened.

CHAPTER FIFTY-TWO

THE MERCHANT SHIP, Newport, slowly made its way through the icy waters about a hundred miles off the coast of Antarctica.

Captain James Murray had been doing this run for a little over two years now.

He looked down onto the front deck of his ship where some of his men were scraping ice off and then pushing it back into the ocean.

It was a never ending process. As fast as they cleaned the decks of the ship, the ocean spray would freeze up again and they'd be right back where they'd started.

He gazed off into the horizon, but there was nothing new to see, just white as the snow drifted down, obscuring his vision.

The bow of his ship cut a tear in the thick ice as it made its way to Kryton Station.

As always, his heart swelled with pride when he looked down on his ship and his crew.

The Newport was a merchant ship, but he ran it like he was still in the Navy. He always believed in discipline and order and he'd learned all of it in his twenty years in the Navy.

Then he had retired, and after only a year of reading books and taking long walks, had become restless again.

Which led him to where he was right now.

His radioman had informed him communication had gone down between his ship and Kryton Station, and they hadn't received anything but dead air for the past two days.

He frowned as he considered the news again.

What would make an entire research station go dark? It couldn't be an avalanche as the station was far from any nearby glaciers or dangerous ice flows and the station was built on a wide open plain.

He frowned even deeper if it was possible. Something was wrong; he could feel it in his gut, but what?

He reached down for his the two-way and called down to the engine room. Upon receiving an answer, he ordered his ship to go from one quarter to one half speed.

When your ship was cutting through two feet of ice at a time, speed was generally not an option.

He felt the ship vibrating beneath the deck plates as it moved faster through the ice.

That was the best he could do. Now all he could do is wait until they arrived tomorrow and see if everything was all right at the station.

* * *

It was late Thursday night when everything went straight to Hell.

The three survivors had been sitting on the floor in the middle of the small building, taking a quick breather while the ghouls seemed to have relented.

Despite Mark being exhausted, he grinned to himself thinking of the ghouls once again like a movie reel.

In his mind, he could see the head ghoul calling for a break and then all the other ghouls stopping their attack and then going and sitting down where they could find a seat. They'd be opening lunchboxes their zombie wives had packed for them as they opened them to take out the bowl of brains or a piece of an arm or leg.

Then they'd relax and eat while they chatted about the human that got away the other day.

Then the ghoul foreman, as Mark thought of him, would call out that the break was over and they would all get up and shuffle back to the walls of the small structure.

Then they would proceed to bang on the walls again, continuing for hours until it was time to go home to their zombie wives and kids.

Sara looked at him and saw him smiling. "Mark, what could you possibly be smiling about?" She asked.

He shook his head. "Nothing really, just tired. Don't worry, this should all be over soon," he said

"One way or another," Fredericks added from across the room where he was curled up in a corner.

"What the fuck do you mean by that?" Mark snapped at him, his temper shortened to the point of breaking from exhaustion.

"I mean, that either we'll be rescued or those creatures will make their way in here and kill us. And quite painfully, I'd imagine."

Mark shot daggers from his eyes as he glared at Fredericks.

"I don't want to hear that kind of talk again, do you hear me? I didn't walk halfway across Antarctica to end up dying in a shack. Especially when we're so close to making it out of here alive! So if you say shit like that again, I'll kill you myself! You got it?"

Fredericks nodded.

The look in Mark's eyes brooked no argument and he knew not to push his luck. But the defiant part of him had to say something.

"I just think if we make it out of here it will be a miracle, that's all."

"That's it!" Mark growled in his throat and then jumped up and ran at Fredericks, in a way happy to fight something that wasn't inhuman.

Just before Mark grabbed him, Fredericks managed to get to his feet.

Mark wrapped his hands around Fredericks' neck and tried to squeeze the life out of him, but Fredericks was able to keep him at bay just enough so that Mark couldn't really apply any real pressure.

The two men rolled around the floor while Sara yelled at Mark to stop it. But Mark was lost in rage and wasn't thinking clearly. He just needed to lash out and Fredericks was the closest thing at the moment.

As the two of them went banging off the walls, they came up against the back window just as a ghoul slipped on the ice outside and fell directly against the loose wood panels covering the window.

The weight of the zombie's body knocked the wood off the frame and into the building where it then struck Mark on the head.

Before anyone inside the room could do anything to stop it, frozen hands and arms thrust through the window and seized Mark by the neck and shoulders.

He was immediately yanked against the window and he desperately reached over his shoulder to try and pry the claw-like hands away from him.

Fredericks immediately began to help, their argument forgotten, when a pale blue face appeared in the window next to Mark and took a bite out of his left arm.

Mark screamed as the ghoul's teeth ripped away skin and clothing, the gnawing teeth cutting into his flesh like daggers.

Mark managed to escape then and he rolled away, coming up to his feet in less than a second. The three survivors beat off the ghouls as they crawled through the window, only the size of the frame slowing them down at all. One after another, they dropped to the floor and then picked themselves up to continue the chase.

Mark knew their cause was lost.

There were far too many attackers and there was no way they could keep the walking corpses out.

That's when Mark glanced up at the ceiling, spotted the panels crisscrossing the ceiling, and had an idea. He piled some of the pallets on top of each other, and after leaning the last one against the wall like a ladder; he grabbed Sara by her arm and pushed her up to the roof.

"But what do I do up there?" She yelled in the chaos that was erupting in the small room.

"Here," he said, as he handed her the hammer. "Whack one of those panels off the ceiling and climb onto the roof! And for Christ's sake, hurry!" He yelled back.

Sara did as she was asked while Mark and Fredericks continued to keep their undead foes at bay. But it was a losing battle and in moments the men would be overwhelmed if they didn't leave now.

Sara yelled down to them. "Okay, I did it, come on up!" She called as she crawled onto the roof, spun around and, reached down for Mark's hand.

Mark grabbed the backpack with the last bomb in it and then pushed a ghoul away from him. Turning, he made a running jump up to the opening in the ceiling. As he jumped, he grabbed Sara's hand, and with her help scurried up onto the roof, as well. Then he turned around and yelled down to Fredericks.

"Fredericks, give me your hand!" Mark pleaded as he watched Fredericks kick a ghoul away from him. But it was painfully obvious Fredericks wasn't going to be coming onto the roof with them.

As Fredericks pushed yet another ghoul away from him, two more went behind him and cut off his escape up the makeshift ladder.

Panicking, he took the only option available to him.

He pushed his way through the crowd of undead and kicked the two by four away from the door. Without hesitating, he pulled the door open and charged into the night.

Mark and Sara went over to the edge of the roof and watched Fredericks as he tried to make a mad dash away from the docks.

But he didn't get twenty feet.

The moment he burst through the door, the frozen dead were on top of him, swarming over him like locusts. Fredericks kicked and punched his way through them while they were slowly tearing pieces of his flesh from his body. As he fought them, his jacket was ripped apart and goose feathers filled the sky to be blown away on the wind where they mixed with the falling snow.

Then Fredericks went down to the snow and he screamed for help.

The ghouls began tearing into him with a vengeance, and as dead hands ripped his abdomen open, his internal organs were exposed to the sub zero temperature and they began to steam in the cold night air.

That was enough for Mark. He might not have liked Fredericks much, but no man deserved to die that way. Taking Sara's hand, he gently pulled her over to the opening in the roof so they could make sure no ghouls attempted to climb up.

Only a few feet away, they could still hear Fredericks' screams of agony as he suffered his last minutes on God's Earth.

Fredericks was in Hell.

The ghouls had a hold of him from every angle, and as their teeth sank into his flesh, he screamed yet again.

How could this be happening to him? He couldn't die; he was the hero of this story.

The story called his life.

He screamed again when a ghoul ripped a piece of his stomach out and began to eat it while he watched.

Fredericks had only a moment of consciousness left on planet Earth when a familiar face came into his field of vision.

Through his pain and anguish, he was able to make out the face of the ghoul hovering over him and his screams froze in his throat when the ghoul's identity came to him.

It was Simpson.

The lab assistant he'd left to die so he could save himself, at what seemed like a lifetime ago.

"No," he garbled through the blood in his mouth. "It can't be you, that's impossible! You're a hundred miles from here!" And then he screamed again as a cold hand reached inside him and pulled out his spleen.

He gazed up at the frozen, bloody faces as they gorged on his insides and yelled at them all with his last remaining breath.

"You can't kill me! I made you!" He shrieked hoarsely just before his voice cut out thanks to a ghoul ripping into his throat with cold teeth and severing his vocal cords.

As Frederick's vision began to fade, he looked up at Simpson who was standing over him, and just before his eyes closed forever in death, he could have sworn he saw Simpson smile.

Simpson watched Fredericks close his eyes and contentment flooded through his frozen heart.

At last, vengeance was his.

Then he pushed the other ghouls away from Fredericks' body until he was actually guarding the body of his sworn enemy.

He stayed like this for a few minutes, waiting for what he knew was coming. When he heard a stirring behind him, he turned around and smiled again.

Now he could savor the ultimate vengeance. Behind him, Fredericks slowly raised himself to his feet, and on torn and ripped legs, shambled away to be with the other walking dead.

Simpson gazed up at the night sky, the snow falling on his face and laughed. Then, he too, went back towards the small building where the two last survivors of Kryton Station remained.

CHAPTER FIFTY-THREE

THE SNOW FELL all around, slowly covering their bodies with a light dusting of white crystals.

On the icy ground below, the undead scraped and moaned as they tried to reach them, but so far they hadn't managed it.

Every now and then a ghoul would attempt to climb out of the opening in the roof, but it was easy work for Mark to use the hammer Sara had used earlier, to knock the pale blue faces back down again.

As he smacked the last one, he was reminded of that game where you have a hammer made of a soft material and you whack the moles as they pop out of their holes.

"Yeah, fifty points for that one," he said as it fell back down to the cement floor to join the others he'd killed.

It had been about an hour since they had climbed onto the roof and they were freezing. The thin coat Sara wore and Mark's shirt did nothing to fight off the frigid chill of the night and Mark had to fight to stay conscious.

If they didn't get warmer clothes soon, they would never see tomorrow.

Mark winced when he shifted his wounded arm to a better position, his face a mask of pain and exhaustion. Sara saw his expression and frowned.

"Mark, we have to talk about it sooner or later," she said as she looked at his arm.

"Why? We both know what it means, so what's the point?" He said and turned away from her.

A pale blue face poked its head out of the opening in the roof and Mark casually whacked the ghoul in the head. The hammer shattered its skull and went in about two inches. When it was withdrawn, there was a meaty sound accompanying the withdrawal. The sound reminded him of when he was a kid and he used to go to the butcher with his father on Saturdays. The butcher's cleaver would make the same sound as it bit into a flank of meat.

Sara wouldn't let up. "Maybe if we can get you help, you won't end up like…"

He knew what she was going to say and said it for her.

"Like Shawn, right? That's who you're talking about. Well, I'm sorry to say that's probably what's going to happen. Look, there's nothing either of us can do about it, so let's just concentrate on staying warm and we'll deal with everything else as it comes, okay?" He stood up to get his blood flowing, looking like he was doing aerobics. But then a wave of dizziness descended on him and he had to stop.

He walked over to the edge of the roof to see what the ghouls were doing.

He was pleased to see they were the same as an hour before. As he scanned the dead faces being illuminated by the moon, he wondered how it would be to be one of them.

Would he still know who he was? Would he still feel pain?

All these things went through his mind when he suddenly saw some familiar faces in the crowd below.

There was Fredericks looking like he had seen better days and when he looked to the right of him, he saw Shawn.

Shawn's face hung slack, like an idiot, and he had his hands out as he tried to push past other ghouls in his way. As Mark watched his undead friend, he saw that Shawn was a few fingers short on one of his hands and his right leg was bent at an odd angle. But it didn't look like Shawn seemed to mind.

Mark watched him for a few more minutes and whispered to the air.

"Don't worry, buddy, I'll be with you soon."

And then he went back to the hole and kicked another ghoul in the face just as it appeared. The ghoul's head snapped back and it fell away.

He inspected his arm and frowned when he saw the blue lines that were starting to crawl up his arm. At the rate the infection was spreading, he wondered if he would be himself when the ship arrived.

He looked down at Sara who was shivering in the cold and decided he needed to do something about their clothing situation right now.

Taking an idea from Fredericks, he waited for the next ghoul to pop its head up. But instead of knocking it away, he reached down and grabbed it by the scruff of its jacket and hauled the body onto the roof with him and Sara.

Sara screamed when she saw what he was doing and crawled away from the opening, but Mark had it under control.

When the ghoul was supine on the roof, Mark cracked its skull with the hammer. One, two, three times he hit the skull, until the corpse lay still.

When he was sure the ghoul was dead for good, he quickly stripped the body of its clothes and then rolled it off of the roof.

He did this two more times to two other bodies, and when he was finished, the two of them were at least wearing the proper outdoor clothing.

They huddled together for warmth as the moon moved across the sky, the falling snow lightening some. They were both lucky that it was only a little below freezing, or they never would have made it as long as they had. Mark found a lighter in one of the jacket pockets and had immediately gotten an idea.

Using some of the wood panels from the roof, he placed them into a small pile, and then using a small amount of the liquid from the bomb, he was able to use the lighter to start them a small fire. Some of the roof had sheet metal on it and he had placed the fire there, so he wasn't worried about the fire burning through the roof.

Together, the two of them huddled together and were able to just stay warm enough not to die from hypothermia. As the hours crept by painfully slowly, Sara took watch to guard the hole in the roof.

Not having to watch the opening, Mark drifted off into a fevered dream.

He opened his eyes to find he was on a beach again with Sara, only this time everything was fine.

She lay next to him on a lounge chair and her tan skin glistened in the sun from the suntan lotion she had put on.

She noticed him looking at her and she leaned over to kiss him.

This time the kiss was warm and welcome. Then he pulled away and gazed at her face.

"I love you," he said softly.

"I love you, too," she said softly with a slight grin.

Then they both leaned back in their chairs and enjoyed the warm rays of the sun.

As he lay there, he began to hear a ship's horn. He tried to ignore it and just enjoy the sunshine, but then he heard it again, louder this time.

When he opened his eyes this time, he was once again aware of where he was. Groggily, he came to a sitting position and looked out over the snow where the dock sat empty and his eyes opened wide when he saw a ship about a mile away.

It was making slow and steady progress, the knife-like point of its bow pushing its way through the ice.

At the rate the vessel was moving, it would probably reach the dock in a couple of hours.

He leaned over and saw Sara standing at the edge of the roof, watching the ship. He stood up and walked over to her.

"Why didn't you wake me when you saw the ship?"

"What would've been the point? Its not here yet and you needed your sleep."

She punctuated her sentence with a whack to a ghoul's head when it tried to scale the side of the building.

Then she had to turn and go back to the hole in the roof, whacking a ghoul that was trying to climb up. First she smashed its hand into a hundred flesh and ice crystals, then she smacked it in the forehead. The face dropped away to crash below.

It was easier for the undead to climb up now as their fallen brethren had been collecting on the floor and now could be used as a makeshift stairway to the roof.

"Still, you could've woken me up," he said as he sat back down. His arm was throbbing and when he shrugged out of his coat to check it, he wasn't happy at what he saw. The blue lines had now completely enveloped his arm where they then continued to his shoulder. He remembered what had happened to Shawn and didn't need to be a medical doctor to know what he'd find if he lifted up his shirt to check his chest. Plus, with his jacket off, he should have been freezing, but he realized he wasn't feeling that bad.

Could it be a side effect of the infection? It would make sense as all the ghouls appeared to be frozen.

He painfully put his coat back on and joined Sara again.

As they watched together, the ship slowly grew closer.

Spotlights went back and forth in front of its bow as the ice was sent flying off to the sides. They could now make out men walking around on the front deck as they did the chores that needed attending to.

The ghouls below also noticed the ship, and some of them began to wander over to the end of the dock where the ship would eventually be moored.

"What do you think will happen when that ship moors?" Sara asked as she watched it plowing through the ice.

"I don't know. We can only hope they figure out what's happening in time before they get overrun by those dead bastards."

Mark put his good arm around her and she reciprocated, and together they stood silently and watched the ship slowly make its way to port.

And hopefully, their salvation.

CHAPTER FIFTY-FOUR

CAPTAIN MURRAY LOWERED his binoculars and turned to his second-in-command, his mouth turned down into a frown.

"I tell you Bob, I have no idea what the hell is going on at that station. From the looks of it, part of the station appears to be on fire and there seems to be people congregating down at the docks."

Lt. Bob Hastings shrugged. "Well, sir, we'll be there in another hour or so," he stated as he watched the fires burning in the distance.

"Tell the men to get ready to give aid to anyone who needs it as soon as we're docked," Murray said as he looked through the binoculars again.

What the hell could have happened over there to do the kind of damage he was seeing? Had they been attacked and if so, then by whom?

He grimaced as he thought about what must have happened to all the people living on the station, many who had become his friends. There had been over two-hundred and fifty people there at this time of year.

He turned and retrieved the radio-mike and set it to intercom so he could address the entire ship.

"Attention, this is the Captain. We'll be mooring at Kryton Station in about an hour. The station's in bad shape. How it happened is undetermined at this time, but I want all men to be armed until we get to the bottom of it. In the next hour, find the time to see the master-at-arms. He'll be issuing weapons. When we moor, stand ready to give aid as needed. That is all."

Setting the radio-mike back in its cradle, he looked out the front windshield of the wheelhouse again.

Well, whatever was going on over there, he and his men would find out soon enough.

*   *   *

Mark and Sara huddled together for warmth on the roof as the icebreaker crawled agonizingly slow towards the docks.

Mark had been racking his brain on how they were supposed to get to the ship without getting run down by the ghouls below them.

He had seen how far Fredericks had gotten and knew they would never make it.

Sara saw the concentration on his face and nudged him softly.

"Penny for your thoughts," she said as she gazed into his eyes.

"I don't think you really want to know what I was thinking about," he said flatly.

"Try me, Mark, I'm a big girl, you know," she said, trying to stay cheerful.

He sighed. "I was thinking about how we could make it to the ship in one piece."

"Yeah, me too. So far, every idea I think of ends up with us getting run down and eaten," she said ruefully.

Mark turned to her. "Then what the hell are we gonna do?"

"I think we should just wait and let fate take its course. After all, it's gotten us this far hasn't it?" She asked as she shifted position. Her leg had fallen asleep and she was just waiting for the dreaded pins and needles to start.

"I love you, you know that, right?" Mark asked out of the blue as he watched her fix her clothing.

She was now looking out at the ship and a smile creased her lips as she turned to him.

"Yes, Mark, I do know that. And I love you, too. Don't worry, we'll get through this, we have to." Then she turned her head and stared off at the ship again. Watching it come closer with each passing minute gave her another piece of hope that they would make it through their harrowing ordeal alive.

Mark continued to watch her as she stared off into the distance. It was good she was optimistic, but as Mark felt his arm throb from his wound, he knew he wouldn't be joining her on that ship.

As he looked down at the undead faces below, he knew he would be staying with them.

Whether he liked it or not.

CHAPTER FIFTY-FIVE

THE NEWPORT SLOWLY pulled up alongside the dock as the crew readied the mooring lines.

For the past half hour, the ship had cut through the ice with ease as it slowly approached the dock.

Captain Murray had stood in the wheelhouse with his binoculars in hand as he continually watched the people who were now standing on the docks waiting for them to moor.

But the more he scrutinized them, the more they seemed a little…off.

They shambled instead of walked and some of them seemed to have life threatening wounds, but yet didn't seem to care. But it was when he spotted a woman who was clearly one of the scientists, as she was wearing a white lab coat that he absolutely knew something was seriously wrong.

At first he could only see her from the right side of her body, but after a few minutes had passed, she shifted position as the other people around her jostled her.

It was when she moved and the left side of her body came into view that Murray could clearly see she was missing her arm from the elbow down.

As he stared in fascination through the binoculars, he could clearly see the fractured limb as she waved it in the air, the white bone jutting through the severed limb.

He lowered the binoculars and watched through the window as his men began to lower the boarding ramp. He decided then it would be prudent to wait a little longer to figure out what was happening at the station, so he reached for the radio to tell his men not to put down the boarding ramp.

But he already knew he would be too late.

He could only watch in horror as his men were systematically ripped apart as the residents of the station swarmed up the boarding ramp.

Merchantman Bill Waters lowered the boarding ramp to the docks as he watched the people milling about, the men and women patiently waiting for the ramp to come down.

It was hard to really make out anyone specifically due to the shadows the ship cast over the dock.

He did find it a little curious why there were so many people about this morning, but he'd seen the fires, too, and figured they just wanted help.

The boarding ramp was about three feet wide and had cargo netting on both sides so any passengers coming on or off the ship wouldn't lose their footing and fall into the icy waters below.

A buddy of his had fallen in about six months ago and by the time they had retrieved the body from under the ice, the man had been nothing more than a frozen piece of meat.

A couple of his buddies were walking behind him as he made his way down the ramp. Then he stopped, remembering he needed to bring the cargo manifest to give to the dock master.

Quickly, he turned and ran back onto the ship to retrieve it as his buddies filed past him, the men continuing down the ramp to greet the people waiting for them.

What Bill Waters didn't realize at the time was that his absent-mindedness had saved his life.

The first man set foot on the dock, and with a big smile, waved to the crowd as they slowly surrounded him. That's when he got a closer look at them. His smile quickly faded to horror when he saw their pale blue countenances and massive bodily wounds up close.

He tried to turn and run, but his buddies blocked his path. They hadn't realized anything was amiss. But when, they too, stepped onto the docks, the men quickly realized they had just set foot into a frozen Hell of undead ghouls.

The walking corpses lunged at the four men, and amid howls of pain and yells for help, they men were quickly ripped apart. With the steaming organs scattered on the wet snow, the frozen dead began to feed on warm viscera.

The only consolation for these men was that the ghouls hadn't had meat for a few days and so they dissected and devoured so much of the hapless men that there was nothing left to be revived.

Finishing the men off, some of the zombies turned to the ramp and began to board the ship, their frozen legs having trouble as they slowly stumbled up the ramp. One or two lost their footing and toppled over the safety netting to be lost in the crushed ice of the churning sea.

But the crewman on the ship had seen what had happened to their comrades, and though they might not comprehend what was truly happening, they did know their friends had just been slaughtered and eaten in front of their eyes. And that made them merciless to the shambling zombies.

As the ghouls came into point-blank range, the crew began firing into the undead crowd.

At first the bullets had no effect on the bodies, but then one of the crewman shot a ghoul in the head, and as it fell over the ramp to the water below, he yelled to the others to, "aim for the head!"

Then it was a massacre as the ghouls could only come at the men one at a time and as each one ran the gauntlet, it was sequentially shot down. Soon, only one man was needed to defend the ship from any approaching ghouls.

Captain Murray had come down from the wheelhouse and now stood by the boarding ramp as he surveyed the carnage before him. He still didn't know what to make of everything until a young crewman of only about eighteen years of age came over to him and pointed at the people still milling on the docks.

"Captain, if I didn't know any better, I'd say those people are zombies."

"Excuse me, crewman, what did you say?" Murray asked incredulously.

"No, really Captain, I'm serious. Me and my friends used to watch this zombie movie about the dead walking and these people that hid out in a mall almost every Friday night, and I'm telling you, those peo-ple are zombies."

Murray mulled it over, thanked the crewman and then sent him on his way.

Zombies? Walking around? Well, maybe there was some kind of outbreak or something that had infected the populace of the station. It sounded like science fiction, but the proof was right there before him.

He was about to order the ramp pulled and release the mooring lines so he could leave before his crew became infected, as well, when he saw small, flickering flames piercing the darkness in the distance that looked like a lot like a signal fire.

He raised his binoculars to his eyes to look further and could just make out two people standing on a ramshackle building at the edge of the docks. They had what looked like a small campfire going and were waving to the ship with their arms swinging widely above their heads. In the flickering of the campfire, Murray was able to make out a man and a woman as they jumped up and down hoping to be seen.

Below them on the ground, the small structure was surrounded by people that Murray couldn't help but call *zombies*.

He removed the binoculars from his face and frowned.

There were survivors out there.

But how the hell could he get to them without losing more of his men?

He was pondering this when he saw the man stop jumping up and down and turn to the woman. He talked with her for a few moments, retrieved something from the roof and then jumped to the ground and began running to the empty spot between the structure and his ship.

He was yelling and waving his arms like a madman as the ghouls turned to the sounds of his voice and began to converge on him.

Murray couldn't believe what the man was doing. Surely he was committing suicide.

Then Murray's mouth dropped open and he witnessed something he thought he would never see in his lifetime.

Mark jumped up and down with Sara and saw the man with bin-oculars look right at them. But he knew there was no possible way the men on the ship could get to them.

The ghouls were blocking the ramp four and five bodies thick, and as he looked down to the ground, there had to be at least fifteen or twenty ghouls surrounding their small building.

Sara hadn't eaten in almost two days and he could feel the infection flowing through his body with every passing minute.

As he stopped jumping up and down, he turned to Sara and stopped her, as well. Her eyes were big and trusting as she gazed into his eyes, her face filled with the hope they would be saved.

"We're saved, did you see? I think that man saw us!" She said with excitement clearly audible in her voice.

"Yeah, I saw him, too, but there's no way for them to get to us. Those dead bastards have got them trapped on that ship. Who knows how long it could take for them to finally reach us," he said with tears in his eyes. Tears that quickly froze as they landed on his cheeks.

Sara saw the tears and didn't understand what was wrong.

"Mark, why are you crying? It's okay, they'll get to us sooner or later," she said trying to console him.

"No, Sara they won't. If what happened to Shawn happens to me, and I can feel it eating away at me, I've only got about another day at most before I pass out and go into a coma. And then become one of those things," he said as he pointed toward the undead faces below them. "And frankly, honey, I don't want to go out like that. So, listen up. I want you to get down on the roof and stay there until it's clear. Then I want you to run as fast as you can to the ramp and get on that ship. You hear me?"

"But, Mark, I don't…"

"Damn it, Sara, just do what I say! And remember… I love you." Then he kissed her softly on the lips.

Before Sara could stop him, he reached down and grabbed the backpack with the last mini-bomb inside and then leapt off the roof and over the crowd of ghouls.

When he landed, he felt something snap in his right foot and pain flashed before his eyes, momentarily stunning him. Then it passed and as he gritted his teeth, he started to run/hop towards the empty space between the ship and the small building with Sara cowering on the roof.

He yelled and screamed as loudly as he was able, wanting to get the ghouls' attention, and in a matter of seconds almost the entire undead horde began to turn and walk in his direction.

Reaching where he wanted to go, he stopped and waited for the zombies to catch up to him. As the first ones came within arms reach, he kicked and pushed them away. He wasn't really trying to defend himself, but just trying to bide enough time for as many of the dead bastards to surround him as he could.

Within moments, they were surrounding him. There were far too many to fend off and they began to bite his arms and body. His clothing was ripped away and he could feel the cold arctic air on his flesh as teeth like small ice cubes sank into various parts of his flesh.

The pain quickly became unbearable, his vocal cords growing raw from his screams and shrieks of pain. He lost an ear first and then a chunk of his neck was torn away, followed by a large piece of his right leg. The skin and tissue on his body was peeled away like a man shucking corn, and he was fast slipping into shock. He could feel his consciousness slipping away into death as his life's blood squirted from his torn and fractured body, and decided it was now or never.

His right hand had been hidden in the backpack and he yanked it out, the pin on the grenade coming with it.

As his head was ripped from his body and the permanent blackness of death began to descend over him, he had one last cognizant thought.

"I love you, Sara, be safe."

And then he saw a brilliant flash of light… and then nothing as his body and all the undead around him were vaporized from the explosion of the mini-bomb.

Within a microsecond, a massive fireball rolled out across the area that Mark had picked for his suicide run, blowing apart the frozen dead and sending the pieces flying across the docks and surrounding area.

On the ship, Murray and his men had to duck down or risk being pelted by flying body parts and debris as the rolling shockwave destroyed everything in its path.

Then it became deathly quiet as the fireball diminished and the soft wind coming off the sea blew the smoke away.

What was left was an eight foot deep hole that had to be at least a hundred feet in diameter.

Nearly ninety percent of the ghouls had either been totally destroyed or put out of action as bodies with no legs or missing arms crawled around the exterior of the blast zone.

Murray sent his men down with guns drawn to finish off the few that remained active and then he sent a party over to the small structure where they found one very frightened young woman.

She appeared to be in shock, and was quickly brought back to the ship where she would be fed and checked out by the ship's physician. She already looked like she had a mild case of exposure to the freezing weather, but it was nothing a warm blanket and a hot cup of soup wouldn't fix. Frankly, it was a miracle she had survived at all.

Then they would ask her what had happened at the station. It was hard to believe that all the people could be dead and only one lone woman would be the only survivor.

But that seemed to be the situation as the ship stayed docked for another hour and continually sounded its fog horn to signal any other survivors they were there.

None came.

Finally, Murray had the ramp withdrawn and the mooring lines thrown off and they set sail back to home port.

As the ship slipped away from the dock, Captain Murray stood in the wheelhouse again and stared at the fires consuming Kryton station one last time. Then he ordered the ship half speed and they put their backs to the Hell they had been witness to.

His last thoughts as the station faded into the dark was if anyone would ever believe what he and his men had witnessed today, or if they would all be called crazy. After all, there was no proof, as all the zombies had been destroyed and the station was in flames, soon to be nothing but ash and burnt out hulks of twisted metal and steel.

He put those ideas behind him and concentrated on his ship and crew. He decided to push the horrific images he'd seen down deep in his mind where they would stay forever, and he planned on telling his crew to do the same.

What had happened on the edge of the world was scientifically impossible, and if they all knew what was good for them, they would remain silent about the events, never speaking of them again.

After all, who would believe them even if they tried?

EPILOGUE

As THE NEWPORT cut through the thick ice, a stowaway pulled himself tighter into the opening in the bow where the anchor would be dropped and winched back up.

The spray of the ice water would hit him and coat his body, then freeze and break off only to repeat the cycle again, but the man just shrugged it off.

He'd been crammed in the same position since he had snuck up into the hole when Mark had blown his undead army to Hell.

Because he was able to reason more than the average ghoul, and had immediately figured out his cause was lost after watching his brethren being mowed down by the men on the ship, he realized he needed a change of tactics.

So he had decided on another course of action and had snuck down onto the ice and had then used a mooring rope to climb up to his present hiding place.

The climb had been tough as his limbs weren't as flexible as they once were, but he'd managed and had then settled down for what he figured would be quite a while.

He amused himself by thinking of what Fredericks looked like when he was ripped apart by his brothers and had then been revived.

That image was enough to keep him company as the ship cut through the ice on its voyage home.

Two weeks later, a new harbor came into view, and by day's end the ship had moored and begun unloading crew and cargo.

He saw the people hustling back and forth on the docks, facilitating the mooring of the ship and then the unloading of its cargo.

From inside his hiding place, Simpson's face cut into a jagged smile as he thought of something he'd heard when he was human.

"If at first you don't succeed, try, try, again."

And that was exactly what he was going to do.

PLAYING GOD: A ZOMBIE NOVEL
by Jeffery Dye

It was supposed to be a regeneration virus to help soldiers on the battlefield—regrowing limbs and healing wounds— but a simple act of carelessness unleashed it on an unsuspecting world.

For the virus was not perfected, and once exposed, the host quickly dies, only to rise again as one of the undead.

As countries are quickly overrun, scientists and military teams battle to contain the outbreak.

There is no other option.

If the infection continues to spread, soon the entire globe will be consumed. And perhaps that will be a just punishment for a mankind that dared to try to play God.

DEAD HOUSE: A ZOMBIE GHOST STORY
by Keith Adam Luethke

The old mansion on the edge of town, aptly named Dead House, has a history of blood, pain, and death, but what Victor Leeds knows of this past only scratches the surface of the true horrors within.

But when his girlfriend is attacked by a shadowy figure one rainy night, he soon finds himself caught up in a world where the dead walk and ghostly wraiths abound. And to make matters worse, a pair of serial killers are fulfilling carefully made plans, and when they are done, the small town of Stormville, New York will run red. The last ingredient to open the gates of Hell, and plunge this small upstate town into madness, is rain.

And in Stormville, it pours by the gallons.

The Lazarus Culture
by Pasquale J. Morrone

Secret Service Agent Christopher Kearns had no idea what he was up against. Assigned on a temporary basis to the Center for Disease Control, he only knew that somehow it was connected to the lives of those the agency protected...namely, the President of the United States. If there were possible terrorist activities in the making, he could only guess it was at a red alert basis.

When Kearns meets and befriends Doctor Marlene Peterson of the Breezy Point Medical Center in Maryland, he soon finds that science fiction can indeed become a reality. In a solitary room walked a man with no vital signs: dead. The explanation he received came from Doctor Lee Fret, a man assigned to the case from the CDC. Something was attached to the brain stem. Something alive that was quickly spreading rapidly through Maryland and other states.

Kearns and his ragtag army of agents and medical personnel soon find themselves in a world of meaningless slaughter and mayhem. The armies of the walking dead were far more than mere zombies. Some began to change into whatever it was they ate. The government had found a way to reanimate the dead by implanting a parasite found on the tongue of the Red Snapper to the human brain. It looked good on paper, but it was a project straight from Hell. The dead now walked, but it wasn't a mystery. It was The Lazarus Culture.

BOOK OF THE DEAD
A ZOMBIE ANTHOLOGY VOL 1
ISBN 978-1-935458-25-8
Edited by Anthony Giangregorio

This is the most faithful, truest zombie anthology ever written, and we invite you along for the ride. Every single story in this book is filled with slack-jawed, eyes glazed, slow moving, shambling zombies set in a world where the dead have risen and only want to eat the flesh of the living. In these pages, the rules are sacrosanct. There is no deviation from what a zombie should be or how they came about. The Dead Walk.

There is no reason, though rumors and suppositions fill the radio and television stations. But the only thing that is fact is that the walking dead are here and they will not go away. So prepare yourself for the ultimate homage to the master of zombie legend. And remember... Aim for the head!

REVOLUTION OF THE DEAD
by Anthony Giangregorio
THE DEAD SHALL RISE AGAIN!

Five years ago, a deadly plague wiped out 97% of the world's population, America suffering tragically. Bodies were everywhere, far too many to bury or burn. But then, through a miracle of medical science, a way is found to reanimate the dead.

With the manpower of the United States depleted, and the remaining survivors not wanting to give up their internet and fast food restaurants, the undead are conscripted as slave labor.   Now they cut the grass, pick up the trash, and walk the dogs of the surviving humans.   But whether alive or dead, no race wants to be controlled, and sooner or later the dead will fight back, wanting the freedom they enjoyed in life.

The revolution has begun!

And when it's over, the dead will rule the land, and the remaining humans will become the slaves…or worse.

KINGDOM OF THE DEAD
by Anthony Giangregorio
THE DEAD HAVE RISEN!

In the dead city of Pittsburgh, two small enclaves struggle to survive, eking out an existence of hand to mouth.

But instead of working together, both groups battle for the last remaining fuel and supplies of a city filled with the living dead.

Six months after the initial outbreak, a lone helicopter arrives bearing two more survivors and a newborn baby. One enclave welcomes them, while the other schemes to steal their helicopter and escape the decaying city.

With no police, fire, or social services existing, the two will battle for dominance in the steel city of the walking dead. But when the dust settles, the question is: will the remaining humans be the winners, or the losers?

When the dead walk, the line between Heaven and Hell is so twisted and bent there is no line at all.

RISE OF THE DEAD
by Anthony Giangregorio

DEATH IS ONLY THE BEGINNING!

In less than forty-eight hours, more than half the globe was infected.

In another forty-eight, the rest would be enveloped.

The reason?

A science experiment gone horribly wrong which enabled the dead to walk, their flesh rotting on their bones even as they seek human prey.

Jeremy was an ordinary nineteen year old slacker. He partied too much and had done poorly in high school. After a night of drinking and drugs, he awoke to find the world a very different place from the one he'd left the night before.

The dead were walking and feeding on the living, and as Jeremy stepped out into a world gone mad, the dead spotting him alone and unarmed in the middle of the street,

he had to wonder if he would live long enough to see his twentieth birthday.

THE CHRONICLES OF JACK PRIMUS
BOOK ONE
by Michael D. Griffiths

Beneath the world of normalcy we all live in lies another world, one where supernatural beings exist.

These creatures of the night hunt us; want to feed on our very souls, though only a few know of their existence.

One such man is Jack Primus, who accidentally pierces the veil between this world and the next. With no other choice if he wants to live, he finds himself on the run, hunted by beings called the Xemmoni, an ancient race that sees humans as nothing but cattle. They want his soul, to feed on his very essence, and they will kill all who stand in their way. But if they thought Jack would just lie down and accept his fate, they were sorely mistaken.   He didn't ask for this battle, but he knew he would fight them with everything at his disposal, for to lose is a fate worse than death.

He would win this war, and he would take down anyone who got in his way.

MONSTER PARTY
Edited by Anthony Giangregorio

Zombies, vampires, werewolves and ghosts are just a few of the monsters in this anthology.

But this isn't any anthology, you see, this is a party.

Or to be more to the point…a *Monster Party*.

Ever wonder what would happen if a werewolf and a zombie squared off? Or perhaps a vampire and a Frankenstein monster? Or better yet, how about a world where every conceivable monster is real and humans are their prey?

If those burning questions have been driving you mad, then look no further than this book.

So go on over to the buffet table, grab yourself a plate (the shrimp looks good) and get yourself a drink, and enjoy the fun ride that is the *Monster Party*.

THE WAR AGAINST THEM: A ZOMBIE NOVEL
by Jose Alfredo Vazquez

Mankind wasn't prepared for the onslaught.

An ancient organism is reanimating the dead bodies of its victims, creating worldwide chaos and panic as the disease spreads to every corner of the globe. As governments struggle to contain the disease, courageous individuals across the planet learn what it truly means to make choices as they struggle to survive.

Geopolitics meet technology in a race to save mankind from the worst threat it has ever faced. Doctors, military and soldiers from all walks of life battle to find a cure. For the dead walk, and if not stopped, they will wipe out all life on Earth. Humanity is fighting a war they cannot win, for who can overcome Death itself? Man versus the walking dead with the winner ruling the planet. Welcome to *The War Against Them*.

DEADTOWN: A DEADWATER STORY
BOOK 8

by Anthony Giangregorio

The world is a very different place now. The dead walk the land and humans hide in small towns with walls of stone and debris for protection, constantly keeping the living dead at bay.

Social law is gone and right and wrong is defined by the size of your gun.

UNWELCOME VISITORS

Henry Watson and his band of warrior survivalists become guests in a fortified town in Michigan. But when the kidnapping of one of the companions goes bad and men die, the group finds themselves on the wrong side of the law, and a town out for blood.

Trapped in a hotel, surrounded on all sides, it will be up to Henry to save the day with a gamble that may not only take his life, but that of his friends as well.

In a dead world, when justice is not enough, there is always vengeance.

END OF DAYS: AN APOCALYPTIC ANTHOLOGY
VOLUMES 1-3

Edited by Anthony Giangregorio

Our world is a fragile place.

Meteors, famine, floods, nuclear war, solar flares, and hundreds of other calamities can plunge our small blue planet into turmoil in an instant.

What would you do if tomorrow the sun went super nova or the world was swallowed by water, submerging the world into the cold darkness of the ocean? This anthology explores some of those scenarios and plunges you into total annihilation.

But remember, it's only a book, and tomorrow will come as it always does.

Or will it?